The Crimson Cavalier

Mary Andrea Clarke

CREME DE LA CRIME

First published in 2007
by Crème de la Crime
P O Box 523, Chesterfield, S40 9AT

Typesetting by Yvette Warren
Cover design by Yvette Warren
Front cover image by Peter Roman

ISBN 978-0-9551589-5-7
A CIP catalogue reference for this book is available from
the British Library

Printed and bound in Great Britain by
Cox & Wyman Ltd, Reading, Berkshire

www.cremedelacrime.com

About the author:
Currently working in the Civil Service, Mary Andrea Clarke has been a regular delegate at crime fiction conferences and a member of Mystery Women since 1998. She has reviewed historical fiction for the Historical Novel Society and crime fiction for Sherlock Magazine, Shots Ezine and Mystery Women. Mary lives in Surrey with her cat, Alice.

The contribution of my late mother has been vital; her belief and encouragement kept me going through the spells of rejection. I wish she could have been here to see the final result.

A major thank-you to Jason Perrott for his invaluable help in pruning the manuscript, publicity photographs and consistent moral support and belief.

Thanks to Jane Baker, Kate Charles, Michelle Spring and Alison Weir for their guidance and encouragement.

My editor Meriel Patrick has been conscientious and thorough and I am grateful for her insight.

A number of people have given encouragement and support on the journey in bringing this book to print. These include Linda Clarke, Gaynor Coules, the late Sandra Gaffney, Lizzie Hayes, Sue Lord, Adrian Magson, Ayo Onatade, Kate Stacey, friends from Mystery Women, the St Hilda's Crime Fiction Conference and David Headley and Daniel Gedeon of Goldsboro Books.

The staff of Dragons Health Club in Guildford deserve a mention for allowing me writing time in their coffee bar, even when I had finished eating and drinking.

Finally, a huge thank-you goes to Lynne Patrick and everyone at Crème de la Crime for believing in me and the book enough to give me this opportunity.

To Mom and Dad, with thanks
for your love, support and belief

1

The pistol didn't waver. There had been no need to fire it; the sight of the stark metal in the black-gloved hand had been enough to instil obedience in the shivering figures beside the carriage. One after another, valuables were surrendered.

"Thank you for your co-operation," the highway robber drawled, passing down the line of submissive faces with an upside-down tricorne for the goods. Watches, fobs, rings went in, the victims quietly submitting to the persuasive glint of the barrel pointed at them, the only sound in the night air the uneasy whinnying of the horses.

At the end of the line the robber faced a young girl in pale yellow, watching with some interest as she slowly drew off her bracelets.

"La, sir, do you mean to rob me as well?"

"Can you think of any reason why I should not?"

"Well, it seems a most ungentlemanly thing to do." The demure tone was belied by the flirtatiousness in her eyes.

Not again, thought the robber. These coquettish girls were becoming a bore. Didn't they have enough eligible men dangling after them? It was always the pretty ones; the plain ladies generally reacted with the indignation and outraged virtue one expected.

Glancing towards the older woman beside the girl, the highway robber saw the scandalised horror which appeared on many a maternal countenance.

"I am no gentleman. Oh, have no fear, madam. I have no designs on your daughter's virtue. I am only interested in her jewels. I beg you will instruct her to hand them over."

The young lady complied, disappointment evident in her face. The older woman reacted promptly, boxing her daughter's ear; the robber's eyes flashed, muscles tensing in anger.

"Do you mean to keep us here all night?" demanded a solidly built gentleman, cheeks red with indignation. "You've got what you came for. Why don't you be off?"

The robber regarded this outspoken individual thoughtfully, raising the pistol to half cock, a thumb hovering in position. "Ah, a hero."

The movement of the weapon transformed the bluster into unease. Dignity vanished as beads of sweat appeared on his face, and his wig, knocked askew when he had been bundled out of the carriage, made for a slightly comic appearance. The moment of silence seemed interminable. Finally, his tormentor put him out of his misery, taking a step back and bowing to the assembled company.

"Thank you for your generosity. You may continue your journey. However, I beg you will be careful. There are a number of highway robbers on this road, and I regret not all are as gallant as I."

The passengers boarded the coach, venturing glances towards the pistol. Nursing her ear, the flirtatious young lady was pushed on board by her angry mother, but not before bestowing a coy smile on the cloaked figure.

"Outrageous!" grumbled the solidly built gentleman, regaining his courage as he settled into a corner of the coach. "Cut-throats holding up innocent citizens."

"I beg pardon," said the robber, having caught these words. "I'm sure none of us is so innocent as we would have the world believe." The pistol once again faced the bombastic passenger. "Probably not even you, my dear sir."

"Insolent puppy!" sputtered the indignant individual. "I'm a respected member of the community. How dare you insinuate I have something to hide?"

The robber's eyes rolled heavenward, inflaming his

opponent even more.

"I'm not without influence," blustered the man. "You'll pay for this, mark my words."

The robber ignored the warning and stowed the evening's proceeds in a black velvet bag secured to a pistol belt. The cheerful crimson scarf which trimmed the tricorne stood out boldly in the moonlight. The sleek chestnut waited patiently as its owner nodded to the driver, weapon focused. "Be off with you, before I find myself tempted to use this."

The driver did not need a second telling. He whipped the horses along the London road at a speed to rival Letty Lade at her most reckless. The chestnut whinnied as the robber pulled it in the opposite direction, hooves pounding as its limbs stretched out to gallop.

The horse's lean muscles covered the ground with easy speed, quickly putting distance between robber and victims. A breeze began to agitate the trees.

"Keep calm. Panic is the road to the gallows."

The robber gave the road a final swift glance and turned the horse towards the woods. The trees always provided good cover, and although necessity varied the route, the lie of the land was familiar enough to ease their escape. Even in the dark, horse and rider moved with easy rapport.

The pace slowed and steadied as they followed a series of turns which brought them back to the road they had started from. The trees thinned, and as they emerged from the cover, the rider pulled up and dismounted, pausing to stroke the animal's neck.

"Sssh! All's well."

The robber twisted the reins securely around one hand, the other stroking the pistol. They were back on the Bath Road, nearer London than when they had parted company with the travellers. A few moments' careful observation revealed no indications of approaching carriage wheels; such a cumbersome equipage would still be some minutes away. The robber remounted swiftly and turned towards London.

The wind grew stronger, and the snap of a branch startled the horse. "Quiet, Princess," murmured its owner. "Not much longer."

Gaps between the trees began to show the occasional house. The horse slowed, grew more cautious. The uneven road gave way to a cobbled street. Eventually, the unnaturally loud clip-clop of hooves slowed still further as they approached a square of apparently unfulfilled ambitions. Several tasteful yet imposing residences had established positions between the same number of vacant, unclaimed sites. The rider slipped down quickly from the animal's glistening back and led it through a passage to the back of a house which stood isolated on one side of the square.

The stables were in darkness. One horse, stalled for the night, gave a slight whinny, but fell obediently silent at a low command.

The rider led the chestnut to an empty stall, casting watchful eyes around for wakeful stable-boys or an over-conscientious groom. All was peaceful, and as the stall's door closed behind them, the rider offered a carrot retrieved from a pocket. The other hand stroked and petted the horse's head. "Good girl, Princess, a fine job again tonight!"

The slower pace of the last part of the journey had allowed the animal to cool, but restoring saddle, bit and bridle to their respective hooks and rubbing down the horse was nevertheless a long task. The animal was eventually settled for the night and the rider slipped out of the stall, fastening the door quietly.

Emerging from the stable still masked, the solitary dark figure looked cautiously about before slipping speedily to the side of the main house. A door was unlocked; the robber glided inside unobserved. The back stairs were visible in the gloom; the robber took them two at a time, and quietly continued through the upstairs hall, heading purposefully towards a particular door.

Opening it without ceremony, the figure strode in.

It was a large bedroom, unoccupied, and the robber visibly relaxed within its sanctuary, removing the black mask once a candle was ensconced on the mantelpiece. The tricorne and gloves landed carelessly on the bed and expert fingers untied the black riband which held back the hair. One or two locks had already begun to escape, and a mane of auburn curls now tumbled about the shoulders of – a young lady.

She stood before a mirror, critically surveying her reflection as she deftly tidied the glossy tresses.

Removing the velvet purse from her belt, she smiled. It had been a good night's work. She turned the bag out on the counterpane of the grand four-poster bed and began to check the contents. It was easy to feel some sympathy with the travellers, though the high-handed manners of the gentleman and older woman tended to keep their share to a minimum.

A barely perceptible scratching sent her hand to a pistol instantly, an accelerated heartbeat drumming in her ears.

"Who's there?" she asked in a low voice.

"It's me, miss."

Relaxing slightly, she let go of the pistol.

"Come in, Emily."

A door leading to the adjoining dressing room opened and a young woman of about twenty entered. Her eyes widened as she saw the little pile glistening on the bed. "Miss Grey!"

Miss Georgiana Grey looked up from her task, her eyes meeting those of her maid. "All quiet here? My cousin hasn't been wakeful?"

Emily shook her head as she closed the door and came further into the room. "Not a sound."

"Good."

Georgiana continued to count, adding steadily to the growing number of piles on her bed.

"What do you think, Emily? I held up Sir Robert Foster's carriage. Can you believe it?"

Emily's mouth dropped open.

"Sir – Sir Robert Foster?" she repeated blankly. "Oh, please, miss, please tell me you didn't."

"You may be very sure I did," responded Georgiana. "Dreadful man. He kept talking pompously about the outrage of it, but made no push to defend himself or his companions." She finished counting. "There, ten pounds. And look at the jewels." Georgiana picked up a striking ring and slid it on to her finger. The dark stone flickered against the reflection of the candlelight, the contrast complementing the fair skin of her hand.

"But he's the worst of them," wailed Emily. "You've heard his talk about making examples. If he were to recognise you, you'd hang!"

"Oh, no I won't," said Georgiana, "not if I don't shoot anyone. For all their brave talk, one magistrate is very much like another. Besides, there are ways of avoiding these things. A well placed bribe can effect quite remarkable miracles."

"Even so, it's reckless."

"Really, Emily, this is hardly an occupation for the prudent," said Georgiana, wandering over to the mirror to untie her cravat. "What difference does it make who's in the coach? Besides, have you forgotten what Sir Robert did to James?"

"Of course not, miss. It's just that…"

"Surely if ever someone deserved to fall victim to a highwayman, it's Sir Robert Foster. And do stop wringing your hands! You look like one of those tragic heroines, waiting for someone to die."

Emily indignantly snatched up the discarded cravat and

folded it carefully. "I beg your pardon, Miss Georgiana," she said stiffly. "I only wish to help."

"Then help me out of these boots."

The removal of a pair of smart gentleman's boots had formed no part of a lady's maid's training, but after nearly two years of practice, Emily rivalled any valet at the task. Seated on the edge of the bed, Georgiana stretched out her stockinged feet and leaned back. She watched her maid thoughtfully. Emily and her brother James had been part of Georgiana's life ever since she could remember. They had virtually grown up together, and Georgiana thought of Emily more as a friend than a servant. Despite her cousin's disapproval, she could not bring herself to obey convention and address the girl as 'Cooper' after their years together.

"Well, Emily?"

"Miss?"

"Say your piece. This dignified silence is growing oppressive."

"I don't know what you mean, miss."

"Oh, yes, you do. You may as well do it now as later."

Emily remained silent, throwing her mistress a baleful look. Georgiana raised an eyebrow.

"If you must have it, miss, I think you're taking too many chances. You've held up Sir Robert before."

"That was a long time ago, and there was a reason for it."

"Yes, miss," said Emily in a more subdued tone. "And I was – am – grateful."

"Oh, nonsense, Emily, I'm not looking for gratitude."

"I know," said Emily. "But you seemed to be the only one who believed James."

"I'm sure Edward believed him," said Georgiana, "even if he didn't feel able to do anything about it."

"Then there was the expense. James's court costs and that fine, and giving your brooch to Sir Robert as a present for his sister–"

"Only because Sir Robert had hinted it might make him lenient. I suppose it depends on one's idea of leniency," Georgiana said reflectively. "Anyway, no matter, I got it back."

"That's always worried me, miss," said Emily. "What if he sees you wearing it? How do you mean to explain having a brooch which a highwayman stole from his sister?"

"Easily. I had it copied before I gave it to him."

Emily seemed satisfied, but still looked worried.

"Yes, well, miss, I still don't like you stopping him again. The next thing you know, you'll be meeting him at some party or other and then there'll be trouble."

"Nonsense," said Georgiana. "How likely is Sir Robert to recognise me as the notorious Crimson Cavalier? I wasn't planning to wear the same clothes to a ball, even a masked one. Though I am rather tempted by this ring. Do you think I should keep it?"

"What about your hair?" retorted Emily. "How many people have hair that colour?"

Georgiana was idly twisting a lock around her finger. Her hair had always been a potential problem. So far she had been lucky. She kept it well tied, and the darkness muted the vivid colour. Descriptions of the Crimson Cavalier's hair varied from to brown to jet black; and Georgiana had been amused to read in one newspaper account that her emerald eyes were now brown.

"True," she conceded. "However, that may yet prove an advantage."

"Miss?"

Georgiana gave her maid a mischievous look. "When do I ever wear red? How likely is anyone to associate this with me?" She gestured at the crimson scarf. "Besides, even if Sir Robert did by some chance guess the truth, can you honestly see that arrogant man telling the world he was held up by a woman?"

"You can't be sure what he'd do, miss. And I don't like you

carrying those pistols!"

Georgiana stared at her maid in open astonishment. "A highwayman without a pistol? I never heard of such a thing."

"It's not as if you ever use them," persisted Emily.

"Well, let's hope I never need to. Do be sensible, Emily. How can I hold up a carriage without a pistol? People can be a little... reluctant when it comes to handing over their valuables. I need some means of persuading them." Her tone took on a conciliatory note. "Wouldn't you be more comfortable knowing I had the means to defend myself if someone were to fire at me?"

"Surely you don't need two?"

Georgiana shook her head. "One could fail just as I need it. I can't take that risk."

Emily looked at her mistress without speaking, her expression still doubtful. Before she could respond, a knock on the bedroom door startled both women. Pushing the weapons under her pillow, Georgiana blew out the candle and moved into the shadows in the far corner of the room. Emily waited until she was safely out of view before opening the door.

"James! What is it?"

The footman raised his candle slightly, peering into the darkness.

"Sir Robert Foster is at the door. He wants to see Miss Georgiana."

Georgiana froze, wondering if she was dreaming. Neither she nor Emily had heard the front door. Emily turned to look at her, Georgiana moistened her lips and nodded.

"At this hour? What does he want?" demanded Emily.

James shrugged. "You don't imagine he would tell me, do you? Shall I say Miss Georgiana's not available?"

"No, James – I'll come." Georgiana spoke up from the corner. "Give him some refreshment. I'll be down directly."

"Yes, miss."

Emily closed the door. Her eyes met Georgiana's. "You can't go down there, miss!"

"It will look decidedly odd if I don't." Georgiana strode towards her wardrobe and whisked through the contents, selecting a simple muslin dress.

"Nowhere near as odd as being accused of holding up Sir Robert's coach."

"What choice do I have? Hide up here in the hope he will go away? I might as well face him. We can't assume he's come to make an accusation. They may have thrown a wheel, or the coachman may have been over-indulging. It wouldn't be the first time."

"You don't really believe that, do you?"

Georgiana did not answer. She stood before her dressing table, watched the reflection of Emily swiftly fastening the buttons of her dress.

"You're sure you weren't followed?" said Emily.

"Of course I wasn't!" responded Georgiana indignantly. She retrieved the pistols from under her pillow and locked them in her nightstand, then handed the key to Emily. "Put this away, would you?"

Pausing on the landing, Georgiana took a deep breath before descending to a hall remarkably full of people. Sir Robert Foster seemed to have taken over her house, barking instructions to anyone who would listen. His two companions stood next to him, apprehension in the eyes of the younger, for which the high-handed and scornful demeanour of her mother amply compensated. A slim, middle-aged woman in a dressing gown of subdued colouring was offering helpful suggestions, largely ignored, her personality as mousy as her light brown hair and pleasantly nondescript features.

The reluctant hostess came forward. "Good evening."

"Oh, Georgiana, I'm so sorry you were disturbed," said the

mousy woman. "I would not have had you woken for the world, but James thought you would wish it."

"Don't worry, Selina," said Georgiana, laying a hand on the other's arm. "James was quite right." She turned her attention to Sir Robert, forcing herself not to look unwelcoming.

"Ah, Miss Grey," said Sir Robert. "I trust you'll forgive us barging in like this..."

"It is a rather odd hour for a social call," Georgiana remarked dryly.

"Yes, yes," said Sir Robert gruffly. "But your house was the most conveniently located."

"I beg your pardon?"

"Sir Robert and his party have run into some difficulty," offered Selina. "In fact, they have had quite a dreadful experience."

"Do you know Lady Winters and her daughter, Miss Louisa Winters?" Sir Robert's voice cut into the explanation. His hungry eyes ran up and down the girl's form.

Lady Winters gave a stately inclination of her head, fiercely poking her daughter in the side. The young lady curtsied, mumbling, "How do you do?" at the floor. She glanced up fleetingly, and, encouraged by their hostess's friendly manner, gave a shy smile which Georgiana returned warmly.

"I see you've met my cousin, Miss Knatchbull."

"Oh, yes, indeed," responded the mousy woman. "So pleased, though the circumstances are rather unusual."

Georgiana turned back to her main quarry. "Sir Robert, I would be very grateful if you would tell me..."

"I should be glad of a cup of tea, Miss Grey," interrupted Lady Winters, sailing towards the drawing room. "My nerves are quite shattered."

"An excellent notion, Lady Winters," said Sir Robert, following in her wake. "Though I should prefer something stronger."

11

"I daresay," remarked Georgiana. "I have asked my footman to arrange for some refreshments. However, this is not a posting-inn. Neither am I accustomed to entertaining visitors at two o'clock in the morning, even those who arrive at my invitation."

Lady Winters and Sir Robert stared in dumbfounded astonishment. And Miss Winters's bottom jaw dropped in an unladylike manner. Miss Knatchbull looked suitably shocked.

"Georgiana! I assure your ladyship, my cousin did not intend to sound uncivil."

"Please don't apologise for me, Selina." Georgiana turned her attention back to the visitors. "Perhaps you would be good enough to tell me why you have disturbed my household at this hour?"

In the stretched-out moment of silence which followed, Georgiana toyed with the possibility of asking her uninvited guests to leave. She rejected the idea as quickly as it was conceived, lest she arouse the suspicion she was anxious to avoid. Instead, she looked towards Sir Robert expectantly, one eyebrow slightly raised. James, approaching at that moment with a tray bearing a teapot and decanter, broke the tension.

"My cousin mentioned you had encountered some difficulty?" Georgiana prompted.

"I should rather say we have, Miss Grey," responded Sir Robert. "We were held up by a highwayman."

Georgiana's eyes widened. She managed to convey just the right amount of shocked surprise into her voice when she responded.

"A highwayman? How dreadful!"

Miss Knatchbull shuddered. "Isn't it horrid? I remember how terrified I was when it happened to us."

"It's disgraceful," said Sir Robert. "Thieves and cut-throats taking over the public roads. Why, if it hadn't been for the

12

ladies, I'd have taught the scoundrel a lesson."

Georgiana suppressed a smile. "I'm sure you would, Sir Robert."

"Wait until he comes before me on the bench. Hanging's too good for the blackguard."

Georgiana couldn't resist. "Don't you have to catch him first?"

It was perhaps as well this remark went unnoticed. Revelling in the fermenting cauldron of his fury, Sir Robert took little heed of anyone else. His next words gave Georgiana a jolt.

"I'm afraid we shall need to trouble you for a horse, Miss Grey. One of ours has gone lame."

Georgiana felt the colour drain from her face. "I'm sorry to hear that, Sir Robert," she replied, wondering how she kept her voice steady. "Unfortunately, I don't think I have anything suitable."

"Now, you needn't worry," said Sir Robert, in a tone not unlike an indulgent uncle. "My man will take care of that."

"What do you mean?" asked Georgiana, praying the dread pressing down in her stomach had not transmitted itself to her face.

"I sent my groom to your stables to have the lame creature tethered and find something to pull our carriage the rest of the way." He held up a hand. "Pray don't concern yourself. I'm sure he'll find one of your people to help him. Your modesty does you credit, but I will say this: considering you don't have a husband to advise you, you've been very fortunate with your choices of horseflesh, very fortunate indeed. You have some remarkably fine beasts. I'm sure that fellow of mine won't have any trouble finding something suitable."

Had Georgiana been of a swooning disposition, there could not have been a more opportune moment to indulge it. She could only grit her teeth and smile, accepting the role of sympathetic hostess which had been thrust upon her. Torn

13

between anger at Sir Robert's high-handed action and fear Princess would be recognised, she listened with polite inattention to her visitors' woes, grateful for her cousin's fluttering concern as her own mind darted from one impossible scheme to another for ensuring neither groom would open Princess's stall.

"That scoundrel had better hope he doesn't meet me again." Sir Robert's booming voice broke in upon Georgiana's thoughts. "I shall know how to deal with him. I'd have done it tonight, only for the ladies." He twisted awkwardly, pulling the folds of clothing at his waist as he hitched his corset into position.

"Oh, indeed, it's a very good thing you did not!" cried Selina. "Why, just think how much more it would have upset her ladyship and Miss Winters."

"Yes," said Georgiana absently. She was finding Sir Robert's verbosity irritating. How satisfying it would be to let him know what a wealth of evidence she had of his cowardice – but of course that would place a rope around her own neck. She had no alternative but to hold her peace and concentrate on solving the immediate problem.

"Yes, they were already very upset," said Sir Robert, lowering his voice and allowing a solicitous note in. "Quite a fright for them, and all their jewels gone. The rogue took a particularly valuable ring."

A chill took possession of Georgiana's brain. Surely she couldn't have…? Her horrified gaze travelled towards her left hand. The mocking sheen of the ring glinted under the edge of the cup and saucer she held, waiting to betray her. She closed her eyes, mentally cursing herself for such an elementary piece of incaution. Her guests' attention was too focused on their own discourse to pay her much heed for the moment; she seized her opportunity.

In a rapid movement of controlled clumsiness, a twist of

her wrist upturned the cup over her left hand. As her guests turned at her cry, she snatched up a napkin from the tray and bound it around both ring and scalded hand.

"My dear Miss Grey, are you injured?" Sir Robert peered at the tea tray where Georgiana's cup had been deposited with little ceremony.

Miss Knatchbull was immediately out of her seat, anxious to assist. She fussed over Georgiana, eager to examine the injury.

"Please don't worry, Selina," said Georgiana. "Clumsy of me. I would be grateful if you'd ring for James. I'm afraid I shall have to leave you for a few minutes while this is bandaged."

"You must allow me to help you," insisted Miss Knatchbull.

"No, I shall manage well enough. Please stay and attend to our guests."

James appeared, and looked in some puzzlement at the disarray. He accepted without question his mistress's request to clear up the mess and bring some fresh tea. His sister, on the other hand, gave a gasp of alarm when Georgiana appeared in her bedroom and unwound the napkin from furiously red skin.

"It's nothing, Emily. Don't worry."

"Nothing! That's a very nasty burn, miss. What on earth happ...?" As she caught sight of the ring, Emily's eyes widened. Georgiana nodded.

"I overturned my tea cup. It seemed best."

Emily looked doubtful. "Your hand looks horribly swollen. You won't get that off for a while."

"I'll manage." Georgiana lifted the jug on her dressing table and poured some cold water into a basin. "Never mind this, I can attend to it. There's something else I need you to do. Sir Robert's groom has gone to the stables to find a horse."

Emily sank down on the edge of the bed. "We're done for."

"Not necessarily, though it's likely he'll have roused Richardson or a stable-boy. Get down there and distract them.

It doesn't matter how. Just keep them away from Princess."

"Won't it be too late?"

Georgiana shook her head. "I don't think so. They'll settle Sir Robert's lame horse before looking for a fresh one. And Richardson will hardly offer my own mount to pull a carriage."

Emily grabbed a cloak, closing the door quietly for all her speed. Georgiana winced as she laid her hand gingerly in the basin of cold water. The scald had served the purpose, but had been more dramatic than she intended. She managed to stretch her fingers as the water cooled the sting. With careful manipulation, Georgiana gradually removed the ring although the action relit the fire in her hand. She held it under water for a few more minutes, tenderly patting it dry with the towel which Emily had thoughtfully left within reach. The task of dressing her injury with one hand proved more difficult than anticipated, and it took some moments to achieve a satisfactory result. Georgiana returned to the drawing room with a bandaged hand and a stream of apologies.

Her guests showed little more than a perfunctory interest in her reappearance. Lady Winters was drinking tea and Sir Robert had made himself comfortable with a generous quantity of wine. Only Miss Knatchbull and the young Miss Winters demonstrated any degree of concern.

James, discreetly waiting in the background, stepped forward and asked if he could pour Miss Grey some fresh tea.

"Yes, please, James. Thank you for tidying up."

"I wouldn't have thought it necessary to thank a servant, my dear," said Sir Robert, as the footman quietly left the room. "He's doing no more than his duty, after all."

As a single woman with her own establishment, Georgiana attracted more than her share of unsolicited advice on how to run her home. "I appreciate your interest, Sir Robert, but I am very well able to manage my household."

Sir Robert frowned. "You know, Miss Grey, that fellow of yours looks familiar. I have an idea I've seen him somewhere before."

Georgiana took a deep breath to quell the rising anger, and spoke with deliberation. "You have, Sir Robert. He appeared before you two years ago. You sentenced him to a year in prison."

The hair on the back of Georgiana's neck bristled as indignation edged through her. She had always felt the injustice of James's conviction. The anger triggered by the travesty of the court had never quite left her, lingering like the cough which James had acquired during his term of imprisonment.

Lady Winters closed her eyes and shivered. "You have employed a cut-throat, Miss Grey? Well! There's certainly no question of us spending the night here. We should undoubtedly be murdered in our sleep."

Georgiana held her breath. "Quite right, Lady Winters, there is no question of you staying overnight," she said stiffly. "Nor is there is any question of James being a cut-throat. He was charged with poaching: the extravagant haul of two trout, as a matter of fact. No doubt you remember, Sir Robert." She smiled sweetly. "He wasn't the guilty party; the culprit threw the wretched fish at him and made his escape, leaving James to face the gamekeeper."

Sir Robert's eyes appeared even more pellet-like. "I do recall something of the incident. You approached me to appeal for the fellow."

"I'm pleased you remember, Sir Robert. I recall you saying justice must take its course, but you did agree to be lenient."

"Of course, my dear, of course. Things could have been worse, you know, whether your man was guilty or not. If I'd sent him to the Assizes, he might have lost his life. Unfortunate if there was a mistake. Still, someone has to take responsibility

– examples must be made." He adopted a confidential tone. "Besides, Miss Grey, these fellows are usually guilty of something."

Georgiana drew in her breath. She had always considered Sir Robert pompous, but this casual dismissal of James's unjust imprisonment showed a callous self-righteousness she would not have expected even of him. It reminded her exactly why she had taken to the road when she saw the kind of justice dispensed in court. She had wanted to teach the powerful a lesson, and had been surprised to discover a talent which had hitherto lain dormant. It had come as a shock to find her illegal activities brought a new excitement to her life which she did not want to relinquish.

Georgiana caught a look of imploring alarm in Miss Knatchbull's eyes. Poor Selina; Georgiana knew she was a trial to her. She often wondered if her cousin would have accepted the role of duenna had she known she would be dealing with a confident young woman used to having her own way. Georgiana held her peace, and gave Selina a reassuring smile

"Of course, when I catch up with that highwayman, I'll make an example of him to drive them all off the roads," Sir Robert informed the company.

"It wasn't just the robbery," said Lady Winters. "His behaviour towards Louisa was atrocious. I've never seen such disgraceful flirting. I quite feared for her virtue."

Georgiana choked on her tea.

"I thought he was rather dashing," said Louisa in a dreamy tone.

"Dashing or not," said Sir Robert, unwittingly saving Louisa from a further slap from her mother, "he must be brought to justice. I'm sure it was that Crimson Cavalier fellow. I'll raise the reward on him. Twenty-five pounds ought to do it."

In light of the retribution Sir Robert threatened, Georgiana found this figure insulting. However, she was spared the need to comment by the arrival of her maid. Emily's demure tone seemed to belong to someone quite other than the forthright girl who had been in attendance upstairs.

"Beg pardon, miss, Sir Robert's carriage is ready."

No one questioned why this message had come from Georgiana's personal maid. The company rose to depart, Sir Robert's waddle more pronounced than when they arrived. He tugged at his corset and turned towards Georgiana. "Thank you so much, Miss Grey," he said, his voice thick with wine.

"Good evening to you, Miss Grey, Miss Knatchbull." Lady Winters breezed past Georgiana, a silent Louisa following behind.

"I'll have the horse sent back as soon as possible," wheezed Sir Robert. "Goodnight, my dear."

As the heavy bolt slid behind her guests Georgiana gave herself permission to feel relief.

"My goodness," said Miss Knatchbull. "What a dreadful experience."

"Yes," said Georgiana. She looked towards her footman, about to enter the drawing room. "There's no need to tidy up now, James. Tomorrow will do."

"But, miss..."

"No, I insist. It's three o'clock in the morning, far too late to worry about it. If Horton or Mrs Daniels say anything, tell them you were following my orders. Go back to bed. I'm sorry you've been disturbed."

James smiled. "Glad to oblige, Miss Georgiana. How is your hand?"

"Sore, but it will do well enough."

"Nasty thing to happen."

"Yes, it was very clumsy of me."

"Goodnight, miss."

"Goodnight, James." Had Georgiana imagined the quizzical

19

look in his eyes? She must have. There was no way he could guess the truth, and Emily was no tale-bearer, not even to her brother.

Georgiana turned towards her cousin, waiting patiently at the foot of the stairs.

"You too, Selina. You must be exhausted."

"Oh, I am well enough, Georgiana. But your poor hand. Is there anything I can do?"

"No, don't concern yourself."

"Good heavens, how can I not concern myself? Isn't that why I'm here, to take care of you?"

Georgiana closed her eyes, not speaking immediately. She knew Selina meant kindly, but sometimes she found it a little overpowering. She had wanted her own life and the need for a female relative to lend her countenance rather curtailed this. Not that there was any escape; she cared little for gossip, but to be ostracised from society could have unpleasant consequences. Selina Knatchbull was generally an inoffensive creature, anxious to please – a consequence of being the only child of a clergyman in reduced circumstances, Georgiana supposed. It was an upbringing which promised few prospects and little reason to put herself forward. However, she was inclined to fuss, a quality which irritated Georgiana intensely. Looking at Selina now, Georgiana responded teasingly, "Really, cousin? I thought you were here to make me respectable."

Selina looked shocked. "Why, Georgiana, I hope I am more use than that."

"Yes, of course, you are, Selina, only do, pray, go to bed. If you are not tired, I am."

"Of course. What a goose I am. Goodnight, my dear."

Georgiana allowed her cousin to go up ahead of her, and picked up the candle from the hall table to follow. Exhaustion and the fire in her hand began to get the better of her.

Emily was waiting in her bedroom.

"You managed it?"

Emily nodded. "I had to promise to spend my afternoon out with him." She eyed her mistress hopefully. "Would that be my normal afternoon, miss?"

Georgiana smiled. "No, of course not, Emily. Did you have any difficulties?"

"Mr Richardson didn't seem too happy about me being there. But I managed to keep them away from Princess. They didn't even notice. You were right about the drink, the coachman had definitely had a drop in."

"Not surprising."

A mischievous grin hovered about Emily's mouth. "He wanted to tell me how he stood up to the Crimson Cavalier."

Georgiana let off a peal of laughter. "The number of brave men on that coach is quite overwhelming. I feel fortunate to have escaped."

Her scalded hand was the only further threat to her night's rest. Georgiana fell asleep immediately, and did not rouse until Emily appeared with her chocolate at ten o'clock.

She stretched her arms, and her left hand rebelled against the movement. She was going to suffer for the impulse of the previous evening. The injury had stiffened overnight and the scald had given birth to a collection of tiny needles pressing against her skin.

"You should send for the doctor," said Emily, opening the curtains.

"Certainly not. I am not such a poor creature."

"It could turn nasty."

"What a joy you are, Emily."

A day of unusual tedium followed; all of Georgiana's servants seemed determined to cosset her into the invalidity she had scorned. An attempt to discuss the household accounts with her housekeeper brought forth all Mrs Daniels's

21

maternal solicitude. Any exertion triggered a willing servant or the over-protective Selina to take the strain from her. Her achievements for the day consisted of writing a letter and reading two chapters of a novel from the circulating library.

By dark the boredom was more unbearable than the pain of her hand. She itched to escape to the road, and ignored Emily's protests about the unwisdom of venturing out on two consecutive nights. Some delicate manoeuvring as she changed her clothes kept the bandage undisturbed. Disapproval piercing the silence, Emily tied the mask into place, and Georgiana stowed her pistols and picked up her hat.

Cavendish Square was quiet, and Georgiana was grateful for the erratic lighting outside its few occupied houses. She met no one as she and Princess picked their way carefully through the streets towards the Bath Road.

The moon was full, and she kept out of its betraying light as she gazed along the length of the road, looking for the Mail Coach.

Her eye caught something in the road, and she peered down for a closer look before slowly encouraging Princess forward a few tentative steps. Her heartbeat increased as she listened for signs of a trap; there was no sound, and she dismounted, looking about cautiously before approaching the inanimate figure which lay face down. She knelt and with one final quick glance around, turned him over towards her.

She looked at her glove. Moisture glistened at her fingertips.

Sir Robert Foster's unseeing eyes stared up at her.

2

Instinctively, Georgiana checked Sir Robert's pockets. Irritated to find her hands shaking, she paused, clenching her fists to regain control. Taking a deep breath, she resumed her task, carefully averting her gaze from Sir Robert's greying face. As expected, nothing of value remained. The area was notorious for highway robbers. Georgiana had often been astounded at the number who seemed to operate in the same area with so little apparent rivalry.

Sitting back on her heels, Georgiana frowned. She knew Harry Smith worked this stretch of the road, but murder wasn't his style. In fact, most highway robbers wouldn't shoot unless provoked. In her experience, co-operative travellers were allowed on their way, sometimes with thanks, and in one case of which she had heard, even an apology.

Georgiana looked back to the recumbent figure in front of her. What was he doing out here by himself? The whole thing was decidedly odd, and the well-born lady of the road could smell a rat.

Swallowing her distaste, Georgiana continued searching the body, avoiding the incriminating red stickiness which gradually spread over Sir Robert's waistcoat. Finding no weapon about his person, she raised her head to look into the still night. There was no sign of a horse. Georgiana could only assume it had bolted when its owner was shot.

With the forefinger of unease tantalising the back of her neck, Georgiana's sense of self-preservation urged her to escape. Yet conscience held her rooted to the spot. She had not liked Sir Robert Foster, but could not bring herself to abandon his lifeless body with no more concern than a broken branch blocking her path. The death had to be reported. How to do so was the difficulty. She bit her bottom lip thoughtfully. Could the thing be done anonymously? Georgiana wasn't sure if this was feasible, but it would be the ideal solution. She had no wish to devise a creative explanation for her presence on the Bath Road at this time of night.

The dark silence was broken by a rattle vibrating through the road. Georgiana stood, sensing her quandary was resolved. As the carriage approached, she moved swiftly to her horse. She took hold of the reins, flinching as she absentmindedly began to twist them around her left hand. The slip cost precious seconds. Georgiana cast a look along the road as she bent to retrieve the ribbons from under the animal's neck. Her reward was the sight of a coach bearing down hard upon Sir Robert's still form, horses protesting against its sudden halt. Georgiana needed no further encouragement. While the darkness was her friend, the least sound could arouse the travellers' suspicions. Tugging the reins insistently, Georgiana began to walk Princess away from the road, towards the few trees offering cover. On the moonlit road, she saw two figures leap from the carriage just as she hauled herself up to the saddle. She turned away, sacrificing speed for stealth. Startled by the sudden brush of low branches, Princess gave a little cry, silencing the babble of travellers' voices. Georgiana bit back her own near scream of frustration. Her erratic heartbeat took on a more insistent quality. She could feel the eyes of the travellers boring into her as they tried to look around in the darkness.

"Who's there? Hello!"

There was nothing else to do. Georgiana urged Princess to a gallop. The cries of "Stop!" and "Murder!" caught her ears.

"Who is it?"

"I'm not sure. One of those highway robbers."

"I saw red on the hat."

"The Crimson Cavalier."

"Untie these horses. Let's get after him."

Georgiana pushed Princess harder, her heart pounding in her ears in time with the horse's heavy footsteps. The report of a pistol cut through the rhythmic sound and Princess reared. Georgiana held her seat with difficulty. The bullet had missed by inches, its whistle remaining trapped in her head. She bent and stroked her horse's neck, offering breathless reassurance.

Concentrated in the shelter of the woods, the hue and cry sounded nearer. Georgiana could not afford to waste time. Taking a deep breath, she urged Princess forward.

Emily had left the candle in the usual place. Its light offered some comfort. Georgiana hastily stabled the horse, rubbing her down quickly, but sacrificing an impulse to do a less than thorough job. She ascended the backstairs swiftly, ignoring the near bursting sensation in her chest. Within a very few minutes, she was locking her bedroom door, flinging her hat across to the bed and turning to face a surprised Emily, engaged in putting away clothes. Her back to the door, Georgiana waited for her heart to steady.

"What's happened?" the maid asked, blank astonishment in her expression as her eyes followed her mistress's movements.

It was a moment before Georgiana's limited breathing allowed her to speak.

"Sir Robert Foster's dead. Murdered. I found his body on the Bath Road." She drew off a bloodstained glove.

Emily gave a horrified gasp.

"No!"

"I'm afraid so. Help me with this, will you? I found him on the road about halfway between here and the Heath. He'd been shot." She winced as the glove dragged over her injured hand.

Emily came to her assistance and watched silently when Georgiana threw both gloves into the fire.

"Were you seen?" Emily asked quietly.

Georgiana nodded. "A coach party. I didn't recognise them." She moistened her lips. "I did hear them mention the Crimson Cavalier. Fortunately, I got away fairly quickly."

Emily paled. "Oh, miss, what are we going to do?"

Georgiana remained silent, looking into the fire as the black gloves took on the glow of orange embers. Her head was spinning. Emily was right. What had begun as an exciting piece of daring suddenly took on a hideous complexion. She pulled off her cravat and began to unbutton her shirt. Emily swiftly removed the boots and within seconds was assisting her mistress into the white cotton nightgown which had been folded neatly under the pillow.

"I need to think," said Georgiana. "The Crimson Cavalier will be blamed for this." She knew she had to keep calm. Panic would be suicidal.

Emily slipped out of the room and returned a few minutes later with a tray bearing a decanter and glass. She filled it and wordlessly handed it across to her mistress. It was accepted with an absent smile as Georgiana sat down on the bed. She drank gratefully, appreciative of the warmth against the shiver she had been trying to suppress. She closed her eyes momentarily and rubbed a cool hand across her forehead. Georgiana was not squeamish, but the shock of finding Sir Robert's dead body had brought a cold reality into her life of adventure. Emily began to tidy away Georgiana's discarded wardrobe.

"You heard no movement outside?" Georgiana said at last.

Emily shook her head. "No." She fell silent for a moment before speaking again. "How well did they see you?"

"Not very," Georgiana responded. "I kept my mask on and got away quickly when I heard the coach. They could only have got a glimpse from the back at best." She paused. "One of them did take a shot, but it went wide."

Emily groaned.

"There's no need to worry," said Georgiana, attempting a reassuring smile. "I'm fine. I think they fired more in hope than expectation. They probably wanted to scare me."

Shaking her head, Emily put away the remainder of the highwayman clothing.

"Well, it scares me, I don't mind saying," she remarked, a worried frown taking shape on her brow. Georgiana glanced at her. Fretting wouldn't help.

"Don't look so anxious, Emily. If they had guessed, surely they would have been here by now."

"Yes, miss." Emily's frown deepened. "But it doesn't mean they won't."

"No." Emily was right, of course. She always talked sense. "I know. One way or another, I shall be blamed." Georgiana took a sip of wine and continued, half to herself. "Even if we manage to keep the Crimson Cavalier's identity a secret, no one will hesitate to shoot me the minute I stop a coach."

"The minute you...? Miss Georgiana, surely you don't mean to go back on the road?"

Lost in thought, Georgiana had been giving her maid little attention. However, Emily's words and anxious expression pierced her mind.

"What? No, of course I can't at the moment." It was to be hoped Emily didn't see through the half-truth. It might be necessary to go back. However, there was no point in both of them worrying about it. She looked towards her maid. "Go to bed, Emily. There's nothing useful to be done tonight."

Emily hesitated, her face reflecting the doubts Georgiana was trying to clear from her own mind.

"Go on," Georgiana urged. "Get a good night's sleep. We'll think about it tomorrow."

Pausing only to remove the hot brick from her mistress's bed, Emily did as she was bid. Georgiana slid under the quilt and lay for a few moments thinking about her dilemma. She had known there would be risks in taking to the road, of course, but that had only added to the excitement. Holding up successive carriages of spoilt aristocracy, often her own acquaintance, offered release from the frustrating restrictions imposed on a woman in her position. The delicious irony had appealed to her sense of humour, especially sharing her spoils with the less fortunate, often neglected, dependents of her victims. The talent she discovered offered a challenge to her ingenuity and she had given very little thought to the possible dangers. Perhaps she had grown complacent. She had certainly never expected any horror such as this. With her brain in turmoil, Georgiana decided she was too tired to consider her problem constructively tonight. She extinguished the candle and turned sideways with eyes closed.

A good night's sleep was not forthcoming, however. Sir Robert's glazed, grey face floated in front of her eyes, dreams of her grim discovery invading what little rest she did get. While Sir Robert's death had not been her fault, she could feel his reproach. Sitting up in bed as dawn broke, she put her hand to her forehead. The night had brought no counsel.

Georgiana reached across and poured some water from the pitcher on her side table, taking a grateful drink before sinking back under the coverlet. It was too early to disturb anyone else in the household. She abandoned all attempts at sleep and stared up at the top of her four-poster bed hoping for inspiration. Emily was right; this looked like the end. It would take every shred of ingenuity she possessed to disentangle herself.

Despite the hour, Georgiana was not surprised to see a well-scrubbed Emily peeping cautiously around the door not many minutes later.

"Come in, Emily. I am awake."

Emily entered the room and closed the door. Georgiana smiled and asked, with a fair idea of the answer, whether anyone else was up. Emily shook her head.

"Well, at least no one's been here looking," said Georgiana.

"Not yet."

"There's no sense worrying until they do," said Georgiana. "We had much better keep calm; it will arouse unwelcome curiosity if we both seem anxious."

"I suppose," said Emily. "Would you like me to fetch your chocolate, miss, or would you rather go back to sleep?"

"I'll have it now, thank you, Emily. I'm not likely to go back to sleep."

Georgiana sipped her chocolate as she reflected on her position. With no one yet beating down the door in search of her, it seemed safe to assume she had not been discovered. However, she knew better than to tempt fate by giving in to waves of relief. She watched Emily take a morning dress from the wardrobe. Even at this moment of crisis, Emily's pride in her work was undiminished. She was unquestionably a first-class maid. Georgiana knew of at least two ladies who had tried to tempt her away. Despite the alarm of the previous night, standards would not be compromised. Looking in the mirror when Emily had finished her labours, Georgiana could not help but be pleased with the result. As she rose from the dressing table, the pale green chiffon morning dress accentuated the effect of the copper ringlets dropped at the side of each smooth cheek, bringing to life the rich green of her eyes.

Emily studied her mistress critically. "You look a bit pale, miss," she ventured.

"Do I?" said Georgiana. "Well, I'll be better once I've breakfasted."

Emily hesitated. "Perhaps a little rouge?"

"That hardly seems necessary," said Georgiana, the barest hint of an edge in her tone.

With her hand still sore from the escapade of two evenings earlier, breakfast was a slow affair. Although James's assistance made matters easier, Georgiana felt the indignity of having her toast buttered for her. The awkwardness of lifting her cup with her left hand gradually became less of a trial, and Georgiana was relieved Selina was sleeping late, freeing her from further fuss. As she perused a letter from an aunt over her second cup of tea, her butler appeared in the dining room.

"Mr Grey has called, miss."

"Oh, bother!" said Georgiana instinctively. What was Edward doing here at this hour? She knew it would be pointless to deny him; Edward was a law unto himself. Nonetheless, the prospect of a brotherly talk over the breakfast table was not one Georgiana found inviting.

"Very well, Horton. Show him in."

Since Mr Edward Grey, apparently in no doubt of his welcome, had already reached the threshold of the room, this instruction proved unnecessary. Georgiana ordered a fresh pot of tea and turned to her brother as the door closed behind Horton.

The resemblance between brother and sister was detectable but not striking. While attentive observers would note an occasional similarity of expression or mannerism, the blood tie between them seemed more distinguished by their differences than any strong likenesses. Edward Grey's light brown hair bore no relation to the stunningly rich auburn locks which made his sister stand out wherever she went. Neither did his pale green eyes offer the sparkle and depth of jewel-like colour which radiated from Georgiana's. Nonetheless, he carried himself well, if a little stiffly, and not the most exacting tailor could fault the cut of his coat.

"Good morning, Edward," Georgiana said as he kissed her cheek.

"Where is Selina?" he inquired.

"Sleeping late. She was rather tired."

Edward's eyes drifted towards his sister's left hand.

"What have you done?" he asked.

"Oh, the silliest thing," she brushed it off. "I knocked over a tea cup. It's nothing."

He studied the bandage. "Have you consulted a physician?"

"No," she said. "Really, Edward, there's no need. Don't fuss so. Do you want some breakfast?"

"No, thank you. I've already breakfasted, at Brooks's."

"Oh." That seemed unusual. However, Edward's movements were not Georgiana's concern. Instead, she turned her attention to the tea brought in by the parlourmaid.

"I'd better pour this. You're obviously not fit to hold it," said Edward, taking charge of the teapot.

"Very amusing," said Georgiana. "What is it you want, Edward?"

"You have a very suspicious streak, Georgiana. Why should you assume I want something?"

"Because it's very often the case that you do. What were you doing at Brooks's at this hour, anyway? Did you abandon Amanda at the breakfast table to feast with your cronies?"

"No, of course not. What a question!" Edward responded hotly, the faintest hint of a flush appearing on his face.

Georgiana smiled as she raised her teacup to her lips. It had never been difficult to rouse her brother to righteous indignation. "I'm only teasing, Edward. I know what an upright citizen you are. How are Amanda and the children?"

Slightly mollified, Edward returned his sister's smile with a degree of genuine warmth. "Very well. You must come and stay with us soon. The children are always asking for you."

"Yes, I should like that," she responded vaguely, her mind drifting back to her own problem.

"As a matter of fact, I have some news for you."

31

"Oh?" No doubt another tale of how Cecily could brush her own hair or how clever young Edward was at Latin.

"You know Sir Robert Foster, don't you?"

His words gave Georgiana a jolt. She moistened her lips, taking a sip of tea before she spoke. Looking across at Edward, she adopted a suitably interested tone, hoping it was sufficiently casual.

"Yes, though not very well. What about him? Has he made an offer for my hand?"

"This is no time for levity, Georgiana. Sir Robert Foster has been murdered."

Georgiana set down her cup, her expression a picture of stunned disbelief. It was a moment or two before she spoke again.

"Murdered? Why, he was here only two nights ago."

"Really?" said Edward in some surprise.

"Yes. It seemed he had been out with friends and they'd been held up by a highwayman. It must have been two o'clock in the morning when they roused the household." She paused, looking thoughtful. "Poor man. What happened? How did you come to learn of it?"

"I've been with some of the magistrates. They think the Crimson Cavalier killed him."

Georgiana gave her brother a measured look. It was better to know the worst now. "Is that likely? Sir Robert and his friends seemed to think the Crimson Cavalier held up their coach the previous night. Would he choose the same victim two nights in a row?"

Edward shrugged. "Sir Robert was found on the Bath Road between the outskirts of London and Hounslow Heath. The Crimson Cavalier has been seen there several times."

"Yes, but that does not mean –"

"A highwayman was seen running away from Sir Robert's body," Edward interrupted, oblivious to Georgiana's having spoken. "There were some people in a coach returning from some party or other."

"But, Edward, it could be any highwayman," she objected.

"These people seemed very sure. They even gave chase, but he escaped. Still, he'll be caught. The reward's been raised to fifty pounds."

A cold, uneasy feeling began to take hold of Georgiana. Why was Edward so concerned with this? She smiled. "So you called to tell me about Sir Robert."

"Well, yes, partly," he said, his embarrassed manner ill-concealing an escaping shaft of pride. "You see, Sir Robert's death has left a vacancy on the magistrates' bench which I may be asked to fill. My help may be needed in capturing the Crimson Cavalier."

"You?"

Georgiana's involuntary exclamation triggered an expression of deep offence on Edward's countenance.

"I beg your pardon, Edward, but how can you possibly go about such a thing?"

"I am acquainted with a Bow Street Runner."

"You – you are acquainted with a Bow Street Runner?" she uttered in strangled accents. "How did that happen?"

"I reported the matter when you and Selina were held up by that highwayman."

"You did?"

"Yes. Opportunities have occasionally arisen to offer help to the magistrates. Perhaps that's why they've suggested me for the vacancy," he said proudly. "I'm sure this Runner will be glad to help."

"No doubt."

This was all Georgiana needed to hear to brighten her day. Her own brother aiming to bring her to the gallows with the aid of a Bow Street Runner. If Edward only knew… Georgiana could picture the look on his face, and despite her own troubles, found it almost impossible to suppress a smile.

Miss Knatchbull's entrance gave Georgiana an opportunity to school her features. Edward rose, moving to pull out a chair for their cousin, who seemed flustered at entering while they were in the middle of a conversation.

"I could not believe the time," she said in apologetic tones. "I do wish you had sent someone to wake me, Georgiana."

"I thought you needed the rest," said Georgiana. "After being disturbed the other night, you still rose early yesterday morning."

"Indeed, but nevertheless..." Selina turned to Edward. "I expect your sister has told you about our excitement the other night."

"She has," said Edward, "though she didn't describe it quite like that."

"Poor Sir Robert," said Selina. "It must have been a dreadful experience. I recall how frightened I was when that highwayman held up our carriage."

"Yes," said Georgiana, "though he was quite harmless, even polite, once we had handed over our jewels."

"That is true," said Selina. "Although it was no less distressing for that. I still can't believe we got the jewels back. I never could understand how you contrived it."

"It's easy enough to advertise for the return of such items," said Edward, to Georgiana's relief. "Quite common, in fact, as long as a reward is offered."

Georgiana waited for him to mention Sir Robert's death, but it did not happen. Clearly he intended his sister to give Selina the news.

"Incidentally," he said, "Amanda wanted me to ask you both to dinner on Friday. You will come, won't you?"

Miss Knatchbull clasped her hands together, clearly enchanted by the prospect. Georgiana felt less enthusiastic. There was something irritating about Edward's casual

34

assumption, and it was typical of him to imagine she had nothing else to do. "I don't know, Edward. I expect to be rather busy this week."

"But, Georgiana…" interpolated Miss Knatchbull.

"Nonsense, Georgiana. What can you possibly be doing? You must come."

Georgiana looked at her brother with sudden suspicion. "Must, Edward? Why?"

"Georgiana, really! What a question. Is it so abnormal for members of a family to have dinner together?"

"Indeed, no," said Selina. "It sounds quite delightful."

Georgiana was still watching Edward. "Every time you invite me to dinner it is with the intention of introducing some eligible suitor or other. Who is it this time?"

"Really, Georgiana!"

"Who?" she demanded.

"Well…" Edward looked towards his sister, as if considering how to respond to her accusation. "Amanda's cousin Bartholomew is paying us a visit."

"Bartholomew Parker?"

"Yes."

"No, Edward, absolutely not. I have no wish to offend Amanda's relatives, but no!"

Selina gave a shocked gasp. Edward persevered.

"Don't be absurd, Georgiana. He's perfectly respectable and would be very glad to see you."

"I daresay, but I should not be glad to see him. Honestly, Edward, why must you and Amanda persist in trying to marry me off?"

"I've often thought Lord Bartholomew seems quite amiable," said Selina, trying to keep the peace.

"Then you marry him," Georgiana retorted.

"Really, Georgiana! I can't see why you are so opposed to marriage," said Edward.

"I'm not particularly opposed to it. I just don't consider it necessary to my comfort. Uncle George left me very generously provided for, as you well know, so I have no need to marry for money. I have a fine home, our cousin for company, excellent servants and am my own mistress. I find that a perfectly satisfactory arrangement."

"But you're three-and-twenty."

"I have no need of you to tell me my age, Edward." She paused. "It's always bothered you, hasn't it, Uncle George leaving me this house and a legacy?"

"You're being absurd, Georgiana. Granted, the man was always eccentric, but why should it bother me?"

"Perhaps because it gave me the chance to be independent and set up my own establishment? Do you imagine I don't know you tried to move heaven and earth to break his will?"

Selina looked from one to the other, desperately anxious to calm the situation.

Edward's colour had heightened, though whether from anger or embarrassment was difficult to tell. "Nonsense."

Georgiana looked at him sceptically. She shook her head. "You've never liked me making my own decisions."

"Perhaps if you weren't so wilful –"

"No, it isn't that. You'd just prefer me to defer to your brotherly wisdom a little more often. Now, fascinating though this conversation is, I'm afraid you'll have to excuse me. I have a rather busy day ahead." Georgiana rose from the table. "Forgive me if I don't see you out. Ah, James," she said to the approaching footman as she left the dining room, Selina and Edward in her wake. "My brother is just leaving. Would you be good enough to fetch his hat and cane? Then send Emily to my room, please, and order the carriage. I'm going out for a while."

"Yes, miss."

"Where are you going?" demanded Edward as James

departed to carry out his instructions.

"That needn't concern you, Edward."

"Nonsense. I can take you wherever you need to go."

"That seems an excellent plan," said Selina. "I shall just fetch my bonnet and pelisse."

"Goodbye, big brother." Georgiana stood on tiptoe to give him a kiss on the cheek. "Thank you for calling. Do give my love to Amanda and the children."

"What about Friday?"

Georgiana paused on the stairs and gave him a despairing look.

"Don't expect me, though Selina may go if she wishes." She turned to go up the stairs, leaving her two relatives staring after her.

Emily was waiting as Georgiana closed the door of her bedroom and leaned back against it, taking a deep breath.

"What is it, Miss Georgiana?"

"We have a difficulty, Emily. My brother had some news for me."

"Oh?" Emily's expression was wary.

"It appears Sir Robert's death has left a vacancy on the magistrates' bench, a vacancy which my brother expects to fill."

"But…"

"Exactly," nodded Georgiana. "My elder brother will be trying to bring me to the gallows. It's as I thought. As far as the authorities are concerned, the Crimson Cavalier is guilty of the murder. It only remains to find him and Edward has a Bow Street Runner to help."

"Lord save us."

"They've even raised the reward."

"What are you going to do, miss?"

"There's only one thing I can do," said Georgiana. "Find out for myself who killed Sir Robert Foster."

3

Emily's mouth dropped open. She looked at Georgiana as though fearing her mistress had taken leave of her senses. It was a full minute before she spoke.

"You're not serious?"

"Of course. You don't think I'd joke about a thing like this, do you?"

Emily blinked. "But trying to find the killer yourself?"

"What else can I do?" said Georgiana. "The authorities have already made up their minds. It's unlikely they'll look for anyone but the Crimson Cavalier. The verdict will be settled before the trial. I can't wait here sewing samplers and paying morning calls until that Bow Street Runner knocks at my door." Georgiana shook her head. "You of all people should know that. I have to make a push to save my neck. You've said yourself often enough, some stroke of ill luck might prompt someone to recognise me. If that happens, I won't have a prayer, and the real killer will melt away somewhere."

"I know," said Emily, a furrow between her brows. "But this is just as dangerous, maybe more. If someone has killed once…"

"Yes," said Georgiana, who had been trying to ignore that aspect.

"In any case," continued Emily, "what can you do? How can you find out anything? You can't go wandering about unescorted asking questions. Even if your cousin were to accompany you…"

"This is no time to worry about social niceties," said Georgiana. She glanced towards her maid, aware her tone sounded irritable. "I haven't quite decided how to go about it… Sir Robert must have had enemies," she continued thoughtfully.

"Certainly one enemy," commented Emily.

"Yes," said Georgiana. "The sentences he administered on the bench would win him few friends. As for the way he treated his tenants…"

"There's not many'll be sorry to see him gone."

Georgiana stood frowning. "I can't imagine someone of the road had anything to do with his death."

Emily gave a short laugh. "Being one yerself, Miss Grey."

"No, seriously, it doesn't make sense. He had nothing of value. I checked. I grant you, he may have been robbed, but there would be no reason to shoot if he handed over everything."

"Maybe he resisted," offered Emily. "Held up by a highwayman two nights in a row could have been too much for him. He complained the night you stopped his coach, didn't he?"

Georgiana smiled and shook her head. "Yes, but it doesn't seem likely. He was full of noise and bluster, perhaps even something of a bully, but the Sir Robert I held up was not particularly brave. I've seen a blancmange shake less."

"Well, I expect some shoot just for the sake of it."

Georgiana looked at her maid and considered the point dispassionately. It was a possibility, but rare among highway robbers. She shrugged.

"You could be right. I'd better have a word with Harry. I can't do that before nightfall." Glancing across at Emily, she asked, "Does that coachman of Sir Robert's still want to take you out?"

Emily nodded, with a slight grimace.

"When are you supposed to be meeting him?"

"Tomorrow afternoon," replied Emily. She hesitated. "Though if the household is in mourning…"

"I don't imagine he'll change his plans," observed Georgiana. "Sir Robert was not an individual one would expect to inspire devotion in his staff. The man may be glad of an excuse to sneak away."

"Perhaps," said Emily doubtfully.

"You know what to do?" inquired Georgiana.

"Oh, yes," said Emily. "Though keeping him at arm's length could be tricky."

"I know. I'm sorry to put you through this, Emily." She paused, looking thoughtfully at her maid. "If you'd rather not..."

"Oh, I can handle any man." Emily gave a shrug of resignation, smiling slightly. "Don't worry, miss. I'll survive."

"The main thing is to learn as much as you can about Sir Robert."

"What about you, miss?"

"I'm going to visit Lady Winters and her daughter," said Georgiana. "Fetch my bonnet and pelisse, would you?"

"Really, miss?" Emily asked in mild surprise as she went to Georgiana's wardrobe. "Whatever for?"

"They were travelling in Sir Robert's carriage. Lady Winters certainly seemed very friendly with him, so it's possible she, or her daughter, may know something, even though they do not realise it."

"Do you think she'll tell you anything?"

Georgiana shrugged. Despite her high-handed manner, Lady Winters was a gossip. Whether she would share any knowledge with Georgiana was another matter. "I don't know, but some sympathy can't hurt. However, I'm not certain I can visit without my cousin insisting on accompanying me."

Emily smiled. "She does feel so responsible for you." The maid brightened as a thought occurred to her. "I could come with you."

"That would be infinitely preferable," said Georgiana, "but, no, Selina's feelings would certainly be hurt. Think how difficult it would be if she considered you had put her nose out of joint."

"Lord, yes," said Emily.

The object of this conversation made her presence felt at that moment, as a voice called Georgiana's name uncertainly from the corridor. Georgiana smiled at Emily, shook her head and opened the door of the bedchamber.

"Here, Selina."

"I'm sorry to disturb you, but the carriage is ready. Are you still intending to go out?"

"Yes. Has my brother gone?"

Selina nodded. "Right after you left us." She hesitated. "He did not seem very happy."

"Don't let it trouble you."

"But it does, Georgiana. I do hate to see family members disagree. It's so uncomfortable."

"Well, never mind. Think how much worse it would be if we lived under the same roof."

Georgiana glanced towards Emily, waiting patiently in the bedchamber with her mistress's pelisse over her arm. Selina stood twisting her handkerchief between her hands, looking nervously at Georgiana.

"Would you like me to accompany you wherever it is you mean to go?" she asked in an uncertain tone.

Edward's gift for avoiding anything of an uncomfortable nature meant that it was unlikely he had mentioned Sir Robert Foster's death to Selina. However, it was inconvenient for Georgiana, making it difficult for her to question Lady Winters and her daughter with her cousin present. Selina continued her handkerchief wringing; there was nothing to be done but accept gracefully.

"Why certainly, Selina, I should be glad of your company. But I have no wish to impose if you have something else to do."

"Impose? Georgiana, what a notion. I'm sure you could do no such thing."

"I don't expect you to be at my beck and call," said Georgiana.

41

"You're my cousin, Selina, not one of the servants."

Miss Knatchbull seemed cowed by this admonition. Georgiana's conscience was pricked, but by taking advantage of her cousin's hurt feelings, Georgiana could perhaps pay her morning call alone. Georgiana shrugged and walked towards Emily for her bonnet and pelisse. "Join me or not as you please, Selina. I must go."

Clearly intimating she was not wanted, Miss Knatchbull mumbled something about needing to sew the flounce of a skirt. She walked slowly towards her room, a suitably affected manner demonstrating the slight she felt. As Georgiana left her own bedchamber, Emily joined her in the doorway, glancing down the hall after Miss Knatchbull.

"She'll be difficult later," observed the maid in a low voice.

"Yes, but what else could I do? Can you imagine what a hindrance she would be in Lady Winters's drawing room when I'm trying to find out about Sir Robert?"

"I'll try to calm her down while you're out."

"Thank you, Emily. You're a treasure."

Emily looked again at her mistress, another thought occurring to her. "Won't Lady Winters think it strange, you calling on your own?"

"Perhaps. But there's nothing odd in visiting to see how they do. My cousin is otherwise occupied, and I will have a groom with me."

Emily nodded. "Good luck, miss."

Georgiana smiled her thanks and went swiftly down the stairs to the waiting carriage.

Lady Winters proved to be away from home. However, the butler understood Miss Winters was in the small parlour if Miss Grey would care to see her.

Miss Grey did indeed care to see Miss Winters. As she watched the butler's retreating form, Georgiana mused on the opportunity provided by the absence of Lady Winters.

Louisa was unquestionably more approachable, but Georgiana doubted whether the girl would be as well informed.

The formal tones in which the butler stated that Miss Winters would be pleased to see Miss Grey contrasted with Louisa's own greeting. She came forward enthusiastically, barely able to contain herself, a warm smile of pleasure lighting up her face. Her pale blue morning dress complemented the cornflower of her eyes, and the daylight set off her soft gold curls. Her sketch book was laid carelessly aside on the sofa.

"Miss Grey! How good of you to call. Mama has gone out, I'm afraid. I'm sure Baxter told you that. Would you like some tea?"

"Thank you, Miss Winters. I should like that very much. I'm so sorry, I'm interrupting you."

"Oh, no, it's of no consequence," said Louisa, gathering up her sketching. "Baxter, would you arrange some tea for us, please?"

"Certainly, miss."

"I don't know where Mama keeps the key to the tea caddy," Louisa confided, "but I'm sure Baxter knows. He seems to know everything."

"Butlers are remarkable like that."

"Yes, aren't they? Won't you sit down?"

Georgiana accepted the invitation with a smile, watching Louisa's efforts to play hostess; it seemed she was unaccustomed to receiving guests on her own. Georgiana sensed knowledge gleaned from close instruction by a meticulous governess.

"My cousin sends her apologies and asked to be remembered to you. I am afraid she is otherwise occupied this morning."

"That was kind of her," said Louisa, blankly.

"We wondered how you and your mother were faring after your unpleasant experience the other night," Georgiana inquired.

"Oh, the highwayman! Yes, we are quite well, thank you." She paused, glancing at Georgiana from under her lashes.

Apparently deciding she could be trusted, the girl continued, "It was a little frightening at first, but he was very polite." A slight blush began to suffuse her porcelain complexion. "Quite gallant, in fact. I'm sure he wouldn't have hurt us. I – I believe it was the Crimson Cavalier. Mama and Sir Robert seemed to think so."

This was ideal. With no need to cast around in her mind for a means of introducing the subject of Sir Robert, Georgiana opened her mouth to speak. She was too late.

"Have you ever encountered the Crimson Cavalier, Miss Grey?"

The question took Georgiana by surprise. "What? Oh, yes, I have come across him."

Louisa looked dreamily past Georgiana, forgetting the tea tray which had been placed between them. "Did you not find him quite charming?"

The maid who had brought the tea goggled as she stood awaiting an instruction to pour. Georgiana smiled at her.

"Thank you. We can manage."

With a look of grudging disappointment, the maid dragged herself away reluctantly. As the door closed, Louisa remembered the existence of the teapot and carefully poured out two cups, handing one to Georgiana with earnest concentration.

"I'm not sure that's precisely how I'd phrase it," remarked Georgiana in answer to Louisa's question.

"I thought he was so dashing and fearless. What do you think makes a man take to the road, Miss Grey?"

The question caught Georgiana off guard. How on earth could she answer it?

"Oh, a variety of reasons, I imagine. Hardship, anger, desperation, boredom."

"Boredom?"

Georgiana knew she was on dangerous ground. "Why, yes," she said, in cautious tones. "I imagine there are times when boredom must play a part."

"I've never thought about that." Louisa gazed ahead, her chin propped on her hands. "I can understand it, though. It must be such an exciting life," she mused. "Can you imagine?"

"Vividly," said Georgiana. "Miss Winters —"

"Oh, please, call me Louisa."

"Thank you. Louisa. I suppose you've heard the sad news that Sir Robert was killed last night?"

"Yes." Louisa's face was immediately composed into solemn expression. "Yes. It was quite horrid, wasn't it? But I'm sure the Crimson Cavalier wouldn't have done it. He was too much the gentleman."

There was some comfort in having one champion, although Georgiana was growing tired of doe-eyed young ladies sighing over the Crimson Cavalier. A highwayman could afford to be blunt. Miss Georgiana Grey had to be more circumspect. She looked thoughtfully at the girl. There must be some way of getting her off the subject.

As Louisa gave her visitor a shy smile, Georgiana realised she was being adopted as confidante. The situation offered mixed blessings, but the peculiarities of her predicament forced her to take advantage.

"He seemed so much more exciting than the gentlemen one usually meets, you know, the *eligible* gentlemen," said Louisa, an alarming glow in her eyes.

"Indeed…" responded Georgiana. This was becoming a trial. How long could one girl enthuse over someone who, in one fleeting encounter, had taken her jewellery at pistol point? The visit was accomplishing nothing. Georgiana toyed with the notion of making her excuses and taking leave.

"Sir Robert wanted to marry me," said Louisa in matter-of-fact tones.

The sudden change of subject caught Georgiana completely off her guard. It took a moment to adjust her thoughts.

Sir Robert was going to marry a girl barely out of the school-room? He had certainly shown an unpleasantly amorous interest in her on the night of the robbery, but marriage? Had Lady Winters encouraged such a match? An avenue which moments earlier had seemed one of stultifying futility became one of promise.

Taking a deep breath, Georgiana discovered in herself a desire for more tea. She leaned forward, cup poised hopefully in Louisa's direction. She was not disappointed and waited until the girl had finished her careful filling of the two cups before speaking. The few minutes grace had given her a chance to mask her surprise as she formulated her sentence.

"Really?" Georgiana asked, keeping her tone to one of mild interest. "Were you in love with him?" She felt the foolishness of the question even as she asked it.

"Oh, no," Louisa responded airily. "But, Sir Robert is – I mean, was – very rich and I believe some of his land is very close to ours. When he told Mama he wanted to marry me, she thought it would be a good match. He wasn't her first choice. She would prefer me to marry my cousin Max. He is my guardian, with Mama, you know."

Georgiana nodded.

"Anyway, that has never come to anything. Perhaps now Sir Robert is dead, Mama will try again to bring it about."

Louisa's casual manner in speaking of her mother's choice of suitors for her daughter was an odd sensation for Georgiana, used to making her own decisions. Even had her parents lived, Georgiana knew they would never have tried to force an unwilling daughter into an unacceptable alliance, and this knowledge contributed to her resentment of Edward's consistent attempts to take charge of her life. Louisa seemed content to accept her fate. Yet it did not fit with the girl who had seemed so uncomfortable in her admirer's presence a few evenings ago. Georgiana looked at Louisa thoughtfully. What could persuade her to acquiesce to the arrangement? Sir Robert's wealth? Or was it fear of her mother?

"Would you prefer to marry your cousin?" Georgiana inquired.

"Oh, no," Louisa giggled. "Max and I are great friends, but he is just like my brother, besides being quite old."

There seemed nothing to say in answer to this. As Georgiana took a sip of tea, she became aware of Louisa looking at her in slightly embarrassed fashion. Perhaps there was something more. Georgiana smiled encouragingly.

"To tell you the truth, Miss Grey, I – I am rather glad Sir Robert is dead. I did not wish to marry him, but Mama, you know…"

"I know," said Georgiana sympathetically. "I should not have wished to marry him either."

"I know I should not say such a thing," said Louisa, with a sigh. "I daresay you are very shocked."

"Not at all," said Georgiana. "I promise I shall not repeat it. We are all acquainted with people we do not like. It is not a crime, unless, of course, you killed Sir Robert."

"Oh, my goodness, no," Louisa responded with a slight laugh. "I should not be brave enough."

Georgiana's forehead creased into a puzzled frown. Brave was an odd word for the girl to use. Georgiana was about to pursue the point when an interruption came in the shape of Lady Winters's butler.

"Excuse me, miss, Mr Lakesby has called. I informed him her ladyship was away from home and you were engaged with a visitor but he was quite insistent on seeing you."

Having made no attempt to wait until he was announced, Louisa's 'elderly' cousin followed hard upon the heels of the butler.

"Thank you, Baxter. You may go."

It was clear the visitor would brook no argument. If the

squeak of delight emitted by Louisa as she jumped up to greet her cousin offended the butler's dignity, his impassive countenance gave no hint as he silently left the room.

For one so advanced in years, Mr Lakesby had not a single grey hair among his brown locks and his face appeared remarkably unlined. Furthermore, his physique suggested regular sparring sessions at Gentleman Jackson's Saloon. Georgiana judged his age at about thirty, although the stern expression directed towards his young cousin was characteristic of someone older. The realisation that Louisa was entertaining did not appear to soften his mood. Nonetheless, his manners remained unimpaired as he turned towards Georgiana, his elegant bearing accentuated by his perfectly cut coat.

"Max, this is Miss Grey. We stopped at her house after we were robbed. Miss Grey, this is my cousin, Mr Lakesby."

Louisa looked from one to the other and smiled with relief, seeming pleased at the apparent success of an unsupervised introduction.

Lakesby bowed slightly towards Georgiana, looking at her more attentively. He greeted her politely, if not with enthusiasm.

"Ah, that Miss Grey. I am very pleased to meet you."

"Mr Lakesby."

"I am slightly acquainted with your brother, Mr Edward Grey."

"Oh?" Edward had never mentioned it. Still, if the acquaintance was slight, that would explain it. Mr Lakesby certainly didn't seem the type of gentleman her brother would have as a friend.

"I'd like to thank you for sheltering my aunt and cousin after their ordeal," he continued. "I am sure my aunt did not trouble to do so."

The hint of a smile lightened the stern expression of his

eyes. Georgiana suspected he featured in the ambitions of numerous matchmaking mamas. No doubt, as his aunt, Lady Winters would feel herself at an advantage.

"I was glad to help, Mr Lakesby. I'm sure anyone would have done the same under the circumstances."

"I doubt it," he remarked dryly.

Georgiana raised an eyebrow. "Are you always so cynical, Mr Lakesby?"

He shrugged. "Realistic. Come, Miss Grey, surely you were not glad to find my Aunt Beatrice and Sir Robert Foster beating down your door in the middle of the night?"

Georgiana eyed him with scepticism. He gave a wry smile.

"Highwayman or not, I should not regard such a visit as a treat."

Georgiana was surprised at his forthright words. She knew she should make her excuses and depart, but felt some acknowledgement was necessary. "Now poor Sir Robert is dead," she sighed. "It is quite shocking. He was most unfortunate."

"Fortunate it didn't happen sooner," observed Lakesby.

Georgiana blinked, genuinely shocked. "I beg your pardon?"

"You seem a sensible woman, Miss Grey. So we will not pretend he was a popular man."

"Max, you should not say such things," said Louisa.

Lakesby turned to his cousin. "It is hardly a secret, Louisa. I should not be surprised to find any number of people more comfortable since his death."

"Mr Lakesby, Sir Robert Foster was murdered. Does that not concern you?"

"Sir Robert Foster's movements have never been my concern. Why should I concern myself now?"

"But, Max—" Louisa began. A stern look stemmed her outburst; it was clear her cousin did not want her to speak.

Georgiana wondered what the girl had been about to say.

"I understand Sir Robert was on the same road where he was robbed the previous night."

Lakesby shrugged. "Foolish of him to go out on that road a second night. A sensible man would have known better."

"Perhaps he was looking for the Crimson Cavalier," offered Louisa.

Lakesby gave a crack of laughter. "Whatever for?"

"To teach him a lesson. He was very angry, wasn't he, Miss Grey?"

"True," said Georgiana. "He had quite a list of retributions ready. Perhaps he did not wish to wait."

"For what? To call him to account?" demanded Lakesby. "Sir Robert Foster was hardly the man for heroics, especially when he could use the magistrates' bench to exact vengeance. In any case, the time for bravery was when the coach was held up. Little point in looking for a highwayman the day after the robbery."

"Very true," said Georgiana, as though she had not previously been struck by this aspect. She decided she was wasting her time and rose to depart. "You must forgive me; my cousin will wonder what has become of me."

The movement showed the edge of her bandage, catching Lakesby's attention. "Miss Grey, I see you have hurt your hand. Not a serious injury, I trust?"

"Oh, no," Georgiana responded. "It was very foolish; I am quite ashamed to admit it. I knocked over a tea cup and scalded myself."

"Very unfortunate."

"It was the night we were at Miss Grey's house," interposed Louisa, "after the robbery. I expect she was tired."

"Yes, I imagine she would have been," he remarked apparently absently, but something in Lakesby's expression belied his tone.

Time to depart, Georgiana thought, and smiled pleasantly. "Well, the situation was rather exceptional. Now I really must take leave of you. Do give my compliments to Lady Winters and tell her I was sorry to miss her. Pray do not trouble to ring for the footman. I can see myself out."

Lingering in the hallway, Georgiana paused by the looking-glass near the door, eyes fixed on her reflection as she twisted a copper curl loosely around her finger, ears pricked for voices in the drawing room, in the hope of learning something to the purpose.

"Louisa, you grow daily more incorrigible. What I did to deserve to be saddled with the care of you…"

"Max, what have I done that is so dreadful?" said Louisa. "I just gave Miss Grey tea. What is wrong with that?"

"Nothing, except for your unfortunate tendency to let your tongue run away with you."

"I don't," she said indignantly.

"Ah, but you do, Louisa. I live in constant fear of your saying something indiscreet with no one to stop you."

"Miss Grey is a perfectly respectable person. The fuss you're making, anyone would think I was entertaining a gentleman alone. Perhaps you and I ought to be chaperoned, Max."

"Perhaps you ought to have your ears boxed. As for entertaining gentlemen alone, if I ever catch you doing any such thing…"

"Should you be jealous?" she inquired.

"I should feel deuced sorry for him, minx."

"Oh, you are a horrible person."

"I daresay. I have no doubt you'd torment the life out of any gentleman unfortunate enough to admire you. However, my sympathy would not prevent me from ejecting him forcibly from the premises."

"What is it you want anyway? You normally have a reason for coming here."

"I have."

At last, thought Georgiana, wondering when they would come to the point. She gave a quick glance down the hall, to ensure no servant was likely to catch her hovering.

"I thought perhaps Mama had sent you to propose," came Louisa's voice. "You needn't. I shall only say no."

"You shall never get the opportunity. It's bad enough having you as a ward. I can think of no worse fate than to be encumbered with you as a wife."

He paused. Georgiana thought she heard footsteps cross the room.

"Now, what's this I hear about you being infatuated with a highwayman?"

4

Georgiana stayed to hear no more. She had regarded Louisa's fascination with the Crimson Cavalier as nothing more serious than a tedious annoyance, so why Lady Winters was sufficiently concerned to ask her nephew to speak to the girl was a small mystery.

Of greater concern was the attitude of Maxwell Lakesby, apparently not a man who accepted things at face value. The notion that he could leap to the assumption that Georgiana was responsible for holding up the carriage which had carried his aunt and cousin was absurd, but she could believe him capable of divining a truth with fewer pieces of the puzzle than most. This uneasy theory made him a person to avoid, no easy matter if she was to pursue acquaintanceship with Louisa. And it was quite evident Lakesby would not allow his cousin to let slip anything he regarded as an indiscretion.

As she stepped into her carriage, Georgiana found her mind resting on Mr Lakesby for another moment or two. The question writ large in her brain was why he would consent to his cousin's marriage with someone he held in such low regard.

Perhaps he hadn't. In fact, had Lady Winters even told him about Sir Robert's offer? Georgiana had no difficulty in believing Lady Winters as the prime force in promoting the project and suspected there would be sparks between aunt and nephew over the subject. Recalling with distaste how Sir Robert's leering eyes had devoured Louisa's petite form, Georgiana wondered at Lady Winters's equanimity in witnessing such behaviour. Could she be hoping to provoke her nephew into a declaration? Or had she just allowed money to win over propriety?

Georgiana's reflections were pierced by a sing-song voice bleating her name. She looked towards the sound and found her fears confirmed.

"Oh, no. Lord Bartholomew Parker. Drive on," she hissed at her coachman. "Now."

The coachman raised his whip, but too late, and Georgiana found herself facing the unwelcome figure of Lord Bartholomew beside her carriage. As usual, he was dressed with exaggerated care. The points of his collar appeared even more extreme in the wake of Mr Lakesby's understated elegance.

"Ooh – ooh, Miss Grey! I was afraid you wouldn't hear me," he gasped breathlessly as he lurched against the side of her carriage, abandoning dignity in his eagerness to catch her attention.

A forlorn hope, Georgiana thought, smiling with forced politeness.

"Good morning, Lord Bartholomew. I trust you are well? Was there something in particular you wanted?"

"Oh, no, that is, of course, there is always one subject – but on that I shall remain silent for the moment. This is not the time or place."

Oh, please not that, thought Georgiana fervently.

The threat of a marriage proposal from Lord Bartholomew Parker had been looming like a damp depression these six months, all Georgiana's best efforts at discouragement steadfastly ignored. She had suspected on more than one occasion that Edward had virtually promised her hand, her own consent only a matter of form. Yet even with the curse of her brother's approval, some artful arrangements on her part had ensured evasion of capture.

"Well, since there is nothing in particular, Lord Bartholomew, I must beg you to excuse me. I am in rather a hurry."

His lordship seemed not to hear.

"I understand you and your amiable cousin will be dining

with us on Friday."

Georgiana looked fully at him. "I beg your pardon?" she said levelly.

"I saw Edward a little while ago and he mentioned it." His confidence evaporated under her withering gaze.

There was something galling about this man's use of her brother's Christian name, even with Edward married to Lord Bartholomew's cousin. Presumably Edward did not object, but it gave his lordship an excuse for familiarity with Georgiana which stretched her patience. Now, Edward had apparently committed her to his wretched dinner party despite her refusal. She looked at Lord Bartholomew, forcing herself to be calm. Edward's high-handedness was not his lordship's fault.

"Edward mentioned it?"

"Why, yes," said Lord Bartholomew. "He said he had called on you this morning. I must say, I am looking forward to it. Amanda and Edward's cook is quite exceptional."

"I am aware," said Georgiana brusquely. "Unfortunately, I shall not be able to join you, though my cousin may. I find I have another engagement. However, I trust you will have a pleasant evening."

The dismay on Lord Bartholomew's face was comical as he clung to Georgiana's carriage. She looked in some irritation at his stricken expression.

"What? Not – not coming?" said Lord Bartholomew. "Oh, but you must. The party will not be the same without you."

"It's very kind of you to say so. However, I am unable to change my plans. Perhaps another time."

"But Edward was most definite that you would be there," his lordship insisted. "You must come."

Georgiana felt her anger rising. Edward was most definite, was he? She could cheerfully strangle her brother for putting her in such a position. Looking at the annoyingly persistent little man fastened to her carriage, Georgiana drew in her breath. She forced herself to stifle an increasingly strong impulse to favour him with her opinion of her brother's encouragement of his suit. Her voice was remarkably steady.

"Unfortunately, Edward was mistaken. We must have been talking at cross-purposes. I told him quite positively I would not be able to dine with you all on Friday."

"Well, why not?" said Lord Bartholomew, growing petulant. "What is this important engagement that keeps you from your family?"

This was too much even for Georgiana's self-control.

"Lord Bartholomew, that is hardly your concern." The irritation in her tone was unmistakable, but Lord Bartholomew remained oblivious to it.

"How can it not be my concern?" he demanded. "When you are aware…"

"Lord Bartholomew, you have said quite enough. Please let me go on my way." Hands clenched tightly in her lap, she struggled to subdue the impulse to slap him.

"But…"

"Can I be of assistance?"

Lord Bartholomew whirled around to identify the owner of the coolly confident voice interrupting his entreaties. Georgiana could barely hide her astonishment. Maxwell Lakesby stood idly swinging his cane back and forth, his expression one of tolerant amusement.

"You need not concern yourself, sir," said Lord Bartholomew. "This is a private matter."

"In that case," said Lakesby, walking down the front steps of the house in leisurely fashion, "may I suggest you refrain from discussing it on the public thoroughfare?"

"It is of no consequence," said Georgiana. "We are quite finished. Lord Bartholomew was just taking his leave."

"I see," said Lakesby.

Unwilling to accept his dismissal, his lordship's mouth was set in mulish lines.

"What about Friday?"

"Friday?" inquired Lakesby, looking from one to the other of the disputants. "My dear sir, there seems to be some misunderstanding. Miss Grey is to give my cousin and myself the pleasure of her company at the theatre on Friday."

"I – I beg your pardon, sir?" sputtered Lord Bartholomew "Miss Grey is to be of your party?"

"Why, yes," responded Lakesby, coming forward.

Lord Bartholomew drew himself up. "May I ask how you are acquainted with Miss Grey?"

"You may ask, but I fail to see why I should be obliged to answer," remarked Lakesby, absently picking a speck of white thread from the sleeve of his perfectly tailored coat.

Lord Bartholomew struggled for words through his indignation.

Lakesby turned to Georgiana. "Is this gentleman your guardian, Miss Grey? Should I have applied to him for permission before inviting you to accompany my cousin and me on Friday?"

Torn between relief at this unexpected rescue and amusement at being in the centre of such a scene, Georgiana had recovered sufficiently to give a composed reply.

"No, Mr Lakesby, Lord Bartholomew is my sister-in-law's cousin. In any case, I am quite at liberty to make my own arrangements." She turned to address his lordship. "Your pardon, Lord Bartholomew, but it is impossible for me to break my engagement with Miss Winters and Mr Lakesby. It has been arranged for some time." Absolutely seconds, she thought.

"I see," said Lord Bartholomew tightly. He returned his attention to Lakesby. "That does not mean, sir," he continued through clenched teeth, "that I may not take an interest in

Miss Grey's welfare."

"No, indeed," said Lakesby. "I trust all Miss Grey's friends are so gallant. Please don't let me detain you further. I will escort Miss Grey home."

Lakesby's tone, though pleasant and conversational, clearly admitted no argument. With Georgiana smiling in a manner that bade him farewell, there was nothing Lord Bartholomew could do but grit his teeth and continue walking. Georgiana leaned back against the seat and let out a sigh.

Lakesby sauntered towards the carriage. Georgiana smiled.

"Thank you, Mr Lakesby. Your timing was fortuitous."

Lakesby bowed slightly. "I'm happy to have been able to help. It would have been most undignified to have driven home with the poor fellow dragging from your door."

Georgiana laughed. "Slow too, no doubt, with an unnecessary weight for the horses."

"Most uncomfortable for them," commented Lakesby. "I trust you have no need of an escort, Miss Grey?"

"No, thank you, that won't be necessary," she replied.

"Very well, I shall wish you good day," he said. "And look forward to your company on Friday evening."

About to give her coachman the instruction to move, Georgiana paused to stare at Lakesby, taking no trouble to conceal her astonishment. "I beg your pardon, sir?"

"Ah, you thought I was bluffing his lordship?" He shook his head. "Not so. I left my cousin on the point of writing to you. I hope you will accept."

"Oh?" Georgiana responded. "Well, I regret, Mr Lakesby, but I am afraid..."

"Surely you do not mean to disappoint her?" His tone was irritatingly disarming. "She seems quite fond of you. Strange." He smiled. "I beg your pardon, how unflattering. I have no doubt you are an excellent person, but I had rather gained the impression you and Louisa were not well acquainted."

Georgiana could hardly believe her ears. Lakesby's entire manner began to irk her. She felt tempted to tell him to go to the devil.

His assurance was unwavering as he stood, looking at her with the ghost of a smile. She answered it with one of her own, of pure uncommitted sweetness.

"Thank you so much for your assistance, Mr Lakesby. Now I really must be on my way. Good day to you."

The coachman wasted no more time, and the neatly matched greys set forth, leaving Lakesby standing, his thoughtful gaze following until the carriage was out of sight.

"Insufferable man!" Georgiana fumed. "Of all the arrogance. How dare he assume…?" She gazed unseeing at the elegant residences along the route. Having Louisa Winters's confidence could prove useful, but Georgiana could not afford to arouse Lakesby's suspicions, and the notion of acceding to his plans infuriated her. She wondered whether he flattered himself she was pleased to be included in his party. Georgiana was not sure; he probably just enjoyed the jape. With some unease she sensed it would be difficult to deceive him. She would have to be careful. Nevertheless, if Louisa wished to pursue a friendship with her, it would be foolish to let slip the opportunity.

Georgiana wore a preoccupied expression as she absently thanked James for opening the front door. She was surprised when he followed her to the drawing room.

"What is it, James?"

"Mr Richardson was concerned about something, miss, and didn't have an opportunity to speak to you."

"Oh?" said Georgiana, puzzling over why her groom should be conferring with her footman.

"He – um." James gave a slight cough. "He noticed some blood on Princess's rein."

Georgiana became aware of her grip tightening on the back of the chair where her hand had rested lightly but a moment

59

earlier. Cursing her own carelessness, she cast about in her mind for an explanation.

"Really? Oh, dear, how remiss of me. I know what must have happened. I went for an early ride this morning. I did not wish to disturb anyone so attended to Princess myself. Unfortunately, I had difficulty managing with my injured hand and it started bleeding. I had not realised it had marked the reins. Do give Richardson my apologies."

"Yes, miss. I told Mr Richardson that was probably the case."

Georgiana looked at him curiously. Surely he couldn't have guessed? She knew Emily would not have betrayed her confidence. However, James was no simpleton. Georgiana knew she was not anyone's first idea of a highway robber, but had occasionally suspected he noticed more than he allowed anyone to think.

Forcing her mind in a different direction, she turned her attention towards her acquaintances on the alternative side of the law. Apparently accepting her mistress's determination, Emily made little protest while aiding Georgiana to dress for her visit to the Lucky Bell as dusk fell. Georgiana knew the risk, but needed to talk to Harry Smith.

For all Emily's fears, caution was her second nature, and she kept well out of sight of the road on her way to the inn known as a highwaymen's haunt. She closed the door quickly on entering its sanctuary. Beyond looking to see who had entered, no one gave her more than a glance. Despite the dusty windows and worn furniture, the tavern had a welcoming atmosphere. The brightly lit candles and comfortable warmth were equalled by the ruddy landlord who asked Georgiana her pleasure without indicating he noticed the mask she still wore.

"Have you seen Harry?" she asked.

"Harry Smith?"

Georgiana nodded.

"Not yet. But I expect he'll be in shortly."

Cedric never asked questions of his clientele, a virtue which made him a popular figure. He was careful about what he answered, too. Representatives of the law had often been frustrated in attempts to find out whether he had seen a particular villain in the vicinity, encountering only a blank stare. His customers were loyal in their turn, freely spending the proceeds of their illicit employment while never leaving evidence to connect him with their crimes. Georgiana was no exception. While she did not drink much, her generosity had prompted Cedric on more than one occasion to remark that she "was a real gent, that Crimson Cavalier".

"The small parlour's free if you want to wait," Cedric said.

Georgiana nodded. "Yes. Send in some wine, would you?"

Accepting the two shillings held out to him, Cedric gave a smile of acknowledgement. Georgiana made her way to the parlour and sat in a comfortable, if threadbare, maroon chair next to the fire. She looked up as a rosy-cheeked maid entered, bearing a tray with a bottle and two ordinary glasses a world away from Georgiana's own delicate crystal. She responded to the girl's pert toss of curls with a silent nod of dismissal. Georgiana had had more than her fill of admirers, though the odd coquettish gesture could still raise an ironic smile. She was used fending off amorous overtures from both genders; at least Harry would be no problem in that respect.

She had not many minutes to wait. The door fell open and a sturdy, badly shaven individual stood in its shadow. He cast her a knowing look.

"Oh, ho! So it's my old friend the Crimson Cavalier. I've been hearing some tales about you, my lad."

"I imagine you have," remarked Georgiana, pouring some wine. "How many of them do you believe?"

"Well, not the one about you killing that old beak. When I

heard that one I says to myself, 'Harry, killing's not his game, your young friend's been made a scapegoat, good and proper.'"

"Thank you, Harry."

"Well, everyone knows the Crimson Cavalier ain't never fired a shot. Gets the gewgaws though. Beats me how you do it."

Georgiana shook her head in wry amusement. "The sight of the pistol is usually enough."

Harry shook his head. "I often gets one as wants to do the heroics. Never had to kill anyone, mind. A shot in the air gives 'em a good scare." He took a drink from the glass Georgiana handed him. "What happened with this cove?"

"I found his body."

Harry gave a low whistle.

"Exactly so," said Georgiana.

"Somebody saw you?"

Georgiana nodded. "A coach party. They gave chase, but I lost them."

"You'd best disappear."

Georgiana shook her head.

"I have to find out who killed him."

Harry's surprise was as great as Emily's, although he expressed it with a greater number of expletives. He scratched his head and looked at her through narrowed eyes.

"How do you mean to do that? And what are you going to do if you find him? Hand him over to the beak?"

"I'll worry about that later," said Georgiana briskly. "I've no desire to hang for something I didn't do."

"If a cove takes up as a bridle-cull, it's odds he'll hang sooner or later," observed Harry. "It's only the devil's own luck keeps him alive in the meantime."

"Is that how it is with you, Harry?" she asked, shaking her head as he held up the bottle.

62

"It's how it is with all of us," he said, pouring himself another drink. "Oh, I've had my share of the devil's luck and no mistake. I've nearly danced at the end of Tyburn's rope."

"Really?" said Georgiana. In all the months she had known Harry, it was the first time she had heard of this. "What happened?"

"Slipped a coin to one of the guards," he said simply. "He got me out in a wine cask. Costly business, but worth it. I'd have made no profit as a gallows-bird."

Harry's turn of phrase was always colourful, but underneath his gruff exterior he had a good heart and demonstrated a sense of protectiveness towards Georgiana which made her a little nervous. Yet he never asked more than she cared to reveal. So it was with all the highway fraternity; none would ask another what they had no wish to tell themselves. Despite the risks, Georgiana found it a breath of fresh air. There had been occasions when common sense told her to give it up; she had even tried to do so once or twice. It did not last; something brought her back.

A knock on the door startled both occupants of the room. Harry moved to answer it in guarded fashion, one hand poised for his pistol. They relaxed at the sight of an urchin of about thirteen years of age. He looked even skinnier than he was as he staggered under the weight of a tray laden with cold ham, cheese and bread, as well as another bottle of wine.

"Mistress sent you some supper," said the newcomer.

"Bess is a rare good'un and no mistake," said Harry. "Set it down there, Tom." He flipped a coin to the boy as the tray was deposited on the table. Tom caught it neatly in a grubby hand. The sight of the food reminded Georgiana that it had been some hours since her luncheon. The fare was simpler than that to which she was accustomed, but it looked wholesome. However, although tempted, she could not afford to remove her mask and shook her head regretfully. Tom lingered, hovering by the door as he looked from one to the other.

"Picked up any worthwhile booty?" asked Harry, sitting down as he helped himself to some ham.

Georgiana produced her black velvet bag and emptied the contents on the table. Harry's eyes widened.

"Very nice," he remarked. He picked up Louisa Winters's bracelet, a loving caress of the smooth white pearls belying his professional manner. "Very nice indeed."

Georgiana was watching him dispassionately. "How much, do you think?"

"I'll have to talk to old Ben," he said putting the items together on the table. "Leave them with me."

Georgiana's gloved hand came down on Harry's wrist. She shook her head.

"Now, Harry, wasn't it you who told me never to trust anyone?"

Harry grinned. "Aye, you're right, my young friend." He rubbed his chin thoughtfully. "Something as good faith?"

"How much?" asked Georgiana. Her upbringing had not schooled her in the handling of money, but she had rapidly developed a businesslike approach. She had no need of profit, but her ill gotten gains could be used well, and Georgiana had no wish to appear as a pigeon ripe for plucking.

Harry looked at her speculatively. "Five pounds?" he offered.

Georgiana nodded. Despite her guarded attitude, she knew she could trust Harry. He counted out the agreed price and scooped Georgiana's haul into his own bag.

"I'll do the dealings with old Ben. He's bound to go higher, nip-farthing though he is."

Tom had watched the proceedings silently. He now spoke.

"You didn't kill that old cove, did you?"

"No, Tom, I didn't," responded Georgiana. "But I need to find the person who did."

"I'll 'elp," volunteered Tom, coming forward eagerly. "Just

tell me what you want me to do."

"Thank you, Tom," said Georgiana. "Nothing as yet, but I'll let you know if I need you."

"I'd do anything for you gents," said Tom earnestly. "But I wish you'd teach me about the bridle-lay."

"Now, Tom," interposed Harry, breaking off a hunk of cheese, "we've told you before. You're too young to take to the high toby."

"But I need to know. Don't want to stay here fetching and carrying 'til I'm old."

"Time comes soon enough, lad," said Harry. "The nubbing-cheat's there for us all in the end. No need to rush to the hanging."

Tom began to scowl and seemed inclined to argue. Harry spoke sternly: "Now be off, and see if Bess can spare us another bottle."

"Not for me. I've lingered long enough already," said Georgiana. She looked steadily at her compatriot as Tom left the room. "You will let me know if you hear anything, Harry?"

"Now, you know I'm no tale-bearer," he said in a reproachful tone.

"I'm not suggesting you become one," responded Georgiana. "But after all, this is my neck."

"Aye, I'd be sorry to see you hang," Harry remarked. "Besides, I don't hold with cold-blooded murder, if that's what it was." He narrowed his eyes, looking at her shrewdly. "I'll keep me daylights open."

Georgiana nodded her thanks and stood up. As she picked up her money, Harry noticed the edge of white linen protruding from under her close fitting black gloves.

"Here, what have you been doing to yourself?" he asked.

"It's nothing. A slight accident."

Harry raised his eyebrows. "You want to be more careful."

"Yes, I know," said Georgiana. She pulled her glove taut and smoothed it over the errant piece of bandage. Giving Harry a brief nod, she closed the door briskly behind her as she melted into the night.

5

The elegant white gloves Georgiana drew on less than an hour after leaving Harry proved more effective in covering the burn on her hand than the practical black ones of the Crimson Cavalier. To her intense relief, it seemed all the guests at the select soirée were blissfully unaware of her injury.

"Miss Grey, good evening. How is your hand? Not paining you too much, I trust?"

Chastened, Georgiana turned and met the steady expression of Maxwell Lakesby. She gave him a cautious smile.

"No, indeed, Mr Lakesby. It is much improved, though a trifle cumbersome."

"Perhaps I can assist," he said, coming forward to relieve her of a plate which threatened to upset a precariously balanced glass of ratafia. "Have you everything you need?"

"Yes, thank you," said Georgiana. "I assure you, Mr Lakesby, I can manage well enough. I have no wish to trouble you."

"I beg you will put it out of your mind. It is no trouble. In fact, I would be honoured if you would have your supper with my party. My aunt and cousin are over at that table."

Surprised by the invitation, Georgiana was instinctively wary. Glancing towards the table she had just left, she met the surprised eyes of her cousin. An oath she had sometimes heard Harry use came into her mind.

"Thank you, Mr Lakesby, but I am afraid I shall have to decline. I must not trespass on your kindness, and my own party will be wondering about me."

"Nonsense," said Lakesby, brushing aside her protests. "Surely your friends can spare you a little while? I know the prospect of my Aunt Beatrice's society is perhaps less than enticing, but that should give you reason to pity me. Between

67

her Friday face and Louisa's limited intellect, I am sorely in need of another companion."

Georgiana hesitated. Lakesby was not as high-handed as Edward, but she was disinclined to fall in neatly with his arrangements, setting aside the snub to her own party of friends and the reaction of her cousin. Georgiana's quandary was not helped by the approach of Selina, looking anxious to protect her charge against whatever designs this stranger might have. Georgiana's urge to stifle Lakesby's confident air found a form of expression.

"Selina, I must make you known to Mr Lakesby, Lady Winters's nephew. Mr Lakesby, this is my cousin, Miss Knatchbull."

Lakesby seemed oblivious to the wariness in Miss Knatchbull's manner as he bowed over her hand, professing himself charmed to make her acquaintance. She responded in kind, unbending so far as to inquire after Lady Winters and her daughter.

Lakesby glanced towards Georgiana before smoothly repeating his invitation to Miss Knatchbull. Taken aback at being asked to leave her party, Selina agreed dear Georgiana's demur was quite proper. However, she annoyed her cousin by saying she thought a few minutes at Mr Lakesby's table would do no harm. Indeed, it was only civil to pay their respects to Lady Winters and her daughter.

"Well, it seems the matter is settled," said Georgiana, begging only a minute to inform their friends.

Louisa was delighted to see Georgiana, smiling and immediately moving her chair to accommodate the new arrivals. Lady Winters appeared less eager. Louisa made no attempt to speak, confirming Georgiana's impression that Lady Winters ruled her daughter with iron discipline. The slap her ladyship had given Louisa on the night of the robbery had made its mark with her. While Lakesby attended to Miss Knatchbull's comfort, Georgiana's mind was focused on how she could persuade Lady Winters to be a little forthcoming about her acquaintance with Sir Robert Foster. She decided to go for a partially direct approach.

"It was shocking news about Sir Robert, was it not, Lady Winters?" she said in a compassionate tone. "Just the day after you were all robbed, too."

"Oh, indeed, yes," chirped Selina, to Georgiana's annoyance. "I was so distressed when my cousin broke the news to me. It made me think of what you said about being murdered in our beds, Lady Winters."

"Sir Robert was not in his bed, Selina," said Georgiana evenly, noting with some irritation Lakesby's attempt to stifle a grin.

"No, but for that dreadful highwayman to lie in wait for him is quite appalling. It does make one wonder what they will do next."

"Selina, you don't know if that is what happened," said Georgiana, a slight mocking laugh in her tone. "Indeed, none of us knows the circumstances, except that Sir Robert was found on the road."

"We know a highwayman was seen running away," interposed Lady Winters with cool authority. "I think that leaves little room for doubt."

"But, surely, Lady Winters..." began Georgiana.

"Can we not think of some more interesting topic of conversation than Sir Robert Foster?" said Lakesby. "The fellow was a confounded nuisance alive; must he continue to bore us rigid now he is dead?"

Miss Knatchbull stared at Lakesby in scandalised disbelief. Lady Winters was more forthright.

"Max, that is no way to speak of one who has recently passed away," she reproved her nephew. "You should show proper respect."

"Sir Robert Foster was difficult to respect," responded Lakesby. "I was not alone in my view. I should be surprised to find above half a dozen people who cared tuppence about him."

Louisa gasped. Lady Winters looked at her nephew with horror-stricken disapproval. Miss Knatchbull looked merely horror-stricken. Georgiana was all attention. She looked intently from one member of the party to another. When she spoke, her tone was suitably solemn.

"You were not a close friend to Sir Robert then, Mr Lakesby?"

"I was not a friend to him at all, Miss Grey. Were you?"

Georgiana believed she noticed a thoughtful expression as he addressed her; she could not accept him at face value. She met the challenge squarely, responding without a tremor in her voice. "No, Mr Lakesby. I have met him but a few times. In fact, I had not seen him for a number of weeks before the robbery in which your aunt and cousin were involved."

"I see."

She found his manner irritating, and tilted her head defiantly. "You must own, murder on the public highway is quite shocking."

"Of course," responded Lakesby politely.

"But when someone of one's own acquaintance is involved, it makes the whole thing that much more dreadful."

"If you say so, Miss Grey."

Georgiana sensed she was being mocked. Annoying though this was, even more galling was the obstruction of her every attempt to coax information from her companions. She turned to Lady Winters.

"Did you know Sir Robert well, Lady Winters?"

"We had been acquainted for a number of years," responded her ladyship loftily. "He and my husband were very old friends."

"That must make his death particularly difficult for you,

70

Lady Winters," said Miss Knatchbull sympathetically. "Such a personal loss."

"Yes," said her ladyship. "Sir Robert has been very kind to Louisa and me since my husband's death. It was sad to lose such a good friend, especially in so shocking a manner."

Hearing of Sir Robert's friendship with the late Sir Archibald Winters did nothing to ease Georgiana's distaste over a prospective marriage with Louisa.

"A modest description, Aunt Beatrice," said Lakesby. He turned towards Georgiana. "My aunt had given Sir Robert permission to approach my cousin with an offer of marriage."

"Maxwell!" intoned her ladyship.

"Really?" said Georgiana, a note of casual interest belying her astonishment at Lakesby's revelation. Her eyes caught a fleeting look of imploring terror in Louisa's expression, as well as stunned disbelief in the face of Miss Knatchbull. "How – how unexpected."

"Unfortunately," Lakesby continued, "she neglected to obtain my consent before doing so, a necessary requirement since I share guardianship of Louisa."

"Maxwell, really!"

Lady Winters's scandalised exclamation left her nephew unimpressed.

"Oh, come, Aunt. Miss Grey and Louisa are great friends, you know. I daresay Louisa has already told her about Sir Robert's offer."

Louisa's colour gradually drained from her face, creeping back with rosily overpowering hue

"I – I…" the girl faltered.

Georgiana felt obliged to support Louisa. "Not at all, Mr Lakesby," she said smoothly. "You give your cousin too little credit. However, since Sir Robert's death has prevented the happy announcement of a betrothal, I can assure you of our discretion. Isn't that right, Selina?"

"Oh, yes, indeed," said Miss Knatchbull, who had been silently following the conversation with an expression of increasing uneasiness.

Lakesby gave a slight bow in acknowledgement of this. "Thank you. I was certain you could be trusted."

Georgiana looked directly at Lakesby, a slight challenge underlying her disarming smile. As he met her gaze, Georgiana wondered what was in his mind. In contrast with their first meeting, he was openly volunteering information one would have expected kept private. Georgiana cast a surreptitious look towards Lady Winters's granite expression; her ladyship's eyes were threatening to ignite. The relationship between aunt and nephew was clearly not an easy one; Georgiana watched the two thoughtfully, hopeful this could offer an advantage. Lakesby was undoubtedly the sharper witted of the two. His blue eyes missed nothing. Georgiana shrugged off the unpleasant sensation which accompanied this idea. It was not as if he could read her thoughts.

"I am so very sorry about Sir Robert," remarked Georgiana, returning her attention to Lady Winters. "It's most un-fortunate."

"Thank you, Miss Grey. These things must be borne. Louisa is young yet, and if a mother may be allowed to say so, not unattractive. She will have other suitors. I have not despaired of her making an excellent match." She cast a look towards Lakesby as she spoke, which he appeared not to notice.

"No, indeed," said Georgiana warmly.

Determined to drag the conversation back to her own point of interest, Georgiana was thwarted by her cousin.

"I must say, I admire your fortitude in these trying circumstances," said Miss Knatchbull. "I feel quite shaken by Sir Robert's murder myself, and he was the merest acquaintance. Don't you agree, Georgiana?"

"Yes," replied Georgiana. "I wonder who could have been

responsible?"

"Why, it was clearly that cut-throat, the Crimson Cavalier, or whatever he calls himself," said Lady Winters in a tone of superior knowledge.

"Do you think so, Lady Winters?" said Georgiana. "Surely if the Crimson Cavalier held you up, he would hardly expect Sir Robert to be travelling on the same stretch of road with anything of value the very next night? Besides, even if a highwayman was in the vicinity, it does not necessarily make him a murderer."

"Miss Grey has an excellent point, Aunt Beatrice," said Lakesby, to Georgiana's surprise.

"Oh, really, Maxwell, does it matter? If it was not the same highwayman, it was certainly one of that breed. Every one of them should be brought to justice, regardless of which one committed which crime."

"Ah, a blanket approach to justice," murmured Georgiana in a tone audible only to Lakesby. He caught her eye, challenging her to join in his amusement. She struggled to defy him, aware her own thoughts seemed to be echoing his. Yet his manner galled her. He was too sure of himself, and worse, seemed sure of her.

Georgiana's reflections were interrupted by the sound of a familiar voice speaking her name just behind her. She turned to face the surprised and, she thought, slightly shocked, face of her brother.

Blast him! Georgiana thought, although her tone gave nothing away. Unlike her cousin, she did not manage to greet him with pleasure, though her voice was cool and level.

"Hello, Edward. What are you doing here?"

"I was about to ask you that very question." His disapproving glance took in Lakesby, who had risen to face him. Lakesby forestalled Georgiana's introduction.

"Your brother and I are already acquainted, Miss Grey,

73

although I don't believe he has met my cousin. Louisa, this is Mr Grey, Miss Grey's brother. My cousin, Miss Winters."

Louisa curtsied and gave a pretty, "How do you do". Edward nodded in perfunctory fashion before returning his attention to his sister.

"I have just seen Mrs Woolton. I understood you and Selina were part of her party. I had not expected to find you here."

"I saw Mr Lakesby when I went to fetch some supper," said Georgiana. "He very kindly invited us to join his party for a few minutes. Mrs Woolton knows where we are. We shall be returning directly."

"Oh, yes," said Selina, apparently feeling the need to justify their actions. "We wanted to come and pay our respects to Lady Winters and Miss Winters. They have been through quite an ordeal."

"Yes, I daresay," said Edward, looking anything but mollified at this explanation. "However, I did not know you were acquainted with Mr Lakesby."

"Really?" said Lakesby in a pleasant manner. "Then you have not heard how your sister was kind enough to come to the aid of my aunt and cousin after they were robbed by a highwayman."

"I am aware." Edward's tone was curt. "However, I did not know your acquaintanceship was of such duration as for my sister to have a long-standing engagement for your theatre party."

Selina looked towards Georgiana in puzzlement. Georgiana paid no heed.

"Really, Edward, is this necessary?" said Georgiana with a meaningful glance towards Lady Winters.

"Miss Grey, do you mean to come with us?" said Louisa, clasping her hands together joyfully. "Oh, I'm so pleased."

The sight of her brother's grim expression immediately decided Georgiana. She was tired of Edward's attempts to manipulate the strings of her life, a mission in which Selina ably supported him.

"Yes, Louisa, I should be very pleased to come. And you must call me Georgiana."

"Yes, I shall, thank you. I'm so glad you're coming to the theatre with us. Max was not sure you would."

"Oh?" Georgiana gave Lakesby a curious look and was rewarded with an annoyingly bland smile.

"Will your cousin be joining us?" Lakesby asked, with a polite smile directed towards Miss Knatchbull.

Georgiana replied before Selina could speak. "My cousin has already promised herself to my brother and sister-in-law for the evening. Now, Selina, I have no wish for you to upset your arrangements," Georgiana continued smoothly, "and since I shall be with Lady Winters, you need not make yourself uneasy about having to accompany me."

Selina looked from sister to brother, seeming unable to speak, her expression beyond bafflement. Georgiana gave Edward a sweet smile.

"So you see, Edward, there is no occasion to worry," Georgiana said.

Edward made no attempt to reply and quickly found his attention claimed by Lakesby.

"Incidentally, my congratulations, Grey," said Lakesby.

"What? Yes. That is – I'm very much obliged..." Edward faltered.

Both Georgiana and Selina looked at Edward with puzzled eyes. Lakesby addressed his aunt.

"Mr Grey has been appointed to the magistrates' bench, to the seat vacated by Sir Robert Foster's death."

"Indeed?" said Lady Winters. "Well, I hope you mean to do something about all these highwaymen terrorising the roads."

"I certainly do, Lady Winters," said Edward strongly. "I intend to start with the one who killed Sir Robert Foster."

"There is no proof he was killed by a highwayman," Lakesby pointed out. "I daresay any number of people may have profited by his death. You did yourself, Grey."

Miss Knatchbull gasped, beginning to protest such a notion. Georgiana looked from one man to the other. The notion of her staid brother as a killer was too fantastic to believe. Edward's puce colouring suggested he found it less amusing.

"Hardly a fit matter for levity, Lakesby," said Edward sternly.

Lakesby cast a meaningful look at Georgiana. She made a point of ignoring it.

"I had not intended it as such," remarked Lakesby solemnly. "I merely mention how you have benefited by Sir Robert's death."

"If, sir, you are accusing me of having something to do with his murder..."

"I accuse you of nothing," responded Lakesby in innocent accents.

"Why, the idea is preposterous!" Miss Knatchbull interrupted.

"I was at Brooks's with a party of friends on the night Sir Robert died."

"Odd," said Lakesby. "I looked in at Brooks's myself that evening. I don't recall seeing you."

"Nevertheless, I was there."

"Maxwell, is all this necessary?" said Lady Winters in acerbic accents.

"I should say not, Lady Winters," said Edward with offended dignity. "Georgiana, Selina, I will escort you both back to Mrs Woolton. Good evening, Lady Winters, Miss Winters, Lakesby."

Too stunned to object, Georgiana rose and made her farewells.

"Georgiana, I was never more shocked," said Edward, leading his sister back to her original party. "Do you know

76

anything about that man?"

"He seemed very kind and civil," said Selina in a small, apologetic voice.

One thought stood out in Georgiana's mind. Had her brother been lying to her? It seemed impossible to believe, but oddly enough, Georgiana found she did.

6

Georgiana's argument with Edward was more heated than the usual squabbles born of his attempts to dictate her life. She had never seen her punctilious brother in such a passion. Even now, days later, the memory of his white-lipped face remained vivid before her. A lecture on the ill-advisedness of her accepting Lakesby's invitation had swiftly become an excruciating condemnation of her entire lifestyle. Georgiana had long ago learned to shrug off Edward's stern head-shakings, yet his manner on this occasion had been infected with a maliciousness which startled her, breaking the control she held over her own temper. They parted on very ill terms, and Georgiana thought it likely she and her brother would keep to their separate paths for the foreseeable future.

Dressing for Lakesby's theatre party, Georgiana was able to reflect on the disagreement with a coolness only possible after the passage of time. Her mind went to the meeting between Edward and Lakesby. She had not expected them to be friends, but Edward's heated animosity had clearly sprung from something more than her refusal of his dinner invitation. Was there some old quarrel between the two men? Her brother had refused to discuss it and Lakesby remained maddeningly calm. His casual remark about Brooks's burned in Georgiana's brain. She had no reason to assume Lakesby was telling the truth, but something told her to believe him. Yet why would Edward lie? One could almost suppose him to be harbouring some guilty secret. Such a preposterous notion nearly made Georgiana laugh out loud. Nevertheless, she was uneasy. If Edward was not at Brooks's on the night of Sir Robert's murder, where had he been?

Georgiana's eyes were fixed on her reflection as Emily

dressed her hair. As the maid stood back to cast a critical eye over the effect, Georgiana smiled and nodded. Emily picked up the haresfoot and lightly dusted her mistress's cheeks. As this task was finished, Georgiana heard Miss Knatchbull's voice calling from the landing. Georgiana smiled at Emily and rose, answering Selina as she opened the door of the bedchamber. Her cousin stood at the top of the stairs, arms folded across the brown and cream dress she had chosen for the dinner party with Edward and his wife. Georgiana thought she looked well in it and said as much. This drew a smile from Selina, briefly relieving what Georgiana regarded as the unfortunate effect of a disapproving frown.

"You mean to go ahead with this theatre expedition, then?" Selina asked, clearly hopeful of convincing Georgiana of her error of judgement.

"Yes, why not?" said Georgiana.

"When Edward and Amanda have invited you to dinner?" Selina clearly thought no further explanation necessary.

Georgiana smiled. "I think it's wise if Edward and I don't meet for a while. Poor Selina, I should not wish to subject you to a repetition of the other evening."

Selina blanched. Georgiana could sense her indecision, torn between her duty to persuade Georgiana to dine with her brother and her fear of a quarrel between them. Georgiana took advantage.

"You had best be off, Selina. You won't wish to keep the horses standing. Have a pleasant evening."

Georgiana's quick return to her room left no opportunity for further discussion. To her surprise, she was looking forward to the theatre party. She ascribed this to curiosity, having little hope of obtaining much useful information about Sir Robert. It was clear Lady Winters had no wish to discuss the matter if it did not involve the condemnation of highwaymen in general and the Crimson Cavalier in particular. Louisa was a more

79

fruitful source, but with her cousin's restraining presence and her mama's suffocating one, Georgiana expected little this evening.

Georgiana paused a moment before departing to allow Emily to smooth out the skirt of her gown.

"Thank you, Emily. Would you fetch my cloak, please?"

The rich blue of the hooded cloak which Emily placed about her mistress's white shoulders made a striking contrast to the pale blue of her dress. As it was tied securely under Georgiana's chin, Emily nodded, satisfied.

"Would like me to wait up for you, miss?"

Georgiana considered. She hated keeping her servants up late but it was conceivable she might want to confer with Emily, especially if she did manage to learn anything worthwhile. Her maid's own attempts at investigation had so far proved fruitless. From what Georgiana could gather, Sir Robert's coachman had spent his evening with Emily bemoaning his late master's nip-farthing ways and trying to indulge an unpleasantly amorous streak which accorded with his consumption of alcohol. Efforts to question him had been met with a lack of serious attention which, Emily had told Georgiana, made it clear he thought she only cut her eye-teeth yesterday. The evening had finally ended with Emily giving him a resounding slap and telling him to take himself off.

Whatever forthright opinions Emily might voice, there was no question about her support. Georgiana gave her maid a smile. "Yes, please, Emily, if you wouldn't mind. However, I'd be very grateful if you could discourage my cousin from doing so."

Emily looked doubtful. "I'll do what I can, miss."

Mr Lakesby's carriage arrived promptly, and Lakesby stood waiting in the hall as Georgiana descended the stairs. Noticing his eyes resting appreciatively on her, she could not help but be aware of the perfection of his own attire. His impeccably tailored coat of superfine cloth and satin knee-breeches could not fail to draw approval from the most exacting valet, while his immaculately tied cravat demonstrated just the right balance between taste and fashion. Georgiana found herself unconsciously comparing him with Lord Bartholomew Parker.

Handing Georgiana into the chaise, Lakesby nodded to the driver as he stepped in behind her. Lady Winters and her daughter were already ensconced, each responding to Georgiana's cheerful good evening in more restrained accents. Georgiana suspected Lady Winters did not welcome her presence and had no doubt any sign of pleasure from Louisa would incur her parent's deep disapproval. Georgiana turned towards Lakesby. Seated opposite her, he seemed conscious of her plight and gave her a wry grin. Despite herself, Georgiana's green eyes danced as they met his blue ones.

"Charming weather for the time of year, don't you think, Miss Grey?" he remarked conversationally.

"Yes, indeed," Georgiana responded, struggling with a bubble of laughter. Fortunately for the preservation of her gravity, the journey to the theatre was short. Georgiana resolutely folded her hands in her lap and cast her eyes down.

"How is your hand, Miss Grey?" inquired Lakesby in a more serious vein.

"Much better, Mr Lakesby, thank you."

"I'm pleased to hear it."

The evening was fine, if cool, and the bright light cast by the moon accentuated the brilliance of the lamps outside the Theatre Royal in Covent Garden. Descending from the chaise, Lady Winters espied an acquaintance and imperiously beckoned her daughter to her side. Left alone to walk with Lakesby, Georgiana accepted the arm he offered. As they began to ascend the steps, Georgiana halted in surprise at the sight of Sir Brandon Foster some distance away from them.

"Miss Grey, is anything wrong?" inquired her companion.

"No. Nothing at all." She dragged her eyes away from Sir Brandon and turned to face Lakesby, smiling apologetically. "I beg your pardon, Mr Lakesby." She knew his eyes had followed the direction of hers and was not surprised to see his penetrating gaze studying her face.

"You expected Sir Brandon to be in mourning for his father, perhaps?"

"Well, naturally…," she averred.

Lakesby shook his head. "Brandon Foster is an unnatural son, though considering his parentage, it is perhaps to be expected. He was begat by a most unnatural father."

"Even so, sir…"

Lakesby grinned. "I see you make no attempt to disagree with me, Miss Grey. Excellent. I should be most disappointed if you pretended to be one of those missish females who affects to know little about the ways of the world."

Georgiana regarded him steadily, trying to determine whether a pithy retort was in order. She decided to opt for frankness instead.

"Mr Lakesby, are you deliberately trying to shock me?"

"Shock you? No, indeed," he responded. "Because I imagine you are not as naive as my foolish cousin?"

"You should not speak that way about Louisa," Georgiana said reprovingly. "She has a good nature."

"Most certainly she has," said Lakesby. "But her intellect, Miss Grey! Even you must allow it is hardly what one could call superior."

While Georgiana could not argue with Lakesby's words, she was conscious of the impropriety of his having said it. She withdrew her hand from his arm and spoke in cooler accents.

"A superior intellect is not a necessity, Mr Lakesby. I shouldn't think it will harm her prospects."

"Probably not," he replied.

They had by this time arrived in the foyer where they were joined by Lady Winters and Louisa. As they moved towards their box, Georgiana noticed Sir Brandon flirting with a rather giggly girl who had been enticed away from her mother.

"Mr Foster – I beg your pardon, Sir Brandon. I was so sorry to hear about your father's death." The sound of her own voice surprised her as much as it did her interlocutor.

"Were you?" responded the young man carelessly. "You must be the only one."

Georgiana's eyes widened. She tried not to show her surprise too openly.

"I am sure you cannot mean that," she said with an attempt at lightness. "Of course, it has been a shock and you must be feeling rather stunned."

Brandon Foster gave a mirthless laugh. "Must I? The old man was a tartar. Everyone knew that. I don't suppose there's one person who'll miss him."

"Sir Brandon," said Georgiana, genuinely shocked. "You are overwrought."

Brandon Foster shrugged. "Well, I can't pretend I'm sorry he's gone. We've barely spoken for years. The title and the ramshackle country house are all I inherit. He'd cut off my allowance and left his money and town house elsewhere. Some distant relative."

This was news. It was no secret that Sir Robert and his son did not enjoy an amicable relationship, but Georgiana had not realised the severity of the break. Brandon Foster was known to have a difficult streak; he frequented gaming hells, drinking deep and playing deeper, and his creditors were legion. It was common knowledge that his father had refused to advance him further sums, yet his credit still seemed to be good. Georgiana, among others, was surprised he had not been consigned to a debtors' prison.

"I'm sorry to hear that," she said sympathetically. "Things must be difficult for you."

"I'll manage," he said with an unexpected grin. "I always do."

"Really? How?" Georgiana hoped her tone was one of innocent inquiry.

Apparently Sir Brandon noticed nothing unusual. His grin grew broader. He tapped the side of his head.

"Just needs a bit of thought," he said.

Georgiana's eyes widened. Brandon Foster had never impressed her as a man who devoted much time to thought, yet he spoke with a confidence, almost a swagger. Georgiana could almost believe he had planned on his father's death. But the estrangement seemed hardly enough to trigger a murder, nor his inheritance worth risking the gallows.

Lakesby appeared at her side to escort her to the box. "I should not wear the willow for Foster if I were you, Miss Grey," he whispered in her ear. "He is a poor prospect."

"Yes, I know," Georgiana replied absently. "His only inheritance is his title and his father's country house."

"How do you know that?" Lakesby sounded startled.

Georgiana turned and met his questioning look. She felt suddenly taken unawares.

"He – told me," she said, trying to sound casual.

"Really?" He looked searchingly at her. "I would not have imagined you on such terms with him as to be in his confidence," he remarked coolly.

"I would hardly call it a confidence, Mr Lakesby," said Georgiana, irritated. "It was merely something he happened to mention."

"I see."

The rising of the curtain put an end to further conversation. Georgiana was irritated by the sensation of wanting to justify herself. There was no need for her to explain her actions to Mr Lakesby. It took an effort to concentrate on the first act.

This effort was lacking in many parts of the theatre, where interest seemed to lie more with the vagaries of fashion among the audience than the stage. Lady Winters and Louisa bore their share in this exercise, leaving Georgiana to feel quite sorry for Hamlet, having to endure the trials of an inattentive public as well as his father's troubled spirit.

As the curtain came down on the first act, Georgiana caught Lakesby's eye. He was an attentive host, ensuring his guests were comfortable and well provided with refreshment.

Louisa yawned. "Mama, may I take a turn about outside? It is growing very hot in here."

"On your own, Louisa? Certainly not," responded her mother.

"No, not on my own, Mama. Susan and her mother will be there. It is just the corridor outside the box."

Lady Winters's expression remained stern. "Even so…"

"Oh, please, Mama."

"Oh, very well. But don't be too long."

Georgiana caught the merest hint of suspicion in Lakesby's eyes. However, he made no comment nor attempted to detain his cousin. His attention was claimed barely a minute later when a tap on the door of the box brought a message for him. Georgiana found herself alone with Lady Winters. Attempts at conversation bore no fruit and after a very few minutes, Georgiana abandoned the struggle.

"If your ladyship will excuse me, I think I shall follow Louisa's example and get a breath of fresh air," said Georgiana.

Far from raising any objection to this plan, Lady Winters gave a cursory nod. Georgiana made her escape as speedily as dignity would allow. Moving from the box to the corridor, she expressed a sigh of relief. Her eyes adjusted to the light of a generous quantity of candles, burning at oddly irregular intervals. Even the closeness of the corridor was better than the icy atmosphere of the box. She opened her fan and began to walk slowly, glad of the opportunity to stretch her legs. Suddenly she halted, closed her fan and stood with eyes fixed on the odd little tableau ahead.

Louisa stood a few yards away, clearly unaware of Georgiana's presence. Since the girl was engaged in earnest conversation, Georgiana could not be surprised at this. What did surprise her was the sight of Sir Brandon Foster standing close to Louisa. Georgiana's eyes widened as she noticed Louisa give a quick glance about her before slipping a piece of paper to Sir Brandon.

"If I don't end by strangling that girl," came an impatient voice in Georgiana's ear, "it will not be my fault."

Georgiana turned. She felt obliged to defend Louisa and made no mention of what she had seen. However, she did not know how Lakesby could have failed to notice what was undoubtedly a billet-doux.

"She is doing no harm, Mr Lakesby. It is hardly improper for her to speak with Sir Brandon in a public place."

"True enough," responded Lakesby. "But if I know my cousin, considerations of propriety are not paramount."

"You are hard on her, sir."

Lakesby did not answer immediately, but frowned as he looked at Louisa. "I'm not sure I don't prefer her foolish infatuation with the Crimson Cavalier. At least he is unlikely to try eloping with her."

Georgiana tried to read his expression. "Elope?" she inquired. "Surely not."

Lakesby drew his attention away from Louisa to look at Georgiana. "Yes, Miss Grey. My cousin has a comfortable portion and is prey to fortune-hunters."

"Surely she would not…"

"As I said, Miss Grey, my cousin, unhappily, is not always

alive to the consequences of her actions." Lakesby's eyes were back on Louisa. "I beg you will excuse me; I must put a stop to this nonsense. If you would wait here a moment, I shall escort you both back to the box."

"Of course."

Georgiana watched as Lakesby put his hand firmly to his cousin's elbow. It seemed a curiously proprietorial gesture for simply a guardian. While his manner had been almost dismissive of her in some ways, he was clearly fond of the girl. Georgiana was too, and could see that her gold ringlets and delicate blue eyes could go a long way towards compensating for lack of brains.

As the cousins walked towards her, Georgiana caught sight of Brandon Foster's form disappearing towards his own alcove. She thought he looked fairly satisfied with himself. Turning her attention back to Louisa and Lakesby, Georgiana smiled at their approach.

"Are you enjoying the play, Miss Grey – I mean, Georgiana," inquired Louisa.

"Yes, Louisa, and you?" said Georgiana, convinced the girl had not taken in one word in ten of the performance.

"Oh, yes," responded Louisa enthusiastically.

"Well, we shall miss the second act if we do not hurry," said Lakesby. He offered Georgiana his free arm. "Miss Grey?"

Georgiana accepted with a smile and Lakesby managed to settle his party in the box in good time for the second act. As the curtain rose, Georgiana found her mind less on the play than the encounter between Louisa and Sir Brandon Foster. Could the girl be in love with him? From what Georgiana had heard, the female company kept by that young man consisted primarily of opera dancers and others of questionable background. Even if his intentions towards Louisa were honourable, the prospects for marriage were not good. Although the obstacle of his father's rival suit had been removed, Sir Brandon was hardly an eligible suitor.

Georgiana's mind went back to her conversation with Sir Brandon and his confidently expressed view that he would manage. She wondered whether Sir Brandon planned to use the girl to solve his problems.

Georgiana was thankful none of this was her concern.

The supper arranged by Mr Lakesby after the final curtain could not be faulted even by his aunt. The soup was excellent and the guinea fowl was roasted to the perfect stage of tenderness. Georgiana had so far not regretted acceding to the persuasions of Mr Lakesby and his cousin in accepting the invitation.

Conversation was desultory on the drive home; the hour was late and the occupants of the chaise were tired. The sharp jolt of its sudden halt dragged each into immediate wakefulness.

"Stand and deliver!" came a determined voice.

Georgiana closed her eyes, unable to believe what she had heard. The voice coming through from the darkness was unmistakably Tom's. The fool, she thought to herself. After all Harry and I have said to him. He'll get himself killed.

Louisa could not resist peeking out of the chaise, to be pushed back in her seat by the forceful hand of her cousin.

"Stay where you are, Louisa," he said.

Georgiana sat very still, as far back against the seat as she could force herself, not daring to speak. She could not afford even the slightest risk. She had complete faith in Tom's ability to blurt out something crashingly indiscreet. She glanced towards her companions. Lakesby's unwavering eyes were on the masked figure outside. Lady Winters sat simmering in indignant disbelief.

"Now then," said one of the postilions. "Be off with you. We're armed, you know. You'll get no booty here."

"Hand over the gewgaws," said Tom, undaunted.

Georgiana ventured a glance out of the window. Tom's skinny form was cloaked in what she suspected was an old curtain from the Lucky Bell. His hat was too large and his mask tied slightly askew. He appeared lost in the ensemble. Georgiana noticed his pistol shaking slightly. It chilled her to see him in this guise.

"On your way and let us pass, lad," said the postilion, anger beginning to creep into his voice, "unless you want to get yourself shot. I've told you, you'll get nothing here."

"Mr Lakesby, for heaven's sake, stop them," said Georgiana, her hand involuntarily gripping his forearm.

Lakesby looked at her curiously. "Stop them, Miss Grey? My servant is doing the job for which I pay him."

"He's only a boy," she said urgently.

"If he is old enough to hold up a coach, he is old enough to face the consequences," said Lady Winters in withering accents.

"You asked for it," said Tom.

Lakesby looked thoughtfully from Georgiana to his aunt. Georgiana suspected he could be persuaded to support her rather than Lady Winters. She had no opportunity to put further argument to find out.

"I'll give you one more chance," said Tom, "or I'll pop you culls."

Georgiana knew the note of bravado in his voice was intended to mask his fear.

The postilions laughed. "Do you hear that?" said the one who had addressed Tom. "He'll give us one more chance. That has me quaking in my shoes. On your way, Master Jack-Sauce."

Georgiana knew it would be a mistake to taunt the boy. A moment later she was proved right. Georgiana saw him level his pistol. He handled it awkwardly as he battled determinedly to still its misbehaviour. A shot cracked out through the darkness. Georgiana let out a little cry. Before anyone could stop her, she had pushed past Lakesby and out of the coach, to drop on her knees next to Tom's limp form.

"How could you?" Georgiana looked accusingly at the astonished postilion. "He's barely a child."

"But, miss, he..."

Georgiana was paying him no attention. Moving the make-shift cloak out of the way, she swiftly tore open the corner of Tom's shirt as the blood began to spread over it. The ball had gone clean through the shoulder, which was bleeding profusely. Relieved to see it was not fatal, Georgiana began to tear strips off the boy's already ragged shirt, folding them into a pad to cover the wound. She looked up to see Lakesby standing behind her.

"Mr Lakesby, I should be grateful for your handkerchief to bind up this wound."

Lakesby silently obliged, watching thoughtfully as she bound the injury with brisk efficiency.

"I thought he was going to fire, sir," said the postilion, apologetically addressing his master.

"I know," said Lakesby, his eyes still on Georgiana, immersed in her task.

Satisfied the wound was as secure as she could make it Georgiana took Tom's pistol and emptied it in businesslike fashion. She turned to Lakesby.

"We can't leave him here. He'll bleed to death."

"What do you propose, Miss Grey?" Lakesby asked quietly.

"If you would be good enough to have your servants lift him into your chaise, he could be conveyed to my home. I'll arrange for a surgeon."

The coachman and postilions stared at her, dumbfounded. It was Lady Winters, looking out the window in horrified stupefaction, who spoke.

"Allow that ruffian to travel with us? Most certainly not."

"He is injured, Lady Winters," Georgiana informed her. "Hardly in a position to do any harm. Besides," she continued, "look at the condition of him. He's no more than skin and bone. What I'm suggesting is simply common charity."

Her ladyship remained adamant in her refusal, declaring nothing would induce her to travel in the company of such a cut-throat.

"Very well," said Georgiana calmly. She turned to Lakesby. "Perhaps you would be good enough to have one of your postilions ride ahead to my home and ask for my carriage to be sent. I'll wait here with the boy."

"I don't think that will be necessary, Miss Grey," said Lakesby. He looked towards his aunt and spoke with a dangerous calm. "Will it, Aunt Beatrice?"

Lady Winters made no reply. With pursed lips, she retreated inside the chaise. Lakesby turned towards his servants. "Do as Miss Grey asks." His attention went back to Georgiana. He gestured towards the pistol. "Er – shall I take that?"

Realising she had betrayed too much expertise, Georgiana handed it to him with what she hoped was a grateful smile.

"Oh, yes. Thank you, Mr Lakesby."

Tom groaned slightly as he was lifted into the chaise. To Lady Winters's horror, Georgiana positioned the boy's head on her lap, his shoulder cradled protectively by her left hand while the right stroked his head in soothing manner. Smears of blood were daubed in garish contrast to the soft blue of Georgiana's dress.

While Horton's eyes widened slightly at the sight of his mistress arriving home with an injured urchin, his rigorous training curtailed any comment. James, for his part, accepted the situation with calm, gently carrying Tom to one of the spare bedchambers. Leaving the boy in the care of Emily, he immediately set off for a surgeon.

Having seen Lakesby's carriage drive away, Georgiana stood

alone in the hall for a moment. She could not suppress a slight smile as she contemplated her blood-smeared hands and dress. She was certain both Lady Winters and Mr Lakesby would do their utmost to prevent further association between Louisa and herself. It was a pity, but could not be helped. Of more concern to Georgiana, as she walked slowly up the stairs to join Emily, was the fact that she had demonstrated a knowledge of firearms unusual for a lady of her position. It had not escaped Lakesby's notice.

Emily did not look up from her task of cleaning the wound as her mistress entered the bedchamber. Closing the door softly behind her, Georgiana looked at the small figure in the bed. Tom was still very pale and unconscious. Emily seemed to have staunched the flow of blood and placed a clean pad over the wound, and was tying the ends of a fresh bandage.

"He's very weak, miss."

"Yes," Georgiana responded, her unwavering gaze on Tom's face.

Emily looked towards Georgiana as she finished her task. "What happened?"

"He tried to hold up Mr Lakesby's carriage."

"What?" Emily was startled.

Georgiana nodded. "He hadn't a hope of succeeding. As far as I know, this is his first attempt. I don't even know where he got the pistol."

Emily looked at Tom with a thoughtful expression on her face. Before either could speak again, James quietly entered the room followed by a middle-aged man whose expression conveyed his lack of amusement at being dragged from his bed to attend a wounded urchin. The expression soured as he took in Georgiana's bloodstained attire. Irritated by his pompous scrutiny, she raised her eyebrows with an air of superior inquiry. Better men than this grizzled physician had quailed under this unexpectedly withering gaze, and he muttered something about examining the patient. Georgiana asked James to remain with him and signalled Emily to follow her out of the room. She asked quietly whether her cousin had returned home, to be answered with a nod and the news that Miss Knatchbull had retired immediately to bed.

In the sanctuary of her own bedchamber, Georgiana regaled her maid with the full story of Tom's misadventure, prudently excluding any mention of her own handling of the pistol. Removing the blood-spattered dress, Georgiana breathed a sigh of relief. She told Emily she never wanted to see it again and poured some water into the bowl on her washstand. The splash of clean water on her face and arms began to refresh her, but the lingering aroma of gunpowder and blood refused to be banished from her nostrils. She sat down on the cushioned stool and stared at her reflection. Her normally bright complexion looked pale and her face drawn. Yet through this, the germ of anger held in check by her anxiety for Tom began to grow. Travellers had to protect themselves, none knew that better than she, but what had been done to Tom was little better than attempted murder. A frightened boy who could barely hold a pistol was hardly a threat to three sturdy and sober men, four if one counted Lakesby.

With a shawl disposed comfortably around her, Georgiana sent Emily back to the sick chamber. She began to pace her own room, teeth clenched, fists closing and opening with every step. Part of her wanted to teach Mr Lakesby's postilions a lesson, but her sense of justice acknowledged his intervention had probably saved Tom's life. The question now was what he planned to do next. Had Tom been saved from the bullet only to be handed over to the noose?

Emily's soft tread outside the door caused Georgiana to pause in her tracks.

"Well?" she asked as the maid entered.

"James is seeing the surgeon out. The boy will live, but he'll have to rest a while." Emily paused. "Miss, have you thought about this? That boy knows you, doesn't he? If he's to be here for long, he could guess the truth."

"Possibly," Georgiana acknowledged. "However, I don't think Tom is quite sharp enough to suspect any link between the Crimson Cavalier and Miss Georgiana Grey, particularly in his present condition."

"Well, perhaps," said Emily doubtfully.

"The problem is," said Georgiana, "he will be missed. Cedric and Bess can easily find another errand boy, but Harry might be more concerned. He might suspect Tom has done something rash and been taken in charge."

"So he might be yet," said Emily.

"I know," nodded Georgiana. "I wish I knew Mr Lakesby's intentions. The thought of going to him on bended knee… Still, if that is what must be, it must be." She turned her mind to more immediate concerns. "Is Tom comfortable for the moment?"

"As much as he can be, miss. James is going to sit with him now and I'll take over in a few hours."

"He is really my responsibility," said Georgiana. "I should—"

"No, miss," said Emily firmly. "James and I will take care of him. You've enough to worry you at the moment."

Georgiana could not argue with this and was grateful for the respite.

Sleep beckoned.

Her dilemma confronted her soon enough at breakfast in telling her cousin of her charitable impulse. Miss Knatchbull was very much shocked, and while she applauded dear Georgiana's sympathetic nature in wishing to help one less fortunate, she could not help but agree with Lady Winters that ruffians who held up innocent citizens on the public highway deserved punishment.

"Nonsense, Selina, he is only a boy. Wait until you see him for yourself."

"I?" said Miss Knatchbull in horrified accents, a hand at her breast. "Good heavens, I have no intention of seeing him. I am astonished you should suggest such a thing. I recommend you send for the Watch at once, or a Bow Street Runner. Edward is acquainted with one, is he not? I'm sure he could advise you."

"Edward advises me a deal too much already," said Georgiana tartly.

Georgiana had not long to wait before being presented with the next part of her problem. Her butler announced the arrival of Mr Lakesby late the same morning. Ignoring the sudden faltering of her usual determination and the surprised eyes of Miss Knatchbull, Georgiana calmly asked Horton to show in the visitor. She would have preferred to be without Selina's company. Making the best of it, she faced Mr Lakesby with a bright smile and cheerful good morning. He paid his respects to Georgiana and her companion, declined her offer of coffee and made no attempt to open conversation until the door had closed behind Horton.

"Won't you sit down, Mr Lakesby?" said Georgiana.

"No, thank you, Miss Grey. I hope not to take up too much of your time. I merely came to inquire after your patient."

"My maid and footman have been looking after him. The surgeon came to see him last night. He's very weak, of course, and will need a great deal of rest. However, his life is not in any danger."

"Then perhaps he could be moved somewhere else," said Miss Knatchbull with urgent anxiety. "Don't you agree, Mr Lakesby? The matter should be notified to the proper authorities; they will see he receives medical attention."

"Do you think so, Selina?" said Georgiana. "I think it more

95

likely they will put him in prison and leave him to shift for himself."

Lakesby did not respond to Selina's question, addressing Georgiana. "It appears your intervention was most timely for him, Miss Grey."

Georgiana shook her head. "I believe he owes his life to you, Mr Lakesby. Many people would have left him on the road."

"My aunt thinks I should have done. I received quite a sermon on the subject."

"Oh, dear," said Georgiana in remorseful tone. "I seem to have caused you a great deal of trouble."

"Not at all," Lakesby responded. "My aunt does not often read me sermons and I pay her very little heed when she does." He paused, apparently contemplating the top of one of his boots. "Have you had an opportunity to speak to the boy?"

Selina gasped. "Speak to him?"

"No," said Georgiana. "I understand he has not yet returned to consciousness." She shot a glance at him. "Do you intend to lay him in charge?"

"My aunt thinks I should."

"Well, I tend to agree with her," said Miss Knatchbull, folding her hands in her lap.

"Do you allow yourself to be guided by your aunt's judgement?"

Lakesby looked intently at Georgiana. She smiled coolly, as though this was the most normal situation in the world. He contemplated the end of his stick as he addressed her.

"Tell me, Miss Grey, do you think I should hand that boy over to a magistrate?"

Georgiana did not even think to press Tom's case immediately. "Does my opinion matter, sir?"

"I have asked for it."

She regarded him steadily. "He is just a boy, Mr Lakesby,"

she said gently. "Half starved, by the look of him."

"Yet strong enough to take up arms against my postilions."

"Exactly so," said Miss Knatchbull.

Georgiana was wishing her cousin at Jericho. "I imagine he was desperate," she explained, in the teeth of the fact that highway robbery had been Tom's ambition since she had known him.

"Possibly," Lakesby responded. "But highway boys grow into highwaymen if not stopped. The very thing your brother is so eager to stop."

The mention of Edward needled Georgiana. She lifted her chin slightly. "I had not realised my brother's views concerned you, sir."

"By no means," he said. "However, I thought they might concern you."

Georgiana looked away from him. She decided not to rise to the bait. "The boy is wounded, Mr Lakesby."

"An occupational hazard, I imagine."

"Nevertheless, sir, I beg you to have some compassion for him. I'm sure this incident will scare him enough to deter him from further adventures. Is it necessary to send him to the gallows as well?"

"Are you so sure, Miss Grey? How can you be?"

"Well, it stands to reason, sir—"

"Does it? How can we be certain we are dealing with a reasonable being?"

Miss Knatchbull looked alarmed. "For heaven's sake, Georgiana—"

Georgiana's heart pounded in her ears. Her voice was surprisingly level.

"I would stake my life on it, sir."

"You very nearly had to. You may not be so lucky another time."

Georgiana looked sharply at him. Was this some strange

game he felt like indulging, or did he wish to teach her a lesson for the way she had taken charge of the previous night's escapade? She drew a deep breath.

"Mr Lakesby, do you mean to hand that boy over to the authorities?"

Lakesby looked at her thoughtfully. "I should like to think about that."

7

Georgiana stood in the drawing room paying little attention to what her cousin was saying. If Lakesby did intend to surrender Tom to the authorities, why had he not arrived with a Bow Street Runner? Perhaps he was waiting for the boy to recover from his injury? Although Mr Lakesby had certainly demonstrated compassion towards Tom's predicament, Georgiana reflected wryly that she had given him very little choice.

Of equal concern to Georgiana was the attention Lakesby had shown to her behaviour of the previous night. With the immediate danger to Tom past, she was now forced to confront the consequences. She was still irritated with herself for the slip she had made. There had been no need for her to touch the pistol. While the leap from Lakesby's observation to a deduction that she was the Crimson Cavalier required some manipulation of imagination, Georgiana recognised it was possible and within Maxwell Lakesby's capabilities.

But Georgiana had never been one to waste her energy worrying over what could not be helped. She would certainly have to apply her mind to some means of limiting any possible damage. However, at present more urgent matters needed her attention.

One of these imposed on her notice in a very forceful way virtually immediately as Tom's protesting yell permeated the entire household. Georgiana could imagine the pained expressions of Horton and her housekeeper. There was no escape; she would clearly have to deal with the matter herself. She excused herself from Selina, avoiding her cousin's scandalised expression, and reached the door just as Emily entered. The maid wore a harassed air.

"Might I have a word, miss?" asked Emily.

"Of course. Would you mind, Selina?"

"Not at all," said Selina, a little stiffly. She rose in dignified fashion to leave. "I shall be in my room if you need me."

"What is it, Emily? Is he refusing to let James wash him?" asked Georgiana, closing the door after her cousin.

Emily rolled her eyes heavenward. "We've not even got to that, Miss Georgiana. He won't eat his breakfast. Seems to think we're trying to poison him."

"I suppose it's to be expected. He's certain to be scared, waking up injured in a strange house." She bit her bottom lip thoughtfully. "I'd better speak to him."

"You'd better not, miss," said Emily. "What if he recognises your voice?"

"I'll have to risk it," said Georgiana. "We can't have him shouting for all the world to hear."

"I know, miss, but..."

"Neither you nor James are having any success with him, are you?"

"Well, no, miss," Emily acknowledged.

"Then you'd best leave him to me. I know him a little better."

"That's the trouble," said a gloom-laden Emily.

Georgiana looked across at her maid. She smiled slightly.

"I know there's a risk, Emily–"

"A risk?" echoed the maid in disbelief.

"However," continued Georgiana undeterred, "I don't think Tom is quite so sharp as to make the connection between Miss Georgiana Grey and the Crimson Cavalier. If he does notice anything amiss, I'm sure I can think of some tale to satisfy him. Perhaps I could invent a black sheep of a distant cousin."

"Your brother could put him right on that," Emily pointed out. She nodded towards the door. "So could Miss Knatchbull."

"True," said Georgiana. "But it is unlikely Edward's and Tom's

100

paths will cross, and Selina has expressed her determination to have nothing to do with the boy, so we need not concern ourselves with that at present."

The sound of breaking crockery from upstairs ended further protest from Emily. Giving her maid one final, speaking look, Georgiana opened the door and went to Tom's bedchamber.

It was unusual to see James in anything other than perfect control, but there could be no doubt from his exasperated expression that his patience was worn thin. The boy was sitting up in bed, an air of belligerence about him, a challenge in his eyes. He tugged at his bandage with some impatience.

"May I ask what the problem is?" Georgiana inquired in her haughtiest tone.

The mutinous set of Tom's mouth seemed to prevent him from answering. James spoke.

"The boy seems to think we mean him harm, miss."

"I ain't a boy!" objected Tom.

Georgiana and James ignored the remark.

"Really?" said Georgiana, looking towards James.

"He won't eat, miss."

"I see." Georgiana cast a thoughtful look towards her young guest and noticed him wriggle uncomfortably under the scrutiny. She wondered just how afraid he was.

"You can't keep me in this ken," Tom said at last. "You're not a beak."

"True," said Georgiana.

Tom's eyes widened. James looked towards Georgiana in some surprise.

"I can go?" said Tom.

"How far do you think you'd get?" asked Georgiana.

Tom had clearly not considered this point and appeared nonplussed. Georgiana pursued her advantage.

"You are weak from your injury. You should rest."

"I ain't weak. Where's me clothes?"

Georgiana knew Tom would be in fear of the Runners. It also occurred to her that he would expect Harry to be looking for him. She knew this was a strong possibility. Harry was fond of the boy and likely to be concerned about his disappearance. However, Georgiana could not, in good conscience, allow Tom to leave yet.

"The surgeon said you must rest. You needn't worry. You are quite safe."

Tom looked at her suspiciously. Georgiana glanced towards James and back to the boy.

"You'd best have something to eat," she said lightly before leaving the room.

As she walked down the stairs, Georgiana caught sight of Emily waiting anxiously at the bottom. She smiled in what she hoped was reassuring fashion.

"Is all well, miss?"

"As much as we can expect. Come into the drawing room, Emily."

Once inside, Georgiana closed the door and stood with her back against it. One hand rested on the door knob as she looked towards her maid's uneasily expectant face.

"I have to get a message to Harry. He'll be looking for Tom."

"He surely won't come here?" said Emily in horrified accents.

"Unlikely. However, it would be best to put a stop to it early."

Emily said nothing.

"I'll go to the Lucky Bell this evening. I'll just–" Georgiana paused. She had been about to say she would leave a note for Harry when it occurred to her that she didn't know whether he could read.

"If it's just a message, perhaps I could go, miss. There'll be no one looking for me."

Georgiana considered, owning herself tempted. However, it was unfair to involve Emily so directly. If spotted, her presence in the vicinity of the Lucky Bell would be more difficult to explain than her knowledge of Tom's whereabouts. Besides, Emily didn't know Harry by sight, and questions would draw attention. Georgiana shook her head.

"No, thank you, Emily. I'd better take care of it myself. Don't worry," she said in response to the maid's doubtful expression. "I'll just let someone at the tavern know Tom is safe and come straight back."

"Well, if you're certain, miss…"

"Absolutely." Georgiana was firm. She glanced at the large pendulum clock on the wall. "I thought I'd visit Joe Hill this morning."

"Isn't he one of Sir Robert Foster's tenants?"

Georgiana nodded.

Emily screwed up her fresh face. "Miss, do you think that's wise, after what's happened?"

"Well, Sir Robert didn't make any effort for them himself when he was alive. Where's the difference now he's dead?"

Emily still looked perturbed.

"The man needs of a bit of charity, Emily," said Georgiana in a more gentle tone. "You know what a bad time he's had lately with the death of his wife."

"She'd been ill for a long time, perhaps it was a blessing for her."

"Perhaps." Georgiana sounded unconvinced. "In any case, he still has four children to feed. The least we can do is offer what help we can."

"It's good of you, miss," said Emily. "But you have to think about yourself. It's Sir Robert's heir's responsibility now."

"Yes, but he will not necessarily make the tenants a priority. Sir Robert was a very neglectful landlord. There is no reason to suppose whoever he has chosen as heir will behave any differently."

"I suppose that's true," said Emily.

"Of course it is," said Georgiana. She thought for a moment. "I had better see if my cousin wishes to accompany me. I have a fancy to go on horseback, but I doubt if I can persuade Selina to do so."

Miss Knatchbull chose not to go with Georgiana on her charity visit, satisfied she would be accompanied by a groom. However, she was pleased her company had been sought and the two parted on excellent terms.

The folds of Georgiana chocolate-coloured riding habit fell in naturally elegant lines and the hat perched smartly on her head gave an impudent finish to her immaculate bearing. When she had drawn on her gloves, Georgiana unlocked a small drawer in her dressing table and removed a handful of the coins liberated from Sir Robert Foster's person a few evenings earlier. Emily made no comment, but smiled as she handed Georgiana her riding crop.

The neat bay Georgiana chose for her expedition was more docile than Princess and could never be taken for the mount of a highway robber. Her groom rode sedately behind her, holding a carefully balanced basket in position. The pair looked every inch the perfect picture of propriety. Georgiana soon found herself within sight of the ramshackle cottages forming the edge of the late Sir Robert Foster's estate. The buildings were testament to Sir Robert's shortcomings as a landlord. Dismounting, Georgiana handed her reins to her attendant and accepted the basket in exchange. She approached one of the cottages near the middle of the row, where a dirt-smeared blonde girl of about ten years of age stood in bare feet, watching with interest. Georgiana smiled at her.

"Hello, Betsy. Is your father at home?"

The girl nodded, wordlessly leading Georgiana to the cottage. She paused for Georgiana to enter first, managing a shy smile. Georgiana handed the child an apple from the basket, transforming the smile into a big grin.

"Thank you, miss."

"You're very welcome, Betsy. May I go in?"

The girl held the apple in both hands as she concentrated her energies into taking a bite.

"Good day, Mr Hill."

The man looked up from his task of buttoning his son's shirt, surprised at the sight of the visitor. He rose from his squatting position and came forward with a smile of welcome. Although he was about the same age as Edward, a careworn look made him appear older. However, he carried himself well, with brown hair brushed neatly and clothes clean and tidy, even if they had seen better days.

"Miss Grey. 'Tis most kind of you to call."

"Not at all. I wanted to bring a few things for the children." Georgiana put the basket down on the table. "I've already given Betsy an apple. I hope you don't mind."

"No, miss, of course not. Thank you." Joe Hill looked around the house self-consciously. "I'm afraid the place is not very tidy. We weren't expecting visitors."

"That's no matter." Georgiana smiled encouragingly at the dark little boy who looked up at her in brooding fascination. "Would you like an apple?"

The boy looked uncertainly at his father then back at Georgiana. She reached into the basket and held the fruit out to him.

"Thank Miss Grey," said his father.

Thus encouraged, the boy accepted the apple and muttered his gratitude. He ran off clutching it as though afraid someone would try to take it from him.

"They're not used to people being kind to them, Miss Grey. You'll have to excuse him."

"Please don't worry, Mr Hill. I just came to see if there was anything you needed."

"Oh, no, miss, you've been more than kind." With some

diffidence, he began to unpack the basket Georgiana had put on the table. "It's made such a difference since Dora died."

"It's been my pleasure," Georgiana said. Her eyes went involuntarily towards the damp patches on the walls. She had not missed the edge in Hill's voice as he mentioned his wife's death. The atmosphere of the poorly maintained cottage was not conducive to good health. If one was already ailing, it could hasten the end.

"Why, that's a fine cheese, miss, oh, and a ham as well. We shall be living like kings. Why, what's this?"

Georgiana's attention was caught as Hill reached his hand into the corner of the basket, bringing out Sir Robert's gold coins glistening in the palm of his hand. He stared at his visitor.

"Miss Grey, I can't accept this. It's too much."

"Yes, of course you must," Georgiana said hastily. She had hoped the coins would not be found until after her departure. "Please. In truth, they are not from me. They are a present from a… a well-wishing friend, who would be very distressed if you were to refuse."

Hill looked doubtful. "Who is this friend?"

"Someone who would prefer to remain unknown," she said promptly. "Please take it. It may help the children."

"Very well." His hand closed over the coins. "Where are my manners? I've not even offered you anything to drink."

"No, thank you, Mr Hill, that's not necessary. I must be on my way."

He followed her out of the house. "I don't know what's going to happen now old Sir Robert's dead. But I suppose things couldn't be much worse, at least, not unless he decides to turn me and the children out."

"Oh, surely not," said Georgiana, shocked at this possibility.

"In any case," Hill continued, "that highwayman did the world a favour, killing the old man like he did. It may sound un-Christian, but if I was ever to meet him I'd like to shake his hand."

"It may not have been a highwayman, you know," said Georgiana warily.

"Well, I don't know about that. All I know is that it was Sir Robert's fault my Dora's dead. I'll never forgive that."

His tone was hard, but Georgiana felt some sympathy for his point of view. She said what she felt she ought. "I do understand your sentiments, Mr Hill. But bitterness can't help your wife now, or the children."

Hill gave a short laugh. "Perhaps not, but I can't be sorry Sir Robert's dead. I'm not normally a bad-tempered man, Miss Grey, but…"

Georgiana began to feel uneasy. She wondered whether she ought to press the point, but Hill was now smiling at her once again in a pleasant manner. Georgiana returned the smile and after a momentary hesitation, held out her hand. He took it in a warm clasp.

"You will let me know if there is anything I can do?" she said earnestly. "If I can be of any help?"

"Thank you, miss. I shall, though you've been much too good to us already."

"Nonsense."

"Miss Grey?"

A voice from the road behind Georgiana took her by surprise. She looked around to see the tall figure of Maxwell Lakesby astride a magnificent beast worthy of any highwayman. Aware she was still clasping Mr Hill's hand, she dropped it quickly, annoyed to find a blush rising to her cheeks.

"Mr Lakesby. Good afternoon. I had not expected to see you here."

"Just taking the air," he replied, "and you?"

Joe Hill was eyeing the newcomer with disfavour. Georgiana's groom stood impassively holding his mistress's horse.

"Miss Grey very kindly called to offer some help to myself

and my children," said Hill in a tone of some dignity.

"Did she?" inquired Lakesby. "Most commendable."

Seething with anger at the hint of mockery in Lakesby's tone, Georgiana was also aware of the indignation of Joe Hill beside her. She knew his pride would be stronger than any concerns over social niceties. Her first thought was to prevent the unpleasantness she could feel threatening. She turned quickly towards Hill.

"I must be on my way, Mr Hill, and I'm sure the children must need you."

"Aye, I suppose."

"Good day to you."

"Good day, Miss Grey." With a last dark look towards Lakesby, Hill walked slowly back to the house.

"Miss Grey, if you are returning home, I beg you will allow me to accompany you."

"That is quite unnecessary, Mr Lakesby, my groom is with me." Georgiana walked quickly towards where her groom stood with her horse. Taking the reins, she mounted the animal before Lakesby could offer assistance.

"True, but I am sure you will not deny me the pleasure of your company." He glanced towards the cottage. "That man is one of Sir Robert Foster's tenants, isn't he?"

"Yes, what of it?"

"He's not your responsibility."

"He is in need of help, Mr Lakesby, regardless of whose tenant he is. Sir Robert was an appalling landlord. If he'd kept his properties in better condition, perhaps Mr Hill's wife wouldn't have fallen ill."

"Perhaps not. Does Hill blame Sir Robert for his wife's death?"

Georgiana was on her guard. "Why do you ask?"

"It would appear to give him a motive for Sir Robert's murder."

"You don't think he was killed by the Crimson Cavalier?" Georgiana inquired.

"Possibly, but it's by no means certain. You do not think so yourself, do you, Miss Grey?"

"What makes you say that?"

Lakesby gave her a shrewd look. "I rather had the impression you inclined towards his innocence, of this killing, anyway." He continued lightly, "The Crimson Cavalier is a fortunate fellow to have so many young ladies feeling impelled to defend him. I wish I knew his secret."

Georgiana glanced towards him. "I cannot imagine," she said in a tone without interest.

"Are you not among the legions of females bowled over by the highwayman's charms?" Lakesby asked quizzically.

"Hardly."

"You seem to have an interest in whether or not he killed Sir Robert Foster."

"You are mistaken, Mr Lakesby. I am no Bow Street Runner."

"No."

Georgiana cast him a sharp glance. To her annoyance, she felt compelled to justify herself.

"One should keep an open mind. Assumptions are dangerous without proof."

"I see you have your brother's zeal for justice."

"How do you know my brother?" Georgiana asked, seizing the opportunity of steering the conversation away from Lakesby's probing.

Lakesby did not answer immediately. Georgiana had the impression he was giving some consideration to his reply. The thought flashed through her mind that perhaps he was not going to offer one.

"We were first introduced at Oxford, though we have only met very occasionally."

"I see." Georgiana paused, wondering whether she should

voice her next thought. She decided to go ahead. "I beg your pardon, Mr Lakesby, but I would not have expected you and my brother to be on friendly terms. You and he are, if I may say so, very different."

Lakesby smiled. "That is true. No, Miss Grey, it would be too much to say your brother and I are friends. However, I've nothing against him and bear him no grudge."

This struck Georgiana as an odd thing to say. Was there some reason Lakesby should bear Edward a grudge? She was wondering how to pursue this question when he spoke again.

"As I said, we have met fairly infrequently. I last saw him at a shooting party a few months ago, at Lord and Lady Wickerston's."

"I did not know Edward knew the Wickerstons."

Lakesby shrugged. "Apparently so. I don't know them well myself. I accompanied a friend."

"I see."

Lakesby looked searchingly at her. "Your sister-in-law was not present. I believe one of the children had some slight indisposition."

"Really? I wonder what that can have been. I'm sure I don't remember it."

Aware of his intent scrutiny, Georgiana smiled and deftly turned the conversation. "And you, Mr Lakesby? Have you nieces and nephews?"

"No, just my tiresome young cousin. It's more than enough to be saddled with the guardianship of her."

"You are unkind."

"Possibly. However, she can be a confounded nuisance sometimes. I shall be glad when she is safely married and the responsibility of her husband."

"Was there not some talk of you marrying her?" said Georgiana before she could stop herself.

"I?" Lakesby looked at her in astonishment. "Heavens, no. That is some foolish notion of my Aunt Beatrice, concocted when Louisa was a baby. I am amazed she still cherishes it."

"I do not think your aunt is a woman who would easily give up her ambitions."

Arriving outside Georgiana's house, Lakesby dismounted quickly and handed his reins to the groom while he assisted Georgiana down.

"Do you think I have no ambitions of my own?" he inquired with a smile as she stood opposite him.

Not certain how to respond to this, Georgiana took refuge in the conventional. She smiled and thanked him for his escort as she stepped away to enter the house.

"Miss Grey."

Georgiana turned her head, and paused with one foot on the bottom step. Lakesby walked purposefully towards her, lowering his voice so he could not be heard by the groom holding the horses.

"You will be careful?"

"What?" Georgiana was genuinely puzzled.

"I don't know why you're taking such an interest in Sir Robert Foster's murder. Boredom, I daresay. I can understand that. Nevertheless, it's a dangerous game. Whoever killed Sir Robert would hardly hesitate to kill anyone else in their way."

Georgiana looked at him in surprise as she took in the import of his words. While part of her wanted to repudiate what she saw as his meddling and send him about his business, she could not help appreciating his obvious concern for her safety. She moistened her lips.

"Thank you for the warning, Mr Lakesby. However, you have no need to fear for me. I am quite capable of looking after myself."

The ghost of a smile took shape around Lakesby's mouth.

"I've no doubt you are, Miss Grey. Good day to you."

He turned on his heel and walked away to take his horse. Georgiana stood watching him. He inclined his head slightly and rode off as she stared after him in growing puzzlement.

Georgiana found her household calmer than she had left it. Her cousin was conferring with the housekeeper. Tom, it seemed, was sleeping peacefully following a visit from the surgeon, who had recommended a few drops of laudanum. James told her the boy had taken it under protest and had capitulated only as he recognised in the doctor's manner one who would brook no argument. Glad of the quiet, Georgiana walked towards her bedchamber, her mind full of her encounter with Mr Lakesby. Her reverie was shortly interrupted by Emily.

"Everything quite well, miss?"

"Hmm? Oh, yes, thank you, Emily."

Emily studied Georgiana closely. "If you don't mind me saying so, miss, you look a bit distracted."

"Do I?" Georgiana responded. "I beg your pardon, Emily. I met Mr Lakesby as I was leaving Joe Hill's cottage. He… he's noticed the interest I've been taking in Sir Robert Foster's murder."

"Oh, heavens!"

"Don't worry," Georgiana smiled. "He shares your own line of thought, Emily. He told me to be careful."

Emily echoed this sentiment several hours later. As night fell, the Crimson Cavalier stood before her insisting on the need to visit the Lucky Bell to speak to Harry Smith. With the scald on her hand considerably less painful, Georgiana drew on her gloves and reached into the bedside table for her pistol. She knew Emily's eyes followed her.

"In case anyone sees me," said Georgiana.

Emily nodded but her face still wore a dissatisfied expression.

"Truly, Emily, I simply need to tell Harry Smith Tom is safe, and then I shall return home."

"What do you mean to do about Tom when he has recovered?"

Georgiana thought about the boy who had finally given in to sleep after a day spent trying the patience of her most equable servant. "To tell you the truth, I don't know," she confessed. "I don't feel right about sending him back to the Lucky Bell. Perhaps he can be apprenticed somewhere."

Thanking her guardian angel for the lack of any significant moonlight, a masked Georgiana dismounted some yards away from the Lucky Bell, aiming for maximum silence in her approach. She twisted Princess's reins around her right hand and was about to lead her forward when the opening of the tavern door held her fixed. Her eyes widened as she saw Joe Hill emerge from its shelter. He did not notice her waiting in the shadows and began to walk solidly down the road, hands in pockets and shoulders slightly hunched. Georgiana was tempted to follow, but it would be difficult for the Crimson Cavalier to explain an interest in his actions should she be noticed. If Hill decided to stand up to the notorious highway robber, she was certain to be exposed. Georgiana smiled ruefully behind her mask as she tied Princess in the thicket at the back of the tavern. Her safest option was to see what she could learn from Cedric's clientele.

Harry was seated at a corner table in the Lucky Bell, a small glass of dark liquid in front of him. He looked every bit as concerned as she had expected. At the sight of her, he jerked his head towards the door of the small parlour. She nodded and followed him.

"Tom's missing," he said as soon as the door was closed behind them.

"I know," Georgiana replied. "He tried to hold up a coach last night and got shot in the shoulder."

"What?" Harry looked thunderstruck. "The devil he did." He frowned. "If he's been taken up in charge…"

"I don't think he has," said Georgiana. "One of the travellers seemed concerned about his injury. I believe he's safe enough."

Harry's eyes narrowed. Georgiana recounted briefly her part in Tom's rescue, keeping it as vague as she could.

"How do you know this?" Harry asked finally.

"I was about to take the coach myself," she lied promptly. "I was under cover off the road so I saw what happened."

Harry seemed satisfied with this explanation, commenting only that she was risking a hemp necktie being out on the road with the way things were. Georgiana shrugged.

"By the way," he said, reaching into his pocket, "I've seen old Ben. He offered me ten pounds as well as what I'd given you for those gewgaws."

"What?" said Georgiana. "Tell him not to waste my time. Give them back to me. You can have your money. I'll take them somewhere else."

"Hold on," said Harry. "I got fifteen. He'll not go higher."

Georgiana knew she would have to be satisfied with this; Harry was her best hope of disposing of anything. She nodded and accepted the coins held out by his grubby hand, leaving a couple for his trouble.

"What about that other matter?" Georgiana asked, stowing away the proceeds.

"Ah, now, that's quite a tale," said Harry. "Not well loved, our friend the beak. Jim Sykes says he stopped the old man that night, but took off when he had the booty. Says he didn't pop the cull."

Georgiana bit her underlip thoughtfully. "Sir Robert was alive when Jim left him?"

Harry nodded. "Mad as fire, Jim said, but gave up the booty. Seemed to be waiting there."

"How odd."

Harry shrugged.

"Maybe I should talk to Jim," said Georgiana.

"No, that you shouldn't," said Harry with a vehemence which surprised her. Georgiana stared.

"You leave that to me," he continued.

"But, Harry—"

"No buts," he said firmly. "I'll find out what I can. No sense you riding about for all the world to see."

Georgiana was left to wonder whether Harry's insistence sprang from a sense of protectiveness or whether he had something to hide.

"All right," Georgiana nodded. Her own business done, she pondered the best way to broach the subject of Joe Hill. Harry looked questioningly at her.

"Was there something else, my lad?" he asked.

"When I came in, there was a man leaving," said Georgiana. "I thought I recognised him. Do you know who he was?"

Harry shook his head. "Can't say as I do. There's been nobody strange in here this evening."

"Really?"

Harry's eyes narrowed. Georgiana mentally cursed herself. The last thing she needed was to provoke him to suspicion. She let the matter drop. He had proved himself a good friend, but she suspected he could be a dangerous enemy. If he had told her the truth, did that mean Joe Hill was a regular visitor to the Lucky Bell?

Outside the tavern, Georgiana untied Princess and led her back towards the cover of the trees before mounting, her mind all the time on Hill. Georgiana's knowledge of him made it difficult for her to accept his involvement in anything dishonest, yet patrons of the Lucky Bell went there to deal in little else.

The night was mild, with only an occasional breeze

interrupting the stillness. In the minimal light of the half moon Georgiana anticipated little difficulty in slipping home unnoticed. As she drew level with the road, she looked up and down the length of it and began to pick her way across noiselessly.

The lamp of the approaching carriage was dim in the distance, its struggle to grow brighter not keeping pace with its speed. Georgiana knew she could not avoid being seen. Instincts baulking against flight, she drew her pistol, reining in to face the approaching curricle. Levelling the weapon she looked directly at the driver. Maxwell Lakesby was holding the reins.

8

"Stand and deliver!"

The familiar words sounded strange in Georgiana's ears, her voice seeming to come from someone other than herself. Head held high, she met Mr Lakesby's eyes unwaveringly.

"Well, well," said Lakesby. "Held up two evenings in a row. However, you seem rather more competent than your compatriot of last night."

She ignored the compliment. "Your valuables, sir." Georgiana instinctively lowered her voice, trusting it wasn't too recognisable with the muffling effect of the mask.

Lakesby did not move. Georgiana's gaze flickered to his companion, presumably a groom. She wondered whether either would follow the example of the postilion from the previous night. She raised her pistol slightly to encourage co-operation.

Lakesby smiled and tossed her a small coin purse. He then drew off a signet ring and removed a pin from his cravat. He handed both items to his servant and jerked his head towards Georgiana. The man looked at him in puzzlement.

"Go on, Brackett," said Lakesby. "Give them to the gentleman."

The groom shook his head and handed over the items. Georgiana stowed them in her black velvet bag, glad the bandage was no longer on her hand. She nodded her thanks and signalled in dismissal. Lakesby immediately raised his whip.

Georgiana's fleeting glance away from the carriage was enough. The weapon was in the groom's hand and aimed as she started to turn Princess.

"Brackett, no!" came Lakesby's strong tones. He acted as

swiftly as his groom. Lakesby's hand grasped the one holding the pistol, fingers closing firmly around the other man's wrist. The shot went wide, startling Georgiana's horse and setting a collection of birds on a speedy flight path. The groom stared at his master in astonishment. Georgiana gave Lakesby a swift, involuntary glance, reining in Princess and digging in her heels to gallop away.

Georgiana arrived home breathless and stood against the back door for a moment. Tugging off her hat and mask, she ran up the stairs. By the time she reached her bedroom, her coat was flung over one arm and she was already starting to unbutton her shirt. Emily's eyes widened at this disarray.

Georgiana tossed her black velvet bag on the bed. Emily frowned as she noticed the weight of it.

"That can't all be from Harry. Miss Georgiana, you promised—"

"I know," said Georgiana. She paused, put a finger to her lips and silently opened the bedroom door to look into the corridor. Peace seemed unbroken. Closing the door quietly, Georgiana turned to her maid.

"I was afraid I might have woken my cousin. Fortunately, she is not the light sleeper she imagines."

"Miss Georgiana, what happened?"

"I encountered a curricle on the road on my way home," Georgiana said in as light a tone as she could manage.

"You didn't…?" Emily's horrified eyes said she already knew the answer.

"Yes, Emily, I'm afraid I did," Georgiana acknowledged. "I know the sensible thing would have been to take cover until they were out of sight. There was little time to make a considered decision."

"That's all very well, miss, but with this murder…"

"Yes, I know, Emily. I promise, I did not set out with the intention of holding up anyone. I'm afraid I just took advantage of the opportunity." She paused. "The driver of the curricle was Mr Lakesby."

Emily paled.

Georgiana continued. "I already had my pistol out when I realised."

"Did he recognise you?"

"I hope not," said Georgiana with feeling. "Although…" She paused thoughtfully.

"Although what?"

"He stopped his groom from shooting. It was quite deliberate. Mr Lakesby pushed his hand away so the shot went wide."

"Heaven help us!" said Emily.

"Thank you," said Georgiana with a laugh.

"Oh, miss, of course I don't want you shot, but why would Mr Lakesby save you unless he recognised you?"

"Perhaps he has a genuinely compassionate nature. He did assist in saving Tom."

"Maybe," said Emily doubtfully, putting away the clothing her mistress had so hastily discarded. After despatching her for the wine decanter, Georgiana sat at her dressing table with her head in her hands. Raising it after a few moments, she looked at her reflection. She could not rule out the possibility that Lakesby had penetrated her disguise. He had been too co-operative, almost amused. He had also probably saved her life. Georgiana had no doubt that left to his own devices, Lakesby's groom would have lost little sleep over inflicting a potentially fatal wound.

It was not many minutes before Emily returned with the wine, a sight of which filled Georgiana with disproportionate relief. She had not realised how shaken she was until she felt its warmth coursing through her. With the second swallow, her brain began to clear. She glanced towards Emily who was looking at her anxiously.

"What now, miss?"

"All we can do is wait, Emily."

"Until the Runners are knocking on the door?"

"Until we have some idea what Mr Lakesby intends to do."

Emily shook her head. "And if he sends the Runners right away?"

The same thought had occurred to Georgiana. Yet she suspected Lakesby would derive a certain amusement from keeping her on tenterhooks. Besides, although he might have suspicions, he had no real proof. Georgiana could not imagine him taking action without it. He would look remarkably foolish accusing a respectable lady of highway robbery without evidence. Georgiana did not think Lakesby was a man to make himself look foolish. Of course, if she were found in possession of his property, things could be different.

She would have to get rid of her booty quickly. About to tell Emily to retrieve her highway clothes for a return to the Lucky Bell, she paused as another idea occurred to her. The ghost of a mischievous smile played about her lips. Emily looked uneasy.

"What are you planning, miss?"

"Do we have any paper in the kitchen?" Georgiana asked. "Maybe something used to wrap bread or cheese."

"I think so," said Emily.

"Would you see if you could find me some?" asked Georgiana, tipping the contents of her velvet bag on to her bed.

Emily did as she was bid, returning with a piece of plain brown paper. She watched fascinated as Georgiana brushed away the few lingering breadcrumbs. Tearing it in two, she placed the items taken from Mr Lakesby on one of the pieces. She rolled the paper around them and twisted the ends securely. Folding them down, she put the little parcel on the second piece and repeated the process.

"This is all that ties me to the robbery," said Georgiana. "I shall have to dispose of it."

"How?" asked Emily.

"Return it to its owner," said Georgiana promptly.

"What?" Emily was horrified. "Beg pardon, miss, but are you mad?"

"I hope not," said Georgiana cheerfully.

"But how can you do that?" asked Emily.

Georgiana did not answer immediately. A number of ideas were tossing around in her mind. She was not certain of their feasibility. Direct contact with Lakesby was best avoided, so it seemed expedient to engage a third party. Georgiana's problem was in determining whom she dared trust. Emily could be recognised, as could any other member of her household, many of whom offered the added risk of gossip below stairs.

"I'm not entirely certain. Perhaps we could engage one of those street urchins. I doubt they'd ask questions."

"Is that wise, miss? You don't know anything about those children."

"True, but more importantly, they don't know anything about us. Those poor souls are usually near starvation, they'll be glad enough to earn a few coppers."

Georgiana fell silent, looking thoughtful. Emily's own expression was resigned recognition, warily watching her mistress.

"You can't save the whole world, Miss Georgiana."

"I know, Emily, we can only do what we can. It just doesn't seem enough." She grew businesslike again, handing Emily the small parcel with sixpence.

"Try to slip out of the house. Give this to one of those urchins, ask them to take it to Brooks's, to be given to Mr Lakesby."

"Sixpence seems a lot to offer a street urchin."

"Perhaps. It's little enough for what they need. In any case, it may prompt the child to carry out the task. If Mr Lakesby's property is restored to him, he has no evidence of a robbery and no reason to pursue any inquiry."

Emily was able to report success on her errand the next day as far as her part was concerned. Georgiana nodded with satisfaction and tried to busy herself with a number of tasks which needed her attention. Despite her cool demeanour she felt on edge, wondering whether the heavy brass knocker would fall and announce the arrival of Mr Lakesby with a party of Bow Street Runners. Although not entirely surprised it did not come, Georgiana dared not succumb to relief. It was usually fair to assume a traveller would act immediately if they knew where to find the highwayman. However, Lakesby was not like most travellers. She could not be certain whether he had not recognised her, or whether he had some other course in mind.

Georgiana's earliest opportunity of judging Lakesby's behaviour came in the course of a morning call on the following day. For some inscrutable reason, he had chosen to accompany his cousin on a visit to the same elderly acquaintance on whom Georgiana decided to call. He gave her an affable good morning and returned his attention to the elderly lady's middle-aged daughter.

Louisa immediately laid claim to Georgiana, taking advantage of their brief conversation to seek her opinion on a pair of gloves she had seen that very morning. Georgiana had little time to reply and barely an opportunity to invite Louisa to tea before Lakesby called Louisa to take leave of their hostess.

As Lakesby put his hand to his cousin's arm, Georgiana noticed he wore the signet ring she had taken. She had never before been aware of its glint, although she had previously seen it on Lakesby's finger. Wondering whether its owner was deliberately trying to draw it to her attention, she affected not to notice and bid him good day with fair composure.

To Georgiana's surprise, when the day arrived for Louisa to

take tea with her, she appeared without her mother although accompanied by a retinue of servants. Georgiana despatched Louisa's maid to the kitchen to be regaled with refreshment and instructed James to ensure the coachman and groom were similarly well-provided. She then turned her attention to Louisa, happily ensconced in a chair in the drawing room. Miss Knatchbull sat opposite, hands folded.

"I think we can serve ourselves, can't we?" Georgiana smiled.

"Oh, yes," chirped Louisa.

"Pray, let me, Georgiana," said Miss Knatchbull. "You should rest your hand."

"Yes of course, you must," said Louisa, all concern. "How is it?"

"It's perfectly well now," said Georgiana, allowing her cousin to dispense the tea through a flow of inconsequential chat. It was not long before Louisa offered up more interesting subject matter.

"Did you know Sir Robert Foster's funeral is tomorrow?" she asked ingenuously.

Selina was all polite attention. Georgiana's pause was barely perceptible.

"No," said Georgiana. "I had not heard. How did you come to learn of it?"

"I heard Mama mention it. She wants Max to go."

"Oh? Why is that?"

"Georgiana, how can you ask?" said Selina, a hint of reproof in her voice.

Louisa glanced towards Miss Knatchbull before answering Georgiana. "She thinks it would be proper, to show respect."

"Quite right," approved Miss Knatchbull.

"What does your cousin say?" inquired Georgiana. "Does he agree with your mother?"

Louisa sighed. "He does not care to go. I cannot blame him.

It sounds very dreary."

Miss Knatchbull gave a horrified gasp. She opened her mouth to speak but was forestalled by her cousin.

"Yes, I daresay. However, funerals are bound to be sad occasions."

"I know," said Louisa. "But it seems foolish to go and pretend sadness when it is the funeral of someone one did not like and will not miss."

Selina's eyes widened, but Georgiana privately agreed with this sentiment. She could not imagine Lakesby indulging in the hypocrisy of displaying grief for a man he made no secret of disliking.

Louisa was biting on her bottom lip. The girl seemed hesitant, a half-ashamed expression in her eyes. It was clear no confidences would come while Miss Knatchbull was within hearing. Georgiana sought for an excuse to send her cousin from the room.

"Selina, would you be kind enough to fetch my shawl? I am feeling a draught."

"Why, yes, of course, Georgiana, anything you wish." Selina almost jumped from her chair in her anxiety to fuss and be of use. Georgiana hoped that if Emily found Selina in the bedroom, she would realise the errand was a pretext and keep her occupied for as long as she could manage.

Georgiana smiled encouragingly. Louisa returned the smile, but her hesitancy of manner continued. When she did speak, her words were sudden, with a slight breathlessness which seemed unnatural, telling Georgiana of a ball dress illustrated in a ladies' periodical. Georgiana made appropriate noises of interest, her mind speculating on where Louisa's thoughts really were. Such sense of discretion had not seemed in the girl's nature.

Georgiana's mind went back to the meeting with Brandon Foster, particularly the item which Louisa had appeared to have secreted into his hand. Georgiana wondered how close the two were. Louisa had exhibited none of the symptoms of being violently in love which were characteristic of a girl of her age, but Georgiana suspected the intrigue of a clandestine affair would appeal. Louisa's naiveté could easily incline her to take any overtures seriously. Georgiana realised that Sir Brandon's present situation might tempt him to consider marriage with a girl of some wealth, but his wild lifestyle would not make him a welcome suitor for the daughter of any ambitious mama.

"Do you think your mama will persuade your cousin to attend Sir Robert's funeral?" Georgiana inquired.

Louisa shook her head.

"I shouldn't think so," she said. "Max did not care for Sir Robert."

"So I gathered."

"Besides, Max always does as he pleases."

This did not surprise Georgiana. "Why did he not like Sir Robert?" she inquired.

Louisa shrugged. "He never told me. I know he was very angry when Mama consented to Sir Robert's offer of marriage. In fact, he seemed out of reason cross." She paused, as if trying to decide whether to say more. "He does not like Sir Robert's son either."

Georgiana's ears pricked with attention. She wondered whether she imagined the slightly aggrieved tone behind Louisa's forced casual manner.

"Your cousin seems very thorough in his dislikes," said Georgiana, picking up a biscuit. "Does he always encompass the whole family?"

"Oh, no," said Louisa. "But he is not very tolerant, you see."

"Oh?"

Louisa hesitated. Georgiana wondered whether she was

going to remember discretion.

"Max does not consider Mr Foster – I mean, Sir Brandon – a proper person for me to know."

"I see," said Georgiana. "I am only slightly acquainted with him. Do you know him well?"

"Oh, no," said Louisa a little too quickly. "Not very well... that is... I know him a little."

Georgiana was sure Louisa could tell her something if the girl would just come to the point. Georgiana decided to be specific.

"Does he drink?" she inquired.

"Well, yes, I believe so," said Louisa. "But, then, most men do, don't they? Even if they don't let one see them foxed."

"Perhaps it is his gambling your cousin does not like?"

Louisa's eyes widened. "Does Sir Brandon gamble? I know he is often without funds, but I thought that was because of his quarrel with his father." She paused. "It is not his fault; he needs assistance."

This caught Georgiana's interest. Had Louisa been giving Brandon Foster money? If so, she must have a generous allowance. It occurred to Georgiana that if Lakesby suspected this, Louisa's pursestrings could be substantially tightened.

"Miss Grey, do you know what happened about that highwayman who tried to rob Max's carriage?"

An icy hand gripped Georgiana's heart before she realised Louisa was talking about Tom.

"He's the merest boy, Louisa, no more than twelve or thirteen, I imagine."

"Really? I did not notice in the dark, though I suppose he was quite small, and he was masked, wasn't he?"

Georgiana eyed Louisa speculatively, wondering how to phrase her point of concern.

"Has your cousin mentioned whether he means to hand the boy over to the law?"

Louisa's eyes widened. "You mean he has not done so?"

"No," Georgiana replied. "At least, not yet. The boy is upstairs, recovering from his injury. Two of my servants are looking after him."

"Oh, heavens!" said Louisa. "Aren't you afraid, keeping him in the house?"

"Of course not," said Georgiana impatiently. "He's nothing more than a child, and is injured as well as unarmed. He isn't going to do any harm."

"I wish I could share your certainty, Georgiana," remarked Miss Knatchbull, returning at that moment with the requested shawl. "Can you imagine, Miss Winters, a highwayman under our very own roof? I've barely had a wink of sleep while he's been here. Even when I have managed to close my eyes, I have visions of the rogue sneaking around the house, looking for valuables."

"I'm sure you have no need to worry," said Georgiana. "As I said, he's hardly in a condition to persecute us."

"But he will recover," said Selina earnestly, "strengthened by our food and waited on by our servants. Perhaps I should push a chair against the door," she mused.

Georgiana rolled her eyes. "Whatever makes you comfortable, Selina," she said in a colourless tone.

"My dear Georgiana, I shall not be at all comfortable until the cut-throat is out of the house."

"What is he like?" asked Louisa. "Is he really a cut-throat? Is he very handsome? Has he tried to escape?"

"I'm not holding him prisoner, Louisa." Georgiana tried to drag the girl's mind back to the question of Tom's fate. "I believe he's asleep at the moment. I must confess, I have not had very much to do with him since he's been here. However, I am concerned about him being taken off to prison as soon as he recovers."

"Really? Mama says all such creatures should be hanged, to

127

teach them a lesson."

"Quite right," said Miss Knatchbull with a shudder.

"I'm sure he will have learnt a lesson," said Georgiana, beginning to wonder whether she would be better employed in aiding Tom to escape. "He is likely to profit far better by it than on the gallows preparing to be a corpse."

Selina looked horrified by the image offered. However, she had no opportunity to remonstrate, attention being directed to the entrance of the butler.

"I beg your pardon, miss," said Horton, "but Mrs Grey has called with—"

"Oh, no, don't bother to announce us," trilled an unwelcome voice as Lord Bartholomew Parker sailed into the room behind Georgiana's quiet sister-in-law.

"Amanda," said Georgiana in some surprise, "and Lord Bartholomew. This is a…"

"Now, now, Miss Grey, we just had to see you," said Lord Bartholomew.

"I did explain you were entertaining, miss," said the butler.

"That's perfectly all right, Horton. Thank you."

"I'm sorry to disturb you, Georgiana," said Amanda Grey as Georgiana stepped forward to give her sister-in-law a kiss on the cheek. "We won't stay long. Hello, Selina, I hope you are well?"

"Yes, quite well, thank you."

Amanda looked towards Louisa. "I do beg your pardon. You must think us shockingly rag-mannered."

Louisa returned the smile shyly and Georgiana made introductions.

"I'm so pleased to meet you," said Amanda. "I understand my husband made your acquaintance a few evenings ago."

"Oh, yes, that's right," responded Louisa, the barest hint of hesitation in her voice.

Lord Bartholomew was studying her, a frown embedded

between his brows.

"It was your cousin's theatre party which took Miss Grey away from us on Friday evening," he said accusingly.

Louisa looked at Georgiana in some confusion. She in turn gave Lord Bartholomew a glance of annoyance to which he seemed blind.

"What has that to say to anything, pray?" said Georgiana. "It is my own business how I choose to spend an evening."

"Of course," said Amanda swiftly. "Bartholomew did not mean anything. He was just disappointed you couldn't join us, as were we all."

Georgiana looked at Lord Bartholomew for a moment longer before transferring her gaze to her sister-in-law.

"Would you like some tea?" Georgiana asked Amanda.

"No, thank you," said Amanda. "We don't wish to intrude."

"Nonsense, Amanda," said Lord Bartholomew, "your sister will not object to us joining her for tea."

"Oh, no," chirped in Selina, "you would be very welcome. We are always very pleased to see you. Isn't that so, Georgiana?"

Georgiana held her peace.

"No, Bartholomew, we can't stay long." said Amanda. "I have left the children with Cousin Mabel, and she will begin to fret if I do not collect them soon." She smiled at Louisa. "What must you think of us barging in like this?"

"Oh, please, you mustn't worry," said Louisa earnestly. "After all, you are family."

"Exactly," said Lord Bartholomew.

"Was there something particular you wanted to speak to me about, Amanda?" Georgiana asked before he could expand on this.

"Yes. I have an invitation for you," Amanda said. "We are having a small party tomorrow evening and were hoping you and Selina would be able to come. You will also be very welcome, Miss Winters."

"Thank you, Mrs Grey," said Louisa. "I shall tell Mama."

"Yes, of course," said Amanda. "We should be glad to see you both."

Georgiana wondered how small the party would be and whether it was another excuse to throw her into the company of Lord Bartholomew. She was a little comforted by the inclusion of Louisa and her mother in the invitation. After avoiding the dinner party, Georgiana supposed she would have to accept.

Georgiana had barely begun to thank Amanda when the sound of an altercation in another part of the house attracted everyone's attention. There could be no doubt about the reason for the commotion. Tom was awake. Georgiana knew she would have to deal with the matter herself and had no doubt Selina would pour out the whole tale as soon as she was out of the room. She saw no way of avoiding this. Georgiana swiftly excused herself, her astonished guests staring at one another in stupefaction. The expression on Louisa's face said plainly that she would have liked to join her hostess.

Georgiana knocked peremptorily on the door of Tom's bedroom, reluctant to enter and give the boy an opportunity of recognising her.

"Emily?" she hissed. "James? What is going on in there?"

The door was quickly opened and shut as Emily joined Georgiana on the landing.

"For heaven's sake, Emily, what's happening?"

"I'm sorry, miss. He's just woken up. He seems to be feeling better, and is making a fuss about wanting to get out."

"Well, see if you can keep him quiet. I'll send everyone on their way and come back."

Emily nodded. "Yes, miss."

Georgiana returned to the drawing room, bestowing a disarming smile upon its occupants. Lord Bartholomew's horrified face told her she had been correct about Selina. Georgiana was irritated to notice an element of self-satisfaction and pride in her cousin's expression.

"I cannot believe you have a highwayman under your roof, Miss Grey," said Lord Bartholomew. "That seems very unwise. You should not give him such encouragement."

Georgiana made a mental note to hold up Lord Bartholomew's carriage at the first opportunity.

"I'd hardly call it encouragement to nurse an injured boy," she responded evenly.

"But if he is able to hold up a carriage..." said Lord Bartholomew.

"That is what I said, as did Lady Winters. Is that not so, my dear?" interrupted Selina, addressing herself to Louisa.

Louisa looked startled. Before Georgiana could voice indignation at her cousin's tactics, Amanda came to the girl's rescue.

"Of course you are concerned – I am myself. But I can understand Georgiana's compassion for someone injured. Did you say he was just a boy, Georgiana?"

"But what will Edward say?" asked the scandalised Lord Bartholomew.

"Edward has nothing to say to the matter," said Georgiana, beginning to lose her temper.

"No, of course not," said Amanda. "But he will be concerned over your safety. Are you certain you are not in danger?"

"Perfectly," said Georgiana.

"Nevertheless, Miss Grey," began Lord Bartholomew.

"He made a mistake. I'm sure he's learned his lesson," said Georgiana firmly.

"Very well, if you are certain, my dear," said Amanda. "However, do be careful, I beg you."

"Of course," said Georgiana.

With the subject so definitely closed, neither Miss Knatchbull nor Lord Bartholomew could voice their opinions further, leaving each looking profoundly dissatisfied.

"Now," said Georgiana, grateful for her sister-in-law's efforts, "about your party."

"You don't have to give me an answer now," said Amanda, rising. "Send me a note tomorrow if you prefer. We have intruded long enough. Come, Bartholomew."

Lord Bartholomew's chagrin was comical to behold. Selina's was little better, she seeming to mistake a sulk for dignified silence. Georgiana might have laughed out loud had her mind not been occupied with more pressing matters. As Amanda and Lord Bartholomew took their leave, Louisa also made her farewells.

With the door safely closed on her visitors, Georgiana gave her waiting cousin no chance to claim her attention.

"I'm sorry, Selina, I am needed upstairs." Turning quickly, she moved as fast as her cambric morning dress would allow and knocked softly at the door of Tom's bedroom. It was opened by James who gave her just enough room to enter before closing it.

"What is the matter?" Georgiana looked towards Tom, sitting up in bed with a belligerent air about him. In a clean nightshirt, his face scrubbed, he looked a very different figure from the urchin she was accustomed to seeing at the Lucky Bell.

"I want to leave," he said.

"Should I assume you are feeling better?" she asked him.

"You can't keep me here."

"Where do you propose to go, pray?"

Tom said nothing, continuing to glower.

"Well?" Georgiana persevered. "Where is home?"

"The Lucky Bell," he spat out.

"The Lucky Bell," Georgiana repeated. "That's a tavern, isn't it? Do you not think you are more comfortable here?"

"I've heard about that tavern," interpolated James. "It's a haven for thieves, mostly highway robbers, I believe."

"Really?" said Georgiana, hoping James's knowledge did not extend beyond common gossip. She kept her eyes fixed on Tom. "That's where you want to go, is it?"

Tom was indignant. "Me friends are there," he said. "If you don't let me go, they'll come to this ken and get me. Then you'll be sorry." He paused, then continued with a hint of pride in his voice, "I know the Crimson Cavalier."

"I've heard about the Crimson Cavalier," remarked Georgiana in conversational fashion. "How can he possibly know where you are?"

Tom appeared thrown. Georgiana turned towards James.

"Leave us a moment."

James looked dubiously at the boy in the bed.

"Are you sure, miss?"

"Yes. Please do as I ask."

James departed with reluctance, assuring Georgiana that he would not be far if she needed him. Georgiana and the patient were left confronting one another. She sat down on the foot of the bed.

"Why do you want to go back to the Lucky Bell?"

"I told you, I got friends there."

"Ah, yes, the Crimson Cavalier." She paused. "You haven't told me your name."

The boy remained silent.

"Oh, very well," said Georgiana. "But I feel I should mention, you are in a great deal of trouble. Mr Lakesby, whose carriage you stopped, knows you are here. If he chooses to inform the authorities, there's very little I can do."

A doubtful look crossed the boy's face but his tone remained defiant. "Don't need help."

Georgiana remained patient.

"You'd rather hang?"

She received no answer.

"Look, it's plain you are not suited to this sort of work. You could have been killed."

"I wasn't," he said, chin in the air.

"This time."

"I can take care of myself," interrupted Tom, using a phrase Georgiana frequently employed herself. "I done it before!"

"What does that mean?" Georgiana demanded.

Tom met her eyes in sullen silence. Georgiana knew he had been left to his own devices with the death of his mother some years earlier, his father having already deserted them both. It was not clear whether his assertion of having 'done it before' was a declaration of independence or a boast of experience in holding up carriages. Georgiana had never heard anything to suggest Tom had taken to the road. He had never hidden his ambitions in this direction, and Georgiana suspected pride would initially get the better of discretion.

"What have you done before?" she asked. "Should I assume Mr Lakesby's is not the first carriage you've stopped?"

Tom gave no answer. However, Georgiana took advantage of the flicker of doubt she noticed in his eyes.

"A gentleman was killed on the road a few nights ago," she said, moving to the foot of the bed and taking hold of the rail. "Perhaps you heard about it. A highwayman is thought to be responsible."

"It's not true," said Tom hotly. "The Crimson Cavalier didn't kill him."

"I did not accuse the Crimson Cavalier," said Georgiana quietly. "Any highwayman could have done it, as indeed could you."

"I didn't!" said Tom passionately.

Georgiana was not blind to the fear Tom was trying to hide. It was easy to imagine his ambitions leading to the hot-headed action of holding up Sir Robert and equally easy to conceive of something going wrong with that robbery. Whether it had resulted in Sir Robert's death was a question which made Georgiana acutely uncomfortable.

"Did you hold up the gentleman who was killed?" she asked.

"I told you, I wasn't there."

A tap on the door prevented Georgiana pursuing the issue. James did not wait for an answer but slipped quickly inside and closed the door behind him.

"I beg your pardon, miss, but Mr Lakesby has called."

"What?"

"He said he was looking for his cousin, whom he understood to be taking tea with you today."

"She's gone."

"So I apprised him, miss," responded James. "He then asked to see you. I informed him you were otherwise engaged, but he said he would be happy to wait."

"What about my cousin? Could she not entertain him for a while?"

"Miss Knatchbull has gone to lie down in her room with the headache. She asked that no one disturb her."

"Bother," said Georgiana. "Very well, I shall be there directly."

James nodded and departed to convey this information. Georgiana looked towards Tom. "I'll have to talk to him. He may want to see you himself. I don't know that I'll be able to stop him."

The boy remained silent and Georgiana departed, sweeping downstairs to the drawing room where Mr Lakesby awaited her. He was standing by the fireplace, his foot stretched before the hearth. He smiled pleasantly as she entered.

"Ah, Miss Grey. Good day to you."

"Good afternoon, Mr Lakesby. I understand you were hoping to see Louisa. I am afraid she has gone home."

"So I've been told. No matter. I thought I would do myself

the honour of paying my respects to her hostess."

"That's very civil, Mr Lakesby."

"Would you care to come for a drive with me?"

Georgiana hesitated, hoping her astonishment was not too apparent.

"Well, I–"

"Only through the park," he assured her with a smile. "I promise I shall not try to abduct you."

"No, of course not. What an idea," responded Georgiana. "It is just that I am rather busy at the moment."

"Are you?" asked Lakesby. "Can you not spare just a little while?"

Georgiana spoke in guarded tones.

"You forget I have a guest, Mr Lakesby."

"I do not in the least forget it, Miss Grey. Surely you can leave him to your servants? You do not need to attend to him yourself?"

"I've been trying to talk to him, in the hope he might tell me something," said Georgiana.

"Oh?"

Georgiana cast a wary look towards Lakesby. "Have you decided whether you will hand him over to the law?"

Lakesby's tone grew inviting. "Come for a drive and we'll discuss the matter."

Georgiana noticed him twisting his signet ring in a seemingly idle gesture. She knew it was dangerous to go with him, but a voice at the back of her mind told her it would be more dangerous to refuse. She found herself capitulating.

"Very well. I shall have to fetch a bonnet and pelisse. Could you grant me a few minutes?"

"Perfectly easily."

"What about your horses?" inquired Georgiana. "Surely you will not wish to leave them standing?"

"They are being walked up and down. You need not concern

yourself."

"Very well. I shall not detain you long."

Returning a few minutes later, Georgiana drew on her gloves as she walked into the drawing room. She wore a pale green pelisse over her morning dress while a cream coloured bonnet, interlaced with green ribbon, sat perched on her auburn locks. The effect was quite striking. She smiled at Lakesby.

"Charming, quite charming," he said as he came forward. He offered her his arm. "Shall we go?"

"Certainly, I am quite ready."

As Lakesby handed her into the curricle, Georgiana noticed his two matched greys were being held by one of her own stablehands. She experienced a check of apprehension at the realisation that his groom would not be with them. This was a double-edged sword. While the groom might recognise her from the robbery of Lakesby's coach, a third party could buffer her against any suspicions Lakesby himself might have. She took care her manner gave no indication of her thoughts and smiled as she settled herself in the well-sprung equipage. Lakesby did not speak as he climbed up next to her and picked up the reins, giving a nod to the stablehand to stand off.

"What fine animals," Georgiana said by way of conversation.

"Thank you," said Lakesby. "You have not, I think, seen them before."

"No, I believe not."

Georgiana noticed him shoot a quick glance towards her.

"I understand you are something of a judge of horseflesh, Miss Grey."

"I? You flatter me, sir."

"Oh? My cousin tells me Sir Robert Foster remarked on it when they called on you after meeting that highwayman."

Privately, Georgiana considered this an odd thing for Louisa to discuss with her cousin. Her response was cool.

"I have been fortunate," she said, remembering how Sir Robert had expressed his opinion of her horses.

"I'm sure you are too modest," Lakesby said, his eyes on the road ahead. "I understand your stables are quite a matter for envy. I should like to see them sometime."

"What a curious ambition," smiled Georgiana.

"Oh, I don't know."

Lakesby fell silent again, his concentration apparently on his driving. His manner was relaxed, his touch on the reins light, his control firm. Georgiana would not have been surprised to discover he was a member of the Four Horse Club.

"The Crimson Cavalier has quite a fine horse," remarked Lakesby.

"The Crimson Cavalier?" Georgiana was on her guard.

"Yes. One hears these stories about highwaymen having exceptional horses. I have always imagined them as part of the legend, but having met the Crimson Cavalier, I have to own myself impressed."

Georgiana felt her heart beating faster. She wondered Lakesby could not hear it. Her mouth grew dry.

"You've met the Crimson Cavalier?" Her voice held a hint of scepticism.

"Well, perhaps 'met' is not quite the right word. He held up my carriage, not far from where Sir Robert's body was found, I believe."

"Really? That seems a rather dangerous area for highwaymen."

"It does seem to keep the Crimson Cavalier well occupied," Lakesby observed. "However, if he disposes of all his booty in the same manner as that which he took from me, it can't be very profitable for him."

"You have traced your property, then?" Georgiana asked, in a tone of mild interest.

"More easily than one would have expected. It was returned

to me."

"Indeed? How odd."

"Perhaps." He looked steadily at her, the hint of a smile appearing. "Perhaps you could enlighten me, Miss Grey."

9

"I beg your pardon?"

Lakesby smiled. His tone remained pleasant, conversational.

"It was very sporting of you, I thought, returning my property. You'd done your work well; you earned the right to keep it."

Georgiana had sensed an element of suspicion on Lakesby's part, but had not been prepared for such a direct confrontation. She decided to brazen it out, adopting what she hoped was a convincingly perplexed expression.

"Mr Lakesby, I am afraid you have me at a loss. Are you accusing me of being a highway robber?"

"A very good highway robber," he responded, "much better than that young friend of yours."

Georgiana seized on the chance he offered. "You have not yet told me what you mean to do about that boy. Do you intend to notify the authorities?"

"Certainly not. I've no desire to hang a child. However," Lakesby continued, "I would advise the boy to choose another line of work."

"I have suggested that to him."

"A wise undertaking. I'm sure he will listen to the Crimson Cavalier." Lakesby's tone was cool. "He lacks your flair for the business."

Georgiana refrained from volunteering that the Crimson Cavalier had already made several attempts to dissuade Tom from venturing into a career with which he was not compatible. Instead, she looked steadily at Lakesby, the beginnings of a puzzled frown taking shape on her brow.

"Mr Lakesby, I must confess myself at a loss. I can only assume you are having a joke at my expense, though rather an

140

odd one. You cannot seriously mean to suggest I could be some notorious highwayman. The notion is quite preposterous."

"Yes, that's what I thought at first," Lakesby mused. "Yet, you know, it's rather what makes the whole thing so appealing. When I think of my Aunt Beatrice and Sir Robert Foster in such high dudgeon, in your house, not to mention your own brother. I collect he doesn't know?"

"There is nothing for him to know," Georgiana laughed.

"How delightful! The sister of a newly appointed magistrate a common criminal?"

"Oh, not a common criminal, Miss Grey, not by any means. I consider you quite exceptional."

"I thank you for the compliment."

Lakesby laughed softly.

When Georgiana spoke again, her tone was more thoughtful. "I suppose it would be quite a coup, discovering the identity of the Crimson Cavalier. I believe the reward is now fifty pounds."

"I have no need of fifty pounds."

"I am pleased to hear it. Nevertheless, sir, it must be tempting."

"That was for the murder, wasn't it?"

"Was it?"

"Did you do it?"

"What?"

"Did you kill Sir Robert Foster?"

"Good gracious, Mr Lakesby, now you're seeking a murder confession? I really don't know what to say."

Lakesby studied her. "I think you do. However, I don't think you killed Sir Robert."

Georgiana inclined her head in gracious acknowledgement. "You are very kind."

"All the stories I've heard about the Crimson Cavalier have one thing in common. He, I beg your pardon, she, never fires a shot."

Lakesby's tone was maddeningly matter-of-fact. Georgiana looked at him in curiosity. He smiled.

"You needn't fear. I don't wish to see you hang. Your secret is quite safe, at least as far as I am concerned."

"I don't understand."

"I think it's quite fascinating. To think of being able to pull off such a feat. It's quite outrageous and yet you did it. You don't deserve hanging, you deserve congratulations."

It was clear Lakesby would not be easily convinced. Georgiana looked at him with a mixture of wonderment and pity.

"At the risk of sounding uncivil, you appear to have windmills in your head. I cannot imagine how you came to conceive such a notion."

"Can't you?" Lakesby's eyes were facing front, focused on coaxing his horses into a tricky manoeuvre of his curricle. Georgiana folded her hands in her lap, looking at him with patient interest. Lakesby glanced towards her and laughed. "To be perfectly frank, Miss Grey, I am more concerned about this business of you investigating Sir Robert Foster's murder."

"What?"

Lakesby turned his gaze full upon her.

"All these questions you have been asking, I see no other construction which can be put upon them. Am I mistaken?"

"You are mistaken in imagining my interest to be an investigation. It's quite true I am concerned and shocked, but I am hardly the proper person to investigate."

"I see," he said.

Georgiana suspected he saw only too well. Nevertheless, she was determined not to give way.

"I do understand your interest," said Lakesby. "However, I would advise you not to pursue it. Such questioning could be misconstrued and if the killer were to learn of it, even dangerous."

"Thank you, Mr Lakesby," said Georgiana, the barest hint

of an edge creeping into her voice. "It is kind of you to show such concern, but I promise you, there is not the least need. I can take care of myself."

"I don't doubt it. I should not have surrendered my valuables with such alacrity otherwise."

Georgiana sighed. "Oh, dear," she said in a bored tone. "Have we not finished with that?"

"But it's quite fascinating, Miss Grey. The sheer audacity of it. Holding up the carriages of people you have probably encountered in some drawing room and getting away with it. I make you my compliments."

"Thank you," said Georgiana, "but it sounds ridiculously far-fetched."

"That is partly what makes it so fascinating."

Georgiana looked at him with an expression which suggested she was growing tired of the joke. However, an idea occurred to her which gave rise to a slow smile.

"Are you certain that is the reason, Mr Lakesby? Perhaps you are yourself looking for someone who can take responsibility for Sir Robert's murder."

"Why on earth should I do that?"

"Perhaps you killed Sir Robert Foster."

"I?" Lakesby's astonishment seemed genuine. "Why on earth should I do such a thing?"

"You didn't want him to marry your cousin, did you?"

"No, I did not regard him as an eligible suitor. However, if I were to murder every ineligible man dangling after Louisa, there would be no room to move for bodies strewn about London."

While this seemed a little extreme, Georgiana could see his point. Although she gave a small smile in acknowledgement, a thought occurred to her which suggested a reason for him wanting to keep his cousin single.

"It must be difficult trying to sift the fortune hunters

from those with a genuine regard for Louisa," she said sympathetically.

"I have grown accustomed to it. In any case, Louisa is too young to be thinking of marriage, regardless of my aunt's views, and there are some ruthless people in the world." He stole a shrewd glance at her. "As I'm sure you know, Miss Grey."

"Yes, indeed," she sighed mournfully. "Poor Sir Robert's fate teaches us that. Of course, you would not wish anyone to take advantage of your cousin."

"No."

Georgiana cast a look at him from under her eyelashes. "It seems unlikely Sir Robert would have needed your cousin's fortune, though perhaps he would not have made her such a generous allowance as you."

"Perhaps."

Georgiana folded her hands in her lap. On looking towards Lakesby, she was surprised by an expression of genuine concern in his eyes. It took her by surprise.

"I understand you are not doing this for your own amusement, Miss Grey. Perhaps I can help?"

Georgiana was wary.

"Thank you, Mr Lakesby, but I am not certain..."

"I find it difficult to believe you uncertain of anything, Miss Grey," he said lightly. "However, if you are determined to persevere with this business of Sir Robert's murder, I may be able to assist. I am able to gain access to places which could be denied to you." He paused fractionally. "And vice versa, of course."

Approaching her house, Lakesby drew rein and leapt from the curricle. He walked around to Georgiana's side and held out a hand to assist her. As she stepped down, Georgiana regarded him steadily.

"Thank you, Mr Lakesby. It's been... interesting."

"Most definitely. Thank you for your company, Miss Grey."

With a smile which appeared to Georgiana a touch enigmatic, Lakesby bowed over her hand and took his leave. Without further speech, he stepped into the curricle and gathered the reins, quickly driving away. As the curricle disappeared, Georgiana gave herself a mental shake and began to mount the front steps, her mind prey to a turmoil of mixed thoughts. She was amazed at the equanimity with which she had faced Lakesby's disclosure. Georgiana contemplated Emily's reaction. Her maid would be appalled.

Horton opened the front door and received an absent-minded 'thank you' from Georgiana. She slowly drew off her gloves and ascended the stairs in something of a brown study. Emily was waiting in Georgiana's bedroom.

"Is my cousin still in her room?" Georgiana asked as soon as the door was closed behind her.

Emily nodded. "Mrs Daniels had some hartshorn and lavender water sent up to her, but apart from that, no one's been near her." She looked anxiously at her mistress. "What happened with Mr Lakesby?"

Georgiana looked at Emily uncertainly. She decided to opt for a compromise.

"Nothing out of the ordinary. We went for a drive through the park."

"That's all?"

Georgiana felt acutely uncomfortable. Her long relationship with Emily made it difficult for her to lie. Yet telling her of the conclusions Lakesby had drawn would only serve to worry her. Emily was looking at her suspiciously; she smiled in what she hoped was a reassuring fashion.

"We have nothing to fear from Mr Lakesby." Georgiana wondered why she felt certain on this point, but she was sure she was speaking the truth.

As Emily put away her bonnet and pelisse, Georgiana sat

in front of the dressing table, trying to determine her next move. She looked thoughtfully towards her maid as an idea occurred to her.

"Emily, Louisa Winters told me Sir Robert Foster's funeral is tomorrow."

"Oh?" said Emily as she closed the wardrobe door.

"It would hardly be proper for me to go, of course, but I was wondering whether I ought to send someone."

"Really?" said Emily. "Is that necessary?"

"A mark of respect."

Emily's expression suggested uneasiness. "You want to find out something."

"Well, it wouldn't hurt," said Georgiana matter-of-factly. "As far as anyone else is concerned, we are paying our respects." She looked at her maid's solemn eyes. Georgiana's guilt over the secret she kept from Emily took refuge in the irritation in her voice. "Very well, I confess. I would like to know who is there."

Emily's brow creased.

"What is it?" Georgiana asked.

"I'm just not certain what use it will be," said the maid.

"Neither am I," said Georgiana candidly. "But we need to explore every possibility."

"Whom do you mean to send?" Emily still looked concerned.

Georgiana paused. "I could ask Horton," she mused. "I daresay he will be less than enthusiastic, but I imagine he'll oblige. It would have to be him or James, and it hardly seems fair to ask James."

"It's not for me to say, miss."

Georgiana looked at her maid shrewdly. "No, of course not." She smiled. "I'm sure he would be very obliging, but of course he would not wish to go. I couldn't blame him."

"I don't imagine Horton will be very eager," observed Emily.

"Perhaps not. But I'm sure he will not hesitate to do his duty."

"But do you think he'll tell you anything?" asked Emily.

"We'll see," said Georgiana. "Hopefully he'll attribute any questions to feminine curiosity and indulge me."

Emily looked doubtful, but agreed it was worth the attempt.

Turning her attention elsewhere, Georgiana knew she could no longer delay sending a note to Amanda concerning the party planned for the following evening. She sat at her writing desk in the small saloon, her quill poised above the blank paper as she gazed ahead in a state of indecision. The ink had dried on the tip of her pen for the third time when James entered. Still no nearer to formulating a reply, she was glad of the distraction.

"Yes, James, what is it?"

"The boy, miss," James responded with barely concealed impatience. "He's growing restless again." James paused. "He's getting stronger and has decided he wants his clothes."

"Oh, dear," said Georgiana with a sigh. The quill feather brushed against her cheek as she knitted her brows in thought.

"Begging your pardon, miss, but what were you planning to do about him?" inquired James.

Georgiana looked at her footman. Her mind had been otherwise engaged, and there had been no opportunity to consider what would become of Tom. She could not keep him against his will. Yet she had made herself responsible for him and could not afford to risk his trying to turn highwayman again. In any case, she was far from satisfied about Tom's situation with regard to Sir Robert Foster, despite his denials.

"Send him in here to me. I'll to speak to him."

"Yes, miss." James complied, but cast a wary look back into the room before departing.

It was not many minutes before Georgiana and the boy

stood confronting one another, she thoughtful, he defiant.

"How are you feeling?" Georgiana asked.

Tom did not answer.

Georgiana sat down and signalled her guest to do likewise. After a slight hesitation, he followed her example.

"Well, what have you decided?" said Georgiana. "My footman tells me you wish to leave."

"Yes."

"To go back to the Lucky Bell?"

Tom nodded.

Georgiana regarded the boy steadily. "You realise if you return to highway robbery you may not have such a fortunate escape next time?"

"I can take care of myself. Besides, I got friends on the high toby."

"Are you sure about that?"

Tom seemed hesitant this time. The look he gave her was part suspicion, part puzzlement. Knowing Harry to be worried about Tom, Georgiana felt a twinge of guilt over her next sentence. Yet a part of her knew she would have his blessing.

"I have not noticed any indication of your friends trying to find you."

"They don't know I'm in this ken," Tom retorted. "Don't mean they're not looking."

"True," said Georgiana. "Do you think they are likely to find you?"

Tom did not answer. Georgiana began to feel cruel, taunting him in this fashion. She kept telling herself it was for the best, regarding him speculatively.

"Highway robbery strikes me as a profession for which you are not entirely suited."

"I can do it."

"It's easy to believe that until you are tested," said Georgiana. "What gives you the idea you can be successful? Have you robbed someone before your most recent disastrous attempt?"

"I know what you're doing," Tom said indignantly. "I told you, I didn't kill that old cove. You can't hang me for it."

"Fortunately, hanging people is not my responsibility. My brother, however, is a magistrate, so has more influence in such matters."

Although he maintained his defiant stance, the increasing nervousness in Tom's eyes did not escape Georgiana.

"So you say you did not kill this gentleman. Did you rob him?"

Tom did not answer. Georgiana's patience was rapidly depleting.

"Did you see him?"

"I wasn't there," Tom said.

"Where?" asked Georgiana.

"Where the old cove was."

Georgiana was not certain how many people would have known the location of Sir Robert Foster's body. Even if it was common knowledge that he had been found on the Bath Road, its length made it unlikely many people knew the exact position. Tempted as she was to pursue the extent of Tom's knowledge, Georgiana suspected he would not be quite naive enough to be taken in by her ploy. She decided to try another avenue.

"Where did you get the pistol?" she asked with casual interest.

"From one as won't needs it again," said Tom darkly.

For the first time in their conversation, Georgiana felt seriously uneasy. A half-forgotten story she had heard several months earlier flashed through her mind. A highwayman had been hanged and his body spirited away, carried to the Lucky Bell by two others working the same road, before the surgeons could take it for dissection. She also remembered a rumour that his pistol had disappeared. There was some suspicion of a guard having stolen and sold it. The notion of his selling it to Tom, or that Tom could afford to buy it, seemed rather bizarre, though not impossible.

"I'll get it right next time," Tom pursued. "I just needs practice."

Georgiana doubted this; she had rarely seen a weapon handled in less expert fashion.

"It doesn't seem to me to be the type of work which offers much opportunity for practice," she commented in a level tone. "A mistake could cost your life. Surely the incident of the other night was adequate proof of that. Mr Lakesby has agreed not to hand you over to the law. However, if he learns you mean to try your hand on the road again, he may not feel so forgiving." She paused, knowing her next words would be a gamble. "I have another proposition for you. Will you hear me out?"

The boy looked blankly at her.

"An offer," Georgiana elucidated. "How would you like to work for me?"

10

The boy stared at Georgiana, his gaping eyes and dropped jaw resembling nothing so much as a startled fish.

"I beg you will close your mouth," said Georgiana.

The boy obeyed, continuing to stare at his hostess, seeming incapable of any form of speech. Georgiana regarded him steadily.

"Well?" she inquired. "Have you nothing to say?"

"I – I dunno, miss."

Georgiana smiled. This sounded hopeful.

"What is your name?"

There was still an air of suspicion about him but he unbent sufficiently to answer.

"Tom, miss."

"Tom what?"

He blinked uncomprehendingly.

"Have you no surname?"

Tom shrugged. "Not that I knows, miss."

"I see. Well, Tom, here is what I propose. I am in need of a page. You will perform those duties in my household and do as you are told. In return, you shall have a uniform, a bed, food and I shall pay you three pounds a year."

"Lor', miss!"

"There are conditions attached," Georgiana continued, ignoring his startled cry. "You must have nothing more to do with anyone at the tavern, and on no account are you to play any more at being a highwayman."

"I wasn't playing," said Tom indignantly. "It ain't a game."

"I am aware," said Georgiana. "Of you, on the other hand, I am not so certain. If you wish to be taken seriously as a high-wayman, you had better be prepared to take the consequences.

If you prefer, I will hand you over to Mr Lakesby. He may deal with you as he thinks fit."

An expression of panic momentarily banished the look of rebellion from Tom's face. He did his best to regain his air of defiance quickly and Georgiana could not help but admire his spirit.

"Well?" she said. "I'm sure you would be comfortable here. You'd find me fair. If you do as you're told and cause me no trouble, I won't be hard on you."

Georgiana could see him wavering. She pressed her advantage.

"If you go back to, what was it, the Lucky Bell, you'll find nothing but trouble. You'll almost certainly end on the gallows. Mr Lakesby may be persuaded to leniency if you give up further thought of highway robbery. However, if you are determined to persevere, I doubt he will let you escape."

Georgiana smiled inwardly at the incongruity of the words coming out of her mouth. She could imagine Emily's reaction.

Tom looked at Georgiana doubtfully.

"I don't know nothing about being a page."

"You can learn. My servants will teach you." As she considered the members of her household, Georgiana thought about how to break the news to them. She knew none would relish taking this dubious character under their protection. Nevertheless, they were loyal and would do as their mistress bade them, whatever their reservations.

Tom still seemed hesitant. "You'd pay me? And have me to live here?"

"That's right," said Georgiana. She knew what he was thinking. There was no adventure in being a page, yet her suggestion would ensure him comfortable shelter and a fixed amount of money. She could not help feeling some sympathy for his quandary.

Tom chewed his bottom lip as he looked at Georgiana.

"What if I don't like it?"

"Then you may go," said Georgiana, "just as I may send you on your way if I don't find you satisfactory."

Tom considered this. He seemed to find it fair, for he nodded. "All right, miss. I'll do it."

"Excellent," said Georgiana. "I'm sure we shall deal extremely together. I don't expect you to make me regret my decision."

There was just a hint of warning in her voice. Tom seemed aware of it.

"No, miss."

"There is just one more thing. You must not discuss your adventures with any members of the household. They would not take kindly to having a self-confessed highwayman among them."

This brought the sullen expression back to Tom's face.

"I mean it, Tom. There will be no boasting." Georgiana looked at him thoughtfully. "In any case, I'm sure you realise your failed attempt gives you nothing of which to be proud."

Tom saw the force of this argument and sighed.

"No, miss."

"Good. Now, for the moment I suggest you return to your room. Tomorrow you may commence your duties and will move to a room in the servants' quarters."

Tom trotted off obediently. Georgiana wondered how long it would last and whether she would come to regret her impulse.

The servants accepted with at least outward equanimity the news Tom was to join them. Georgiana could only be grateful that by some miracle, word of his adventure had not permeated the household. She did notice a fleeting look of anxiety cross Emily's face, to be banished instantly as the composure demanded of a good servant was restored.

In the privacy of Georgiana's bedchamber, the maid did not hesitate to speak her mind.

"I hope you know what you're doing, miss, taking in that boy."

"So do I," said Georgiana.

Emily looked at her in alarm. Georgiana laughed.

"I think he will do very well, Emily."

"You think, miss?"

Georgiana grew solemn.

"Seriously, Emily, I don't believe there's anything to fear. If Tom was likely to recognise me, surely he would have done so by now. Besides, he won't see the Crimson Cavalier again."

Emily was shaking her head. "Perhaps, but why must you needs reform the boy?"

Georgiana smiled. "It is a little ironic, isn't it, under the circumstances?" She lapsed into thoughtful silence. "Emily, have you considered the possibility that Tom might have killed Sir Robert?"

"What? At his age?" Emily saw Georgiana was serious. "You don't really think so, do you?"

"I'm not sure," responded Georgiana slowly. "He seemed to be hinting at greater experience than we know."

Emily spoke slowly, her brow furrowed in thought. "You think he held up Sir Robert's carriage?"

"It's a possibility, don't you think?"

"Well, yes," said Emily. "It doesn't mean he did the murder, though, does it? Why would he?"

"I don't think he would have done it deliberately. The pistol may have gone off by accident. It was clear when he stopped Mr Lakesby's carriage he was struggling to handle it. I had every expectation of it firing."

Emily had no difficulty accepting the force of this argument. "What about the pistol, miss? If he was only an errand boy in that tavern, no one would just give it to him, would they?"

154

"I've been thinking about that," said Georgiana. "Do you recall my telling you about a highwayman hanged a few months ago?"

"I remember." Emily nodded. "Sid something, wasn't it?"

"That's right. He was cut down and taken to the Lucky Bell, before his body could go to the surgeons or the gibbet."

Emily shuddered. "I don't know which is worse."

"Well, never mind that now," said Georgiana, pushing out of her mind images of sharp medical dissecting knives or birds pecking the flesh of dead criminals. "I remember someone mentioning his pistol was missing. There was talk that one of the jailers had stolen and sold it."

"To a boy of Tom's age? Is that likely, miss?"

"Perhaps not likely, but possible."

"Would he have the money?" Emily sounded doubtful.

"I don't know. If the pistol was stolen the thief may have been glad to take what he could get. People with stolen goods to dispose of usually know the Lucky Bell is the place to do that. I'm sure crooked jailers are no exception."

"You think Tom may have used it to hold up Sir Robert?"

Georgiana nodded. "He denies being there, but there's a nervousness about him which makes me unsure. Perhaps he stopped Sir Robert and the robbery went wrong."

Emily mulled over this possibility. "Do you think it will help to keep him here?"

"I think it would be safer to have him under my eye."

"What about Mr Lakesby?" asked Emily. "What are you going to tell him?"

"Nothing for the present. He's agreed not to turn Tom over to the authorities. In any case, I've got nothing but suspicion at present."

"While we're on the subject of Sir Robert's murder, miss—"

"Yes?"

"Well, I saw young Betsy Hill this morning. Cook had an

155

extra loaf and some fruit, so I thought I'd take it down to them."

"Yes?"

Emily hesitated. "Well, Betsy mentioned her father was away from home most of the night Sir Robert was killed."

Georgiana mused on the possible significance of this. Joe Hill's hatred of the dead man had been open and unashamed. Would this have been the case if he had carried out the murder? Georgiana found herself wondering if there was more concerning him than the problems caused by the poor state of his cottage. She was torn between sympathy and suspicion.

"I do feel for Joe Hill," she said at last. "He has every reason for hating Sir Robert." She paused. "I wonder if he could have done it. I would never have thought of him as a killer, but I suppose, given the right provocation..."

"He's certainly had that," observed Emily. "If the problems with his cottage were the cause of his wife's death..."

Georgiana looked towards her maid, her expression thoughtful. "Emily, do you have some reason to imagine they weren't?"

"Oh, no," said Emily, "it's just..." She paused, considering how best to put her thoughts into words. "It's just that none of Sir Robert's cottages are in good repair. He's always been neglectful. Why would Mrs Hill suddenly get ill and die like that? I'm not saying she didn't but, well, it seems a bit odd when it's not happened to anyone else."

"That is an excellent point. But even if it wasn't the cause of her illness, such an atmosphere can't have been conducive to recovery."

"No," said Emily.

Georgiana sat thinking. "The damp in that cottage is quite bad. I wonder if it is worse than any of the others."

"I'm sorry, miss. I didn't mean to complicate things."

"Don't worry, Emily, you were right to mention it. Joe Hill was far from being the only one with a grudge against Sir Robert. However, I find myself wondering whether it could have originated before his wife's illness."

"Oh?"

"Yes," said Georgiana thoughtfully. "If Mr Hill already had reason to be angry with Sir Robert, what could be more natural than to blame him for the death of his wife?"

Emily considered this, nodding slowly.

"I did hear Mrs Hill used to clean house for Sir Robert. Perhaps something happened at that time?"

"Perhaps," said Georgiana. "I wonder if there's any way of finding out." She sighed. "Neither must we forget Sir Brandon, the despair of matchmaking mamas. When he mentioned his father's will, he said he would manage and always does. He seemed quite proud of himself, as if he'd come up with some ingenious idea."

"Perhaps he's a highwayman," Emily said lightly.

Georgiana smiled. "The thought did cross my mind. Can you imagine his father's reaction?" She continued in more serious vein. "He seemed quite unconcerned about his father's death, and he's showing interest in the girl Sir Robert was proposing to take as a second wife." She frowned. "I thought Louisa passed him a note at the theatre, but it has since occurred to me that perhaps she gave him some money."

Emily looked surprised at this. "I don't suppose her ladyship or Mr Lakesby would be too pleased about that."

"I imagine not," said Georgiana, "particularly if she does it often." She paused. "In fact, if Mr Lakesby has control of Louisa's inheritance until she comes of age or marries, perhaps it would suit him to keep her single."

Emily's eyes widened.

"Helping himself to her inheritance?"

"Possibly," said Georgiana. "From what I've seen of him,

I wouldn't have thought it, but one never knows. He may have debts of his own, perhaps thought a little borrowing from his cousin's inheritance would help, to be returned later. Louisa is young, plenty of time to pay it back."

"So Mr Lakesby may not have been too happy about Lady Winters wanting her daughter married so soon. I must admit, I should not like to make an enemy of him. I hear he's a good shot."

"Oh?" Georgiana looked inquiringly at her maid.

"Apparently," Emily said with casual unconcern. "There's a story he hit a diamond out of a playing card for a wager. I don't know how much truth is in it."

"Which card?" Georgiana could not resist asking.

"I don't know. A five, I think."

Georgiana smiled. "A colourful tale."

"Oh, I know, but I still think he's not a man to be crossed," replied Emily.

"If Louisa had married Sir Robert, I wonder how he would have treated her," mused Georgiana.

"He might have spoilt her with trumpery bits of jewellery," grinned Emily.

"So he might," responded Georgiana. "Hideous heirlooms which would not cost anything." She glanced towards a clock. "It is getting late. I had better see how my cousin is. Emily, I think I will go to Amanda's party tomorrow."

Even with her decision made about the party, Georgiana found her mind more focused on Sir Robert Foster's funeral. The following day, she waited impatiently for the return of Horton, who had accepted as natural the request to represent the household. She allowed some time for him to refresh himself with some soup and a mug of ale before sending for him.

"Did it all go smoothly?" Georgiana asked.

A quickly suppressed flash of surprise crossed the butler's

countenance, but he responded in an impassive tone. "Yes, miss."

"Were there many people there?" Georgiana inquired as casually as she could.

"A fair number, miss."

"Really?" Georgiana had not expected this. Sir Robert was hardly a man who would be extensively mourned.

"I believe most were members of his household, miss," continued Horton. "His son was there, of course. Lord Bartholomew Parker and Mr Lakesby were present, as was Mr Grey."

"Lord Bartholomew Parker?" asked Georgiana in astonishment.

"Yes, miss."

"And Mr Lakesby?"

"Yes, miss."

Georgiana sat dumbfounded for a moment. She became aware of Horton watching her and roused herself enough to give him a grateful smile. "Thank you, Horton. That will be all."

"Very good, miss."

When Horton departed, Georgiana lapsed into thought. Mr Lakesby and Lord Bartholomew Parker at Sir Robert Foster's funeral? Why? Edward's presence also came as a surprise, but knowing his sense of duty and correctness, this was more easily explained. It seemed unlikely Lakesby would have allowed himself to be persuaded by his aunt. Lord Bartholomew Parker was even more of a mystery. Georgiana had no idea he was even acquainted with Sir Robert.

Georgiana was still pondering this point as Emily put the final touches to her hair for the evening. She had not seen Edward since their quarrel at Mrs Leeman's soirée several days earlier. She knew neither of them would refer to the incident, and Selina would certainly also avoid doing so.

Edward's manner was a little stiff as he greeted Georgiana,

although he unbent sufficiently to give her a kiss on the cheek. Lord Bartholomew flitted among the guests gorgeously arrayed in a waistcoat of fuchsia and gold which contrasted outrageously with his pale knee-breeches. His shirt-points were starched just enough to prevent any independent movement of his head, and his cravat was arranged in the extravagant style of the Waterfall.

Looking around the room, Georgiana caught sight of Louisa, standing near her mother's elbow. The sight of Mr Lakesby approaching his aunt and cousin with refreshments prompted Georgiana to glance towards her brother. He and Amanda were still occupied in greeting their guests. Georgiana wondered about Edward's reaction when Lakesby presented himself at the door. Amanda would be warm and welcoming, of course. However, Georgiana had no doubt her brother would be seething inside, especially if Lakesby, as she suspected, had walked in coolly, showing no doubt of his welcome.

Georgiana cast her eye towards Lakesby again. He was occupied in talking to his cousin, but seemed aware of Georgiana's glance and looked towards her. The slow smile he gave her showed more in his eyes than on his face and held a conspiratorial air. She looked away quickly and found Lord Bartholomew at her elbow. He handed her a glass of ratafia.

"I cannot believe that man had the impertinence to show his face here," said Lord Bartholomew.

"Is there any reason he should not?" said Georgiana.

"Well, I mean to say…"

"What do you mean to say, Lord Bartholomew?" said Georgiana, surprised at the note of challenge in her own voice. "I imagine Lady Winters and her daughter needed an escort. I see nothing improper in Mr Lakesby obliging them."

"I'm so glad my action meets with your approval, Miss Grey," said a cool voice behind her. "Ah, Lord Bartholomew, your servant, sir."

Lord Bartholomew nodded stiffly, whether as a deliberate gesture or the result of his starched collar points, Georgiana could not be sure. At any rate, he did not seem pleased to see Lakesby.

"I did not know you were acquainted with my sister-in-law, Mr Lakesby," said Georgiana to cover the tension.

"No, I wasn't until this evening, although I knew her by sight. She is quite charming."

"I am surprised to see you here this evening if you were not acquainted with my cousin." said Lord Bartholomew.

"Yes, I am a little surprised myself," responded Lakesby coolly. "However, as Miss Grey has been astute enough to realise, my aunt required my escort and can be very persuasive."

The charm in Lakesby's voice was equalled only by the smile he bestowed on his listeners. Lord Bartholomew remained unimpressed, his brow clouded. Georgiana, for her part, returned Lakesby's smile, if a little absently, as her eyes began to wander around the room again. As her gaze reached her brother, she blinked, trying to focus. She seemed unable to move any other part of her body.

Amanda and Edward had finished greeting their guests, but he remained close to her side as she stood in conversation with an acquaintance of her mother's. Like his sister, Edward was also looking around the room. As Georgiana's glance fell on him, she noticed his eyes come to rest on one guest. More of a shock to Georgiana was the spark which came into her brother's eyes. She looked towards the object of his attention. There could be no doubt Lady Wickerston returned Edward's look, barely perceptible as it was. Georgiana's head reeled; she felt the colour drain from her face. She was dimly conscious of Lord Bartholomew's voice echoing somewhere in the background, but had no idea what he said. She became aware of a slight touch on her arm and Lakesby's voice penetrated her mind.

"Miss Grey, I am sure you must be in need of some further refreshment," he said, taking her half-empty glass from her. "This looks rather tired. Allow me to fetch you some wine."

"Yes. Yes, thank you." Georgiana allowed herself to be led to the refreshment table followed by the dismayed expression of Lord Bartholomew.

"This will help," said Lakesby as he handed her a glass of wine.

"Thank you," said Georgiana.

Lakesby smiled. "I know it's a surprise, but in fairness one could hardly expect your brother to discuss his inamorata with his sister."

Georgiana stared at him, thunderstruck. "You know?"

Lakesby nodded. "I've had my suspicions, though your brother has been fairly discreet as these things go."

"He always seemed so devoted to Amanda."

"I'm sure he is," responded Lakesby.

"How can he be when...?" Georgiana looked at Lakesby. "Does Lord Wickerston know?"

Lakesby shook his head. "I don't think Wickerston sees much beyond the bottom of his current bottle."

"I don't understand," said Georgiana. "How can you...?"

Lakesby smiled. "I'm afraid I was not entirely truthful with you, Miss Grey. Your brother and I are better acquainted than I led you to believe."

"What?" Georgiana stared, further astonishment visible in her expression.

"This is not the time or place," said Lakesby. "Your cousin is watching us, concerned for your virtue, no doubt."

Possibility of further conversation was ended with the approach of Selina Knatchbull, smiling pleasantly. Dumbfounded yet fascinated with what she had learned, Georgiana remained silent while Lakesby greeted Miss Knatchbull and listened with all appearance of interest to details of the headache which had laid her low the previous day and the benefits of lavender water and hartshorn in such circumstances.

"I must say, Mr Lakesby," said Miss Knatchbull in earnest accents, "I was very shocked to hear about your carriage being held up the other evening. There seems no end to these highwaymen terrorising the roads."

"Well, it was not a successful attempt," said Lakesby lightly. "It was a pity the boy was injured, but no doubt your cousin is ensuring he is well nursed."

Selina shuddered. "I do wish Georgiana had not brought him back to the house. I cannot begin to tell you how my nerves have suffered."

"That is unfortunate," said Lakesby sympathetically.

"I shall be glad when you hand him over to the authorities, Mr Lakesby," Miss Knatchbull said.

"I see no need for that," Lakesby said. "The boy would be hanged and there was no real harm done."

"But – but – surely he needs to be taught a lesson?" said Miss Knatchbull, a tremor in her voice.

"Your cousin assures me he has learned his lesson. Is that not so, Miss Grey?"

"Yes, indeed."

"Besides," continued Lakesby, "no lesson will benefit him once he is dead."

Miss Knatchbull was stricken to silence, an unusual circumstance which filled Georgiana with as much amusement as gratitude. Lakesby began a flow of trivial conversation. Georgiana played her part, her cousin's presence precluding any possibility of asking what she really wanted to know: the truth about his acquaintance with Edward and his attendance at Sir Robert Foster's funeral. Hopes of persuading Selina to interest herself with another guest were abandoned when Edward joined the group, clearly not happy at the sight of his sister in Lakesby's company. Between the memory of their last encounter and her new discovery, Georgiana felt a spirit of mischief take hold of her. Involuntarily, she glanced towards Lakesby. To her annoyance, he seemed to be deriving huge enjoyment from the situation.

"Well, Georgiana," said Edward. "I'm glad you decided to come. Amanda and I are always pleased to see you."

"Thank you, Edward."

Edward turned towards Lakesby. His expression, while not openly disapproving, said plainly he took this guest's presence on sufferance. Lakesby's pleasant smile and manner seemed to wear away at Edward's thinly stretched levels of toleration.

"It was most kind of your wife to invite my aunt and cousin this evening, Grey," said Lakesby in friendly fashion.

"Not at all."

"Very agreeable company," Lakesby pursued.

"I'm sure my wife will be glad it meets with your approval." Edward's voice was clipped, unwelcoming. The vein in his temple began to throb with ominous regularity.

"Most certainly. Please give her my compliments." Lakesby bowed to the ladies and strolled away. Brother and sister faced one another, their cousin glancing nervously from one to the other, apparently uncertain whether or not she too should move away.

Edward spoke first.

"I am glad you decided to come, Georgiana."

"Yes, Edward, so you said." Georgiana felt the temptation to taunt her brother. It was not Georgiana's business that he had a mistress, but for the lady to be invited to a party at the home he shared with his wife seemed in extremely poor taste. The knowledge that Edward's life didn't stand up to scrutiny made Georgiana want to laugh out loud, particularly when she thought of the constant moralising to which he subjected her.

"I must say, this is all very pleasant," commented Selina. "Amanda is really very clever at arranging such things."

Edward turned towards his cousin with a smile. "Yes, indeed. She will be pleased you said so, Selina."

As they were talking, Georgiana's eye strayed towards Lord Bartholomew Parker, deep in conversation with another guest. She noticed him casting one or two surreptitious glances in her direction. The unhappy thought came to her that if she was to learn anything about his attendance at Sir Robert's funeral, she would have to engage him in conversation.

"By the way, Edward," said Georgiana, still looking in Lord Bartholomew's direction, "I didn't know Lord Bartholomew was acquainted with Sir Robert Foster."

"What?"

"I heard Lord Bartholomew and you both attended Sir Robert's funeral."

Selina put her handkerchief to her mouth, seeming ready to faint. Edward looked slightly shocked, as though he considered the subject unsuitable for feminine sensibilities.

"I believe Sir Robert was some distant relation of Bartholomew's. As for myself, having taken over his seat on the magistrates' bench, I felt it my duty to attend."

"Yes, of course," Georgiana brushed aside Edward's reasons. "Amanda never mentioned the connection."

"Sir Robert was not related to Amanda. He was on the other side of Bartholomew's family" Edward looked at his sister, his light green eyes drawing together in suspicion. "Why should that concern you?"

"Oh, it doesn't," Georgiana said hastily. "I was just curious."

Edward continued to regard her mistrustfully. "I thought you were not interested in Bartholomew. Goodness knows, I've tried often enough to persuade you otherwise."

"Oh, for heaven's sake, Edward, don't start that again," said Georgiana in exasperation. "I told you, I was just curious as to how he came to be at Sir Robert's funeral. Don't make such a fuss about it."

Edward's brow grew dark and intent as he regarded Georgiana.

"With whom have you been discussing Sir Robert Foster's funeral?"

"What?" Georgiana was taken aback by his tone.

"Lakesby, I suppose," he said petulantly. "Really, Georgiana, it is most unseemly. I have to say, your choice of friends leaves a great deal to be desired."

"My choice of friends! Well, I like that, Edward. What concern is it of yours?"

"Furthermore, Selina and Bartholomew tell me you have a wounded highwayman under your roof. What on earth possessed you to do such a thing?"

"Selina and Lord Bartholomew would do better to keep to their own concerns," Georgiana said, with an angry look towards her cousin.

"Georgiana, please," interposed Selina.

Georgiana was halted by the timely arrival of Amanda at Edward's side. Despite her cousin's presence, Georgiana knew her anger had nearly betrayed her into impropriety. But she had no wish to hurt her sister-in-law, and held her tongue.

"Georgiana, Edward, please," begged Amanda. "No more quarrelling."

"Oh, yes," said Selina. "I'm so sorry, Amanda. I did try."

Edward pursed his lips, continuing to glower. Georgiana took a deep breath and managed to smile at her sister-in-law. What would Amanda say if she knew the whole truth?

"If you'll excuse me, I must pay my respects to Lady Winters and her daughter," said Georgiana. She sailed off, her cousin close at her heels, much to her annoyance. Georgiana just caught the hushed voices behind her as Amanda gently admonished Edward.

"Why can you and Edward never seem to meet without quarrelling?" pleaded Selina.

"It takes two to quarrel, Selina."

"I don't know what has come over you lately, Georgiana. I daresay Edward is right and it is Mr Lakesby's influence."

Georgiana stopped in her tracks. "Edward said that?" she demanded.

Miss Knatchbull quailed before the expression in her cousin's eyes.

"Well, no, not exactly. It's just that... Well, you have changed. What was all that talk about Sir Robert Foster's funeral? As for bringing that ruffian home, I daresay it was Mr Lakesby who persuaded you, since he is going to let the rascal go free."

"Not at all," said Georgiana coolly. "In fact, it was I who asked him not to hand over the boy."

11

Lady Winters greeted Georgiana civilly, although the icy edge in her voice indicated she had not forgotten their last encounter. Louisa gave a bright, beaming smile. She seemed particularly cheerful this evening, almost as if she was brimming over with the desire to exchange confidences. Georgiana wondered whether the girl had something of interest to impart, or whether this was an impression created by her own over-hopeful imagination.

"I must say, Miss Grey, it was very civil of your sister-in-law to invite us this evening," remarked her ladyship.

"Amanda was pleased to include you, Lady Winters," responded Georgiana.

Her ladyship turned her attention to Selina, one or two paces behind Georgiana, her pallor giving a suggestion of the shock her cousin had just inflicted upon her.

"Miss Knatchbull, are you quite well?"

"Oh, yes, your ladyship, thank you. It is most kind of you to ask. I was laid low with the headache yesterday, but am feeling much better now."

"Hmm. Perhaps you had better go home early," remarked Lady Winters. "You don't look at all the thing."

"Well, if your ladyship thinks so, but indeed I am perfectly well."

Having dispensed her advice, Lady Winters apparently lost interest in the well-being of Miss Knatchbull and spoke again to Georgiana.

"I hope you mean to ensure that young ruffian gets what he deserves, Miss Grey. Charity is all very well in its place, but you can't go taking pity on every villain who meets with some misfortune. They have only themselves to blame, and it is nothing but a waste when they will be hanged in any case."

"I see," said Georgiana.

"It's perfectly acceptable to feel sorry for the unfortunate," said her ladyship. "I do myself."

Georgiana wondered how she prevented herself reacting to her ladyship's self-congratulatory manner. "Do you?" she said, icily polite.

"However," continued Lady Winters, "young men gadding about on the public highways terrorising innocent travellers deserve no sympathy, whatever may befall them."

Georgiana bit back the impulse to retort. As Mr Lakesby approached with refreshments, Georgiana could imagine his desire to taunt her by seeking his aunt's opinion of young ladies on the public highways. Georgiana kept her eyes resolutely from him.

"I am sure you are right, Lady Winters," she responded quietly.

"I am very glad to hear you say so, Georgiana," said Selina.

"A glass of lemonade, Miss Knatchbull?" interposed Lakesby.

Georgiana looked at him. Despite his help in distracting Selina's attention, she could cheerfully have throttled him.

"I heard you attended Sir Robert's funeral today," she said.

"Did you, Max?" asked Louisa in some wonderment.

"Yes, Louisa."

"How odd," said Louisa. "I always thought you did not like him."

"No more did I," said Lakesby. "However, it seemed the thing to do."

"Very proper, Max," commented Lady Winters. "One should always pay one's respects to the departed."

"I thought so, Aunt Beatrice. In fact, Miss Grey's brother was also there, as was her butler."

"I am pleased to hear it, especially when one considers the

way Sir Robert died," said her ladyship with a shudder. "It is truly appalling."

Fearing another sermon on the outrageous behaviour of highwaymen, Georgiana decided she could no longer delay facing Lord Bartholomew. She sensed Lakesby knew her thoughts as he followed her quick glance towards where his lordship stood. She detected the ghost of a smile in Lakesby's expression. Georgiana was not sure whether she was more irritated by the thought of having to talk to Lord Bartholomew or the fact that Lakesby apparently considered it a source of amusement. She decided to take herself off before she said something indiscreet, suggesting her cousin stay and talk to Lady Winters.

Lord Bartholomew seemed pleased by Georgiana's approach, although she wondered whether she imagined a vaguely suspicious shadow crossing his face. She shrugged it off and gave him a smile of warm concern. "Lord Bartholomew, I felt I must express my condolences. I had no idea until today you were related to Sir Robert Foster. I am most truly sorry for your loss."

His lordship appeared taken aback by her sympathy and, for once, did not have a response ready to gush forth.

"What? Oh. Yes. Thank you," he said as he seemed to collect his thoughts. "Thank you very much. It is most kind of you, though he was only a very distant relative, you understand. We were not close."

"Even so, it must have been very distressing for you," said Georgiana sympathetically, "for such a thing to happen in your own family."

"Oh, yes, the scandal will be quite dreadful."

"Ye-es," she responded. She regarded him speculatively, considering how best to continue. "How is Sir Brandon faring after his father's death?"

"Oh, well enough, I believe," said Lord Bartholomew airily.

"Brandon and I don't deal much. He's always spent a lot of time at his father's country house."

"Indeed?" said Georgiana. "Still, I imagine things must have been difficult in view of the situation between him and his father."

Lord Bartholomew looked at her in puzzlement.

"I understand there was a rift between them," pursued Georgiana gently.

"That had nothing to do with me," said Lord Bartholomew, his agitation accentuating his sing-song voice. One or two people glanced towards him.

"No, of course not, Lord Bartholomew," said Georgiana. She changed her tactics. "How was Sir Robert's funeral? I know it must be a difficult time for the family."

"Oh, yes, yes," said Lord Bartholomew. He paused. "I had not expected to see your butler there, particularly since Edward attended. It was most kind of you to send him." Lord Bartholomew's hand stretched out to touch Georgiana's arm as he spoke. Instinctively, she recoiled.

"It was the least I could do. I felt I must pay my respects." Georgiana sighed. "Poor Sir Robert. Such a dreadful thing to happen."

"Yes," said Lord Bartholomew. "I'm sure we'll all feel much safer once they catch that highwayman."

"Assuming a highwayman is responsible," interpolated the voice of Lakesby at Georgiana's elbow. "Please excuse the interruption."

Eyeing the newcomer with disfavour, Lord Bartholomew seemed disinclined to do this.

"You seem to be bearing Sir Robert's death with fortitude," remarked Lakesby. "However, I suppose if your connection was but a distant one..."

"The family tie is strong, sir, no matter how distant," said Lord Bartholomew, with a look towards Georgiana.

"Quite true," said Lakesby. "Well, we must hope Sir Robert's murderer is soon brought to justice."

Lord Bartholomew took a deep breath. He looked at Lakesby as if uncertain whether he was being mocked before returning his attention to Georgiana.

"Perhaps you will do me the honour of taking a drive in the park with me soon, Miss Grey? I have just acquired a new curricle and an excellent pair of matched bays."

"Perhaps," said Georgiana, who had heard Lord Bartholomew was a thoroughly cow-handed whip. The notion of him in charge of such a dashing sporting vehicle gave rise to an incongruous sensation of amusement and dread.

"I wonder you dare, the roads being as dangerous as they are," remarked Lakesby in mock awe. "Perhaps you should wait until Sir Robert's killer is caught."

"Are you suggesting I am a coward, sir?" demanded Lord Bartholomew haughtily.

"No, indeed," laughed Lakesby. "Pray, do not call me out. It is a long time since I indulged in a duel; I am sadly out of practice."

"Then I shall thank you to keep a civil tongue in your head," Lord Bartholomew snapped, turning on his heel.

"What on earth was the meaning of that?" said Georgiana in astonishment.

Lakesby was looking at Lord Bartholomew's retreating form, a slight smile playing about the corners of his mouth.

"Do you know anything of Lord Bartholomew's income, Miss Grey?" he inquired.

"What an indelicate question," said Georgiana. "I know it is fairly modest, but other than that, no. Why should I?"

"That is what I thought," remarked Lakesby. "It wouldn't strike you as odd, then, that he is in the happy position of being able to afford a curricle and pair?"

Georgiana looked at him warily. "I suppose it is rather, now you mention it. Perhaps he has had a piece of good fortune."

"I should be very interested to know what it was," said Lakesby. "You see, but a few short evenings ago, he was close to tears at having to pledge some hideous piece of jewellery to cover his losses at play."

Georgiana's eyes widened. "Really? Possibly his luck has turned."

"Perhaps," said Lakesby, "though in my experience, it rarely turns for long. From what I hear, Lord Bartholomew is not usually very fortunate at the tables."

"Then I imagine it's best to make any purchases while one is winning." Georgiana paused. "I must say, I had not taken Lord Bartholomew for a gambler."

"No? What did you imagine his interests were?"

Georgiana grinned. "Frankly, Mr Lakesby, it's not a subject to which I give a great deal of thought."

He responded with an answering smile. "As I suspected. Do you intend to go driving with him?"

"Good heavens, no!" said Georgiana. "I should expect to be overturned inside of ten minutes."

Lakesby smiled again. "I am glad you have so much sense."

A shadow cast between them prevented her responding. She glanced towards her brother in some irritation.

"Come, Georgiana, you must circulate. Amanda didn't invite you so you could be monopolised by Mr Lakesby all evening."

"No, I am sure she did not," said Lakesby with a smile. "I must beg your pardon, Grey. I have been quite selfish in taking up your sister's time when there must be others wanting the pleasure of her company. Miss Grey, your servant."

With a slight bow, he departed to rejoin his aunt and cousin. Georgiana watched his retreating form with a twinge of regret. She turned back to her brother.

"Time to do my duty?" she inquired.

"I'm sorry you regard meeting our friends as a duty, Georgiana," said Edward stiffly. "Amanda and I wished you to come this evening because we thought you might enjoy it."

"Indeed I am," Georgiana smiled.

Edward's eye went towards Lakesby with disfavour. "So I noticed. You should know better, at your age, than to spend so long in the company of one man. It is giving rise to comment."

"Is it? I must say it's always struck me as rather a pity when people lead such dull lives they must needs comment on those of others."

"Georgiana, really!"

"Well, I'm sorry, Edward, but I don't see that my actions should be of concern to anyone else, including you," said Georgiana crossly. "It is bad enough I have Selina plaguing the life out of me."

Edward drew in his breath. His voice, when he spoke, was heavy with dignity. "Selina has your welfare at heart, as have I. You are my sister, Georgiana. It is only right I should be concerned about you."

"Yes, of course it is, Edward. I am sorry." She smiled. "It is just that you can be so excessively over-protective at times. It does become rather overbearing. I am not a child, you know."

"It is bad enough Lakesby has to be here at all—" Edward began.

"Yes, I must confess, I was rather surprised to see him," said Georgiana. "I thought you did not like him."

"I do not," Edward responded irritably. "However, Lady Winters sent a message to Amanda asking if it would be acceptable to bring Lakesby as an escort. I don't know why Amanda couldn't have found some excuse to refuse."

"Lady Winters is a difficult woman to refuse."

"I daresay, but Amanda might have made some effort. She

could have offered to send our carriage for them. To have to endure that man in my own house is quite outrageous."

Georgiana forced herself to curb her reaction. A slight clenching of the fist was all the expression of anger she allowed herself. She was not sure whether she was more annoyed over Edward's peevishness about his wife, or his remarks about Lakesby.

"Tell me, Edward, what exactly is the matter with Mr Lakesby? I'm sure I have never heard anything derogatory about him."

"I should hope not," said Edward in shocked accents.

"Is it women?" asked Georgiana curiously. "Has he had a succession of mistresses?"

"Georgiana!"

"Well, is that not very common among gentlemen?" she asked in a tone of innocence. Her brother's pompous manner made her unable to resist the opportunity of taunting him.

"Young ladies should not know of such things."

"Should not know of them or not speak of them?" Georgiana quizzed him. "Oh, do stop being so tedious, Edward, and tell me. I shall only find out some other way."

"I hope you will not."

"I'm sure I shall." Georgiana's eyes danced. "Perhaps I shall ask Mr Lakesby. He has already told me you and he are better acquainted than I realised. I'm sure he will be glad to give me the details if you will not."

Edward's eyes widened in horror. He refused to oblige her, however and rapidly turned the subject, suggesting she pay her respects to a particular aunt of Amanda's.

"Yes, of course, I shall do so, but first I should like you to introduce me to Lady Wickerston. I have the liveliest curiosity to meet her."

Edward paled. "Why?"

"Why not? I hear she is very amusing."

"I do not think you would find her so. She is really quite a dull creature. I am sure you and she would not deal together."

For Edward to describe anyone as dull struck Georgiana as just as incongruous as her own insistence that Tom discontinue his career as a highwayman. The mischievous spirit continuing to prompt, she grew even more determined to get her own way.

"Really? She does not look at all dull. In fact, she seems quite charming. Ah, here is Amanda. I'm sure she will oblige."

To Edward's chagrin, Amanda was only too happy to accede to her sister-in-law's request and Georgiana had the satisfaction of seeing her brother grow acutely uncomfortable. As Amanda led her towards Lady Wickerston, Georgiana happened to catch Lakesby's eye across the room. He raised his glass in silent appreciation.

Amanda was the perfect hostess. "Lady Wickerston, may I present my husband's sister, Miss Grey. Georgiana, Lady Wickerston."

Georgiana regarded the woman who stood smiling before her. She was a striking figure, tall and fair, with intense blue eyes which could command attention in any gathering. Oddly enough, her apparel was sombre, a long-sleeved dress of muted grey with a white lace collar, serious rather than severe. Georgiana was amazed at her ladyship's easy manner and lack of embarrassment at being introduced to her lover's sister by his wife. Returning the smile, Georgiana expressed herself delighted. Satisfied that the two women seemed disposed to like each other, Amanda took herself off, her attention claimed by another guest.

Georgiana and Lady Wickerston were left facing each other. It was Georgiana who spoke first.

"I am sorry we have not met earlier, Lady Wickerston. I believe you have been acquainted with my sister and brother for quite some time?"

"Yes, about a year, perhaps slightly more," responded her ladyship. "An aunt of mine is a friend of Amanda's mother."

"I see," said Georgiana. The woman's easy familiarity with her brother's wife made her feel vaguely uncomfortable. Her eyes flickered quickly in Edward's direction. Even before she looked, she knew he was staring at her.

The thought crossed her mind, swiftly growing as it took root, that nothing would provoke Edward more than to see a friendship develop between his sister and his mistress. Georgiana wondered whether it could be managed. Lady Wickerston was clearly an intelligent woman; she would be wary of any overtures Georgiana might make. She could imagine Edward's horror. A quick glance across the room told her he was not the only one watching. She felt Lakesby urging her on. The temptation was irresistible.

"A delightful party, don't you agree, Lady Wickerston?" said Georgiana with a smile.

"Yes, indeed. I have not been out much of late. However, as Amanda said this was to be quite a small gathering, I thought it would be acceptable."

"Oh?" Lady Wickerston did not strike Georgiana as a person who shied away from social contact. "I trust you have not been ill?"

"Oh, no," her ladyship responded almost too quickly. "No, I am perfectly well. But there has recently been a death in my family. Not a close relative, you understand," she added hastily, "an uncle I saw very occasionally. However, it is only proper to pay one's respects, particularly in view of the way he died."

"Yes," said Georgiana, "of course. I am so sorry." The coincidence was too absurd, but her brain was already anticipating what Lady Wickerston would say next.

12

Georgiana would never have believed a small party at Amanda and Edward's house could be so eventful. On the following morning, her mind was awash with all she had learned.

By an ingenious piece of social manipulation, Georgiana had managed to obtain the escort of Lord Wickerston in to supper. The arrangement gave Edward anything but pleasure and yielded little to Georgiana in terms of worthwhile information. Lord Wickerston was disappointingly discreet. If he did suspect anything about an intrigue between his wife and Edward Grey, he was not revealing it to Edward's sister. Furthermore, he was a far from lively supper companion. He had something of the morose air of Brandon Foster, with a harder edge which hinted at the dangerous. He made little attempt at conversation, giving credence to Lakesby's words by constantly refilling his wine glass and only once or twice thinking to offer the decanter to Georgiana.

In an evening which had given up a succession of surprises, Georgiana could not decide on the greatest. To all appearances, Edward was happily married to a wife of his own choosing. He was too conscious of his position to be interested in women of the class of opera dancers, and Georgiana had taken for granted his faithfulness to Amanda. Even the knowledge of her own double life had never led her to question this. She didn't know why she should have supposed Edward would not succumb to temptation: he was no different from other men. However, for him to take up with a married woman of quality, accepted as a guest in his home, was a slap in Amanda's face.

The situation would certainly explain Edward's odd behaviour about his movements on the night of Sir Robert's death. If he had been with Lady Wickerston instead of at

Brooks's, he would naturally not wish to divulge this. She wondered how she could persuade him. Confronting him with the truth might startle him into openness, but somehow Georgiana thought it unlikely. Perhaps she could blackmail him? But while the notion appealed to her sense of humour, blackmail against her own brother was going too far.

More pressing was the revelation of Lady Wickerston's relationship to Sir Robert Foster. Her ladyship had said she and her uncle had not been close. Nevertheless, it was possible there were expectations from his estate. While neither she nor her husband looked in desperate need of funds, Lord Wickerston's clear fondness for the contents of his wine cellar was surely expensive.

Georgiana wondered whether Sir Robert could have discovered the affair between Lady Wickerston and Edward Grey. She suspected he would not have hesitated to exploit the knowledge. While Georgiana found it difficult to believe her brother involved in Sir Robert's murder, she could not rid herself of the uneasy sensation that he knew more than he was willing to disclose.

Georgiana's thoughts moved away from her brother's situation to that of Lord Bartholomew Parker. She found it odd he had never mentioned being related to Sir Robert Foster. If anything, he seemed at pains to distance himself from the connection. While Georgiana could not blame him, she had always known Lord Bartholomew to be a stickler for the conventions. This lent some logic to his attendance at Sir Robert's funeral. However, close or not, it surprised her that he seemed to be continuing his life normally, without any withdrawal for a suitable period of mourning.

Georgiana's mind wandered to what Lakesby had said about he and Edward being better acquainted than either had first indicated. Why had they found it necessary to keep this information secret? The notion danced in her head that they could have been involved in some scandal together, to be rejected almost immediately. Georgiana could not see Edward and Lakesby involved in anything together. Perhaps it was some old quarrel? A duel between them would certainly explain their reticence, but Georgiana could not imagine the subject of such a dispute. She decided to quiz them both, curious as to how different their accounts would be.

In the midst of these reflections a tap came on the door, followed by the tentative entrance of her cousin, softly speaking Georgiana's name. It was not often Selina visited Georgiana in her bedchamber in the morning. Georgiana's concern that there might be something wrong was allayed by the timid smile she received from her visitor.

"Come in, Selina. How are you?" said Georgiana cordially.

"Oh, I am quite well, though a little tired from our late night. Still, it was an enjoyable party, was it not?"

"Yes, indeed, very pleasant," said Georgiana. She had not thought the hour especially late, even allowing for the erratic nature of her nocturnal activities. However, Selina's upbringing in the rectory had been a quiet one, and Georgiana did not imagine there had been much in the way of party-going.

"I do not think Edward was very pleased to see Mr Lakesby last night," remarked Selina, "nor to see you spend so much time talking to him."

"Nonsense," said Georgiana. "We exchanged a few words. I did not spend the evening in his pocket, so if Edward means to accuse me of impropriety..."

"Oh, no, indeed, I am sure he does not," Selina said quickly.

"I can't imagine why he has such a dislike of Mr Lakesby," said Georgiana. "Admittedly, I would not expect them to have much in common, but Edward seems almost venomous about him."

"I believe they were acquainted at Oxford," said Selina. "Perhaps Edward knows something to Mr Lakesby's detriment."

"Or perhaps Mr Lakesby knows something to Edward's," replied Georgiana.

"Georgiana!"

"Well, really," said Georgiana with some impatience. "I daresay it is all a piece of work over nothing. If gentlemen were ostracised for every youthful folly committed at Oxford…"

To Georgiana's surprise, this drew a smile from Selina. "Oh, dear me, yes, usually quite harmless, I suppose. Of course, I can't imagine Edward indulging in any larks."

"No, I expect he was a very dull dog."

Selina gave a little cry of reproof at this, to which Georgiana paid little attention.

"Do you have any plans for today?" Georgiana asked her cousin.

"Perhaps I shall do some sewing. Do you have anything you would like me to mend?"

Georgiana mentioned a couple of loose buttons and promised she would ask Emily to fetch the items of clothing. Sewing had never been a passion of Georgiana's, but she knew Selina enjoyed it and how much it meant for her to be useful. Georgiana was glad to have her cousin occupied.

Considering what to do next, Georgiana resolved to explore as many possibilities as she could in her efforts to find Sir Robert's killer. She had not forgotten her need to speak to Tom again, but as he was just learning his new duties as page, she resolved to leave him for the moment. Remembering what Emily had said about Joe Hill, she decided a visit might be useful.

"I thought I would go to the Hill cottage and see if they need anything."

"Oh, yes, I'm sure they would appreciate that. Poor Mr Hill and all those children. I often feel I should do more." Georgiana feared for a moment Selina would offer to accompany her, but she left the room in search of her sewing basket.

Conferring with Emily before she left, Georgiana learned Hill had not been to work on the previous day. This struck Georgiana as odd. The money she had given the family would not last forever, and he could not afford to lose a day's pay. Perhaps he was unwell. Georgiana thought about the late Mrs Hill. Emily had made a good point. The cottage had been in poor repair for years, a common occurrence with Sir Robert's properties. Had something suddenly changed to account for Mrs Hill contracting a fatal illness?

Betsy opened the door to Georgiana and gave a bright smile of greeting. Despite their poverty, the door was always open to acquaintances, and Georgiana never felt less than welcome. She considered the possible consequences if Joe Hill had killed Sir Robert. She dreaded to think what would become of his children if their only surviving parent went to the gallows.

"Good morning, Betsy," said Georgiana. "I heard your father was not at work yesterday, and was afraid he might be unwell."

"Thank you, miss." Betsy always seemed older than her ten years. Since her mother's death, there was a careworn look about the child which always made Georgiana wish she could do more for the family.

"Would you like something to drink, miss?"

"No, thank you, Betsy. I don't wish to be any trouble; I don't intend to stay long. Is your father at home?"

The girl nodded. "Shall I fetch him?"

"If he feels able to receive a visitor."

Joe Hill appeared in hastily dressed state within a very few minutes. Despite the smile with which he welcomed his visitor, he seemed flustered. Georgiana rose from the table where she had been seated, looking searchingly at him. He was pale, certainly, but she could discern no other signs of illness. Georgiana knew this was not in itself conclusive, but it struck her as odd. Joe could not afford to lose one day's pay; to lose two was unthinkable.

"It's most kind of you to call, Miss Grey, most kind."

"How are you, Mr Hill? Is there anything you need?"

"No, thank you, miss. I'm well enough. It's just the old trouble plaguing me again. Confounded nuisance, it is, begging your pardon, miss."

Georgiana knew the 'old trouble' was an injury to his leg from some years previously. While resolutely pushing aside the suspicion that it surfaced at moments of convenience, she could not help but recall there had been no sign of a limp as he had walked away from the Lucky Bell.

"Betsy told me your maid had called with some bread and fruit," Hill said. "It was very good of her. It's wonderful how everyone in your house thinks of us, especially since Dora died."

"Not at all," said Georgiana. "We're only too glad to help."

Hill did not seem to know how he should continue the conversation and Georgiana found herself unable to postpone broaching the subject she would have liked to avoid. Her glance went involuntarily towards Betsy.

"Betsy, why don't you run outside and play?" Hill said to his daughter, as though aware Georgiana did not wish to speak in front of her.

The child obeyed, giving Georgiana a cheerful smile as she passed. Hill returned his attention to his visitor, gesturing towards her recently vacated chair.

"Won't you sit down, Miss Grey?" he asked.

"Thank you, Mr Hill. I hope you can help me." As Georgiana seated herself, she gave some thought to her next words. "My brother has just been appointed to the magistrates' bench."

Hill appeared puzzled, as though not certain why Georgiana was telling him this. "Well, I hope you'll give him my best, miss."

"Yes, of course. Thank you. He is looking into the matter of Sir Robert Foster's death and I was a little concerned, because I gather you were away from home on that evening."

Hill stiffened. Georgiana could sense his withdrawal.

"That's true," he said.

"Would you mind telling me where you went?"

"That I would, Miss Grey. You've no right to ask me such a question."

"No, of course, I understand that," said Georgiana. "But things would be better for you if you could prove where you were when Sir Robert died."

Hill eyed Georgiana with growing suspicion. "Are you accusing me of something, miss?"

"No, indeed," said Georgiana.

"Then I don't see why you should be wishing to know," Hill replied. "With respect, Miss Grey, it's not you who's the magistrate."

His tone was polite but unmistakably final, warning against any further attempt to continue this questioning. Georgiana was not easily daunted.

"My intention is not to pry, Mr Hill. However–"

"I think perhaps you should go, miss."

"Now, Mr Hill, do but listen–"

"I'll not be accused of murder in my own house, not even by you, Miss Grey." Hill stood up as he spoke.

"I'm not accusing you of anything," Georgiana protested. "However, if you can't account for your whereabouts, it is likely someone will make accusations."

"Why should anyone accuse me? I thought it was that highwayman who did it."

Georgiana thought carefully about how to phrase her reply. "The Crimson Cavalier is certainly a strong suspect, but there are others who could have had reason for wanting Sir Robert dead."

"Are you saying I was one of them?" Hill demanded.

"You must admit, Mr Hill, you had no reason to be fond of him." Georgiana paused. "I know Sir Robert was a neglectful landlord…"

"Neglectful?" cut in Hill in a heated tone. "He was beyond neglectful, miss, he was downright nasty." Hill stopped and took a breath before continuing. "You can see the walls are damp. Well, then the door started getting cracked, with bits breaking off the bottom. Made the wind fair rush through. That's when Dora started coughing."

Recalling the cough James had developed in prison, Georgiana could understand Hill's animosity. She glanced towards the door.

"Aye, it's right enough now," he said, noticing the direction of her eyes. "I knew Sir Robert wouldn't do anything about getting it fixed, so I did it myself. Took time from work to do it." Hill's face grew grim with the memory. "Sir Robert wanted to put the rent up. Said if we wanted to live in luxury we'd have to pay more. We didn't have the money, and he said we'd have to get out unless…" Hill stopped abruptly, his face flushed.

"Unless?" prompted Georgiana.

"I'd rather not discuss it, miss. It wouldn't be seemly."

"What? Good gracious, Mr Hill, what on earth…?" Georgiana paused, enlightenment dawning. "Mr Hill, would I be correct in assuming Sir Robert made advances to your wife?"

The look of mortification on Hill's face gave Georgiana all the answer she needed.

"Advances? Oh, aye, he made advances right enough. Treated her like a common tart, tried to bargain for her. Said if she'd oblige and be a bit friendly with him, he'd let us stay here, even hinted he'd let the rent go by."

"I see," said Georgiana.

"Was the same when she used to clean house for him.

185

She told me he was always leering, always suggesting…"

"I understand," said Georgiana.

"Used to come home in tears, she did. I wanted her to leave, but she was worried we wouldn't be able to manage without the money, miserly though it was. In the end it got too much for her and she did leave. That's when he put our rent up," Hill concluded bitterly.

"I see," said Georgiana quietly.

"Do you, Miss Grey?" he asked with a touch of sarcasm. Suddenly he sighed, looking defeated. "I beg your pardon, Miss Grey. I've no right to be getting angry with you. Only when I think of how she died…"

It was easy to see why he blamed Sir Robert for his wife's death. "In your situation, Mr Hill, I think anyone would be angry."

"Anger's one thing, murder's another," said Hill with some hostility. "I didn't kill him."

One thing still niggled at Georgiana. "Then why are you being secretive about where you were on the night Sir Robert died?"

Hill looked steadily at her. "Begging your pardon, miss, but that's a private matter."

Georgiana grew exasperated.

"For heaven's sake, do be sensible. I'm trying to help you."

Hill rose.

"Thank you for calling, Miss Grey," he said stiffly, his face pale. "I won't take up any more of your time."

Georgiana tried another approach.

"Perhaps you will tell me instead what you were doing in the Lucky Bell."

Hill checked in the act of moving to open the door. He looked back at Georgiana, dumbstruck, then shook his head.

"I'm surprised at a lady like you knowing about that place, miss."

"Never mind that," said Georgiana.

Hill continued to hesitate, his colour rising. His voice, when he finally spoke, was awkward and apologetic. "I – I went for a walk. Even with four children, a man gets lonely. I was – I was looking for company. That's why I went to that tavern. I'd been a couple of times: one of the girls there was quite friendly."

Georgiana nodded.

"I had a drink with her, but I got to thinking about Dora. It wasn't just that I felt I was betraying her, it seemed I was no better than Sir Robert Foster, trying to bargain for that girl's company the way he tried to bargain for Dora's. I finished my drink and walked home. I'm not proud of myself, Miss Grey, that's why I kept quiet. Anyway, I knew it would look bad, me being out on the night Sir Robert died. I don't know anything about that, miss, I swear it."

Georgiana left the cottage in thoughtful frame of mind. Untethering her horse, she suddenly felt the weight of the task she had set herself. There seemed to be complications everywhere she looked. She was so absorbed she did not at first hear her name called from the road; she noticed Lakesby only as he rode up to her.

"You were in quite a brown study, Miss Grey. I was just on my way to visit you," he said pleasantly. As he dismounted, he studied her face. "Are you quite well?"

"I beg your pardon. Yes, I am in excellent health."

Georgiana frowned. Lakesby was watching her closely.

"Should I assume your inquiries are not progressing as you might wish?" he inquired.

Georgiana glanced towards him. "Inquiries? Mr Lakesby, are you speaking of Sir Robert's death?"

Lakesby smiled as he aided her to mount then returned to his own horse. He glanced towards the Hill cottage as they rode away. "Is Mr Hill one of your suspects?"

"My suspects? What a curious turn of phrase," said Georgiana. She continued almost absently, "Although he was not at home on the night Sir Robert died."

"Neither were many people. I was not myself."

"No," said Georgiana, eyeing him cautiously.

Lakesby laughed. "I see I am also a suspect, Miss Grey. Pray, don't concern yourself that I might be offended by the notion."

Georgiana had no such concern, but refrained from volunteering this information.

"Do you think Hill might have had something to do with it?"

Georgiana hesitated a moment before speaking.

"He blames Sir Robert for the death of his wife. Sir Robert had increased the rent. The Hills couldn't afford it, of course, and Sir Robert threatened to evict them." She paused. "Unless Mrs Hill grew more friendly and... obliging."

"I see."

"With his wife's death as well, I think Mr Hill holds Sir Robert responsible for all his misfortunes."

"It's easy to understand why." Lakesby looked closely at her.

"He denies being near the scene of the murder."

"As I said, Miss Grey, any number of people might have been away from home when Sir Robert was killed. I suppose it's possible to check the truth of his story?"

"I expect so," said Georgiana.

They fell silent for a moment or two longer before Georgiana decided it was time for a change of subject.

"You were at Brooks's on the night of Sir Robert's death, were you not, Mr Lakesby?"

"Indeed, I was. I even spoke to one or two people, should I be in need of witnesses."

"Do you expect to need them?"

"One never knows."

They rode on in silence for a moment or two, Georgiana thoughtful, the horses walking alongside companionably. Lakesby did not press her to conversation.

"Did you learn anything at the funeral?"

"Nothing," Lakesby responded. "Brandon Foster was his usual delightfully morose self and Lord Bartholomew scurried away as soon as he'd done his duty. Your brother gave me a civil bow. The rest were servants, who may not have been very fond of Sir Robert, but I hardly imagine they had reason to kill him."

Since Lakesby had mentioned Edward, she decided it would be a good moment to ask about their acquaintance.

"Mr Lakesby, what did you mean when you said you and my brother were better acquainted than you had led me to believe?"

Lakesby gave a wry smile. It was a moment before he spoke. "I think I mentioned we met at Oxford."

Georgiana nodded.

"I daresay this will surprise you, but we became good friends," he continued. "Not what you expected, I'm aware. I don't need to tell you Edward was always serious, though not quite so serious as he is now. I wouldn't say he was ripe for kicking up larks, but he sought diversion as much as anyone. He even pulled me out of the occasional scrape."

"Really?" This was a side of her brother with which Georgiana was unfamiliar.

"I can't say he liked it, but it didn't stop him helping. He would certainly lecture me about it afterwards."

"Now that sounds like Edward."

Lakesby smiled. "There was one occasion which was different from the others. I expect he would tell you I carried things too far."

"What happened?" said Georgiana.

Lakesby gave a twisted smile.

"It was absurd, the sort of thing that seems harmless, but when blown out of proportion…" He grimaced, shaking his head at the memory. "Edward and I were at the same college. A cousin of mine asked me to look after his pet dog, one of those tiny creatures that one could almost hide in a drawer. Alas, the noise of the thing…" Lakesby's eyes rolled. "As it happened, one of the professors had a cat in his rooms. Edward was helping look after my cousin's pet, we took turns with the thing so one of us did not have it all the time. We thought this might mean less chance of being found out. Unfortunately, despite our precautions, the dog escaped from his rooms, through a window, I think. Of course, it found the cat which created no end of trouble. The poor creature was chased through the college, and they finished in the Master's Lodgings, knocking over a valuable vase. Edward, in a bout of honour, confessed to our part in the affair. We were both sent down for the remainder of the term."

"I see," said Georgiana, eyes ahead, a smile playing about her lips. "I do remember Edward once arriving home a few days early; he said there had been some confusion over dates."

"I believe he found some obliging friends to lodge with in the meantime."

Georgiana glanced towards Lakesby. "You and Edward quarrelled?"

Lakesby nodded. "Being sent down was a stigma to Edward. He blamed me and hence never forgave me."

"How absurd," said Georgiana. "Granted the outcome was unfortunate, but to end a friendship over it seems quite an over-reaction."

Lakesby shrugged. "I daresay he imagines I've moved on to worse follies. In any case, this is hardly relevant. There are certainly enough people with motives for murder. Your footman, for instance."

"James?" said Georgiana in some surprise. "Don't be absurd,

Mr Lakesby. Of course James didn't do it. What would he have to gain, pray?"

"Revenge," responded Lakesby promptly. "I seem to recall hearing he'd suffered Sir Robert's wrath from the bench."

"How could you know that?" she demanded.

"My valet is very well informed."

"I see, servants' gossip," remarked Georgiana.

"Poaching, wasn't it?"

"Yes," said Georgiana eyeing him warily.

"He must have lost, what, a good year of his life in prison? That kind of experience can make a man bitter."

"James is not the vengeful sort."

"I'm pleased to hear it. It is not often one hears of someone turning the other cheek. Most refreshing."

His mocking tone irritated Georgiana. "If you have nothing more constructive to say, Mr Lakesby–"

"I beg your pardon," said Lakesby in more serious vein. "I daresay you are right and your footman is not responsible."

"Thank you," she responded coolly.

"I must say," Lakesby remarked, turning the subject, "I was most impressed by your efforts to trying to strike up a friend-ship with Lady Wickerston. It was unfortunate your brother looked rather bilious."

Georgiana wrestled with her conscience for a moment or two. The grin which appeared on her face indicated her conscience as the loser.

"Did Lady Wickerston explain why she was attending a party if she was supposed to be in mourning for her uncle?" inquired Lakesby.

"My sister-in-law had told her it was to be a small affair, so she considered that would be acceptable."

"I see," said Lakesby.

"Besides," Georgiana continued, "she was apparently not close to him."

"I suppose her sombre attire was some concession."

"Yes," said Georgiana absently.

They had by this time reached Georgiana's house. After the barest hesitation, she invited Lakesby in for some refreshment. He declined.

"However, I beg you will give me the pleasure of coming for a drive with me tomorrow."

Georgiana hesitated.

"Come, Miss Grey," Lakesby continued in a persuasive tone, "I'm sure you would find it enjoyable."

"Very well. Thank you, Mr Lakesby."

Lakesby escorted Georgiana up the steps to her front door and they took leave as Horton opened it. Entering the hall, she was about to draw off her gloves when the eye-catching sight of a jewel-encrusted cane resting on the hall table sank Georgiana's heart. There could be no mistaking Lord Bartholomew Parker's flamboyant taste.

"His lordship insisted on waiting, miss," said Horton as though reading her thoughts.

"I see," said Georgiana in a colourless tone. "Very well, Horton, where is he?"

"In the drawing room, miss. Miss Knatchbull asked for tea to be served. Would you care for some fresh?"

"No, thank you, Horton. That won't be necessary."

"Very good, miss."

Georgiana made her way to the drawing room, still in her riding habit. She found Lord Bartholomew settled in an armchair looking very much at home. His attitude irritated her, not helped by the sight of her cousin appearing all welcoming affability. Georgiana wondered whether Lord Bartholomew could be persuaded to transfer his attentions.

"Ah, here is Georgiana," Selina said.

"Good day, Lord Bartholomew."

His lordship sprang up and came forward. "My dear Miss

Grey! We were growing quite concerned."

"Indeed? Why?" Georgiana's tone was frosty.

"Well, you have been away so long."

"I had to visit someone. I had already mentioned it to my cousin. I'm sure she told you. Didn't you, Selina?"

"Why, yes, but you have been such a time," said Selina.

"I would have set out to meet you," said Lord Bartholomew, "but I was sure you would be back at any minute."

"That was not necessary."

"I suppose your groom was an adequate protector," he said sulkily.

"Certainly," replied Georgiana. The devil at her shoulder prompted her to continue. "However, I met Mr Lakesby and he rode back with me."

Selina looked quickly towards her cousin. The colour drained from his lordship's face.

"Was there some particular reason you called, Lord Bartholomew?"

Lord Bartholomew tried to pull himself together. "Indeed there was. I have brought my new curricle and pair. I thought we could go for a drive."

Georgiana frowned.

"Oh?" she asked in surprise. "I did not notice your curricle outside."

"No, I asked for it to be taken to the stables when I realised you were out. Your cousin said it would be in order."

"Did she?" said Georgiana, with a meaningful look at her cousin. Selina seemed to shrink into her chair.

"Well, thank you for your invitation, Lord Bartholomew," said Georgiana. "However, as you see, I have just returned from my ride and have not had an opportunity to change. Perhaps some other time."

"I can wait for you," offered his lordship, "and not just today."

Georgiana cringed.

"It looks a fine vehicle," put in Selina.

"Does it?" said Georgiana without interest. "Then you go, Selina. I'm afraid I have another engagement."

"Perhaps tomorrow morning then?" pursued Lord Bartholomew.

"Mr Lakesby has already invited me to go for a drive with him tomorrow. You must excuse me."

"Mr Lakesby?" said his lordship in shocked accents. "You are going out with Mr Lakesby again?"

"Yes." Georgiana was aware of Miss Knatchbull's eyes upon her.

"Oh, this is too bad, Miss Grey, much too bad. One would almost think you were trying to avoid me. And for you to be encouraging Mr Lakesby in this fashion is most unseemly."

"Really?" Georgiana's tone was pure ice.

His lordship did not speak but continued to look sulky. Georgiana smiled sweetly.

"I must beg your pardon, Lord Bartholomew, but as I said, I am obliged to go out. I have an appointment with my dressmaker."

Georgiana rang the bell. Lord Bartholomew had no choice but to accept his dismissal.

James answered her summons.

"Lord Bartholomew is ready to leave. Will you be good enough to show him out?"

"Yes, miss."

His lordship departed in something of a dramatic huff. Georgiana turned to her cousin.

"For heaven's sake, Selina, what are you thinking, encouraging him to hang about in this fashion?"

"What do you mean, Georgiana? It was good of Lord Bartholomew to call and it seemed only civil to allow him to wait. I had not expected you to be so long."

"I'd have been a considerable time longer, had I known he was here," Georgiana answered tartly before going upstairs to change.

On her return to the drawing room, there was no sign of Selina. Assuming she had retreated to her room, Georgiana rang the bell. This time her butler answered.

"Could I have some tea, please, Horton?"

"Certainly, miss."

"By the way, I thought today was James's day out."

"It should have been, miss, but he changed with young Frederick and took last Tuesday evening instead."

"I see."

"Will that be all, miss?"

"Yes, Horton, thank you."

Georgiana sat thinking after Horton had departed. Tuesday was the night Sir Robert Foster had been killed.

13

Seated at her dressing table, Georgiana looked at her reflection. Lady Winters had invited her to dinner. The single string of pearls Emily had fastened about her throat complemented the rich auburn tones of her hair, brought to life by the pale yellow silk of her gown.

Georgiana had been surprised to receive Lady Winters's invitation. She could only assume Lakesby's lie about Tom's fate had put her in favour with her ladyship. There could be an interesting reaction if either she or her nephew were to learn the boy's true fate. She had no doubt Lady Winters would cut her acquaintance very speedily. She was not sure about Lakesby. Part of her thought he might find the situation diverting.

Tom had settled down surprisingly well to life as a page. While there were mistakes and failures in matters of etiquette which caused Horton to roll his eyes heavenward, the boy had proved enthusiastic beyond Georgiana's expectations. In many ways, he was a breath of fresh air in the household. Miss Knatchbull's initial silence on receiving the news was broken only when she asked in a weak voice if Georgiana wished to drive her from the house. Resisting a temptation which would oust her from Society, Georgiana assured her cousin she desired no such thing. She then sat listening patiently as Selina voiced her fears of everyone being murdered in their beds before quietly pointing out the unlikelihood of this event since Mr Lakesby had taken away the boy's pistol.

"There are knives in the kitchen," said Selina.

"Good heavens, Selina, can you seriously imagine that boy waking up in the middle of the night and going to the kitchen in search of a knife to murder everyone in the house? Why should he do such a thing, pray?"

"To rob us," said Selina darkly.

"Well, I hardly think he'd need to do both. Besides, I'm sure his duties will keep him far too busy to be waking up in the night."

Georgiana had so far managed to avoid a lot of direct contact with Tom. This was not too difficult. Both Emily and James kept a close eye on him without quite intimating he could not be trusted.

The thought of James made Georgiana frown. Horton's words were circling inside her head. The knowledge that James was out on the evening of Sir Robert's murder disturbed her. It also created a barrier between herself and Emily. Georgiana wondered if Emily knew of her brother's absence from home. If she did, it was unlikely she'd say anything, even to Georgiana.

As Emily finished her task, she stood back to survey the effect. Satisfied, she fetched a cream shawl from the wardrobe and draped it around her mistress's shoulders. Georgiana rose.

"Thank you, Emily. I don't expect to be very late home."

"Yes, miss."

Selina was waiting for Georgiana in the hall, pulling her shawl tight as she looked nervously about her, as if expecting Tom to spring out with a pistol in his hand.

Amanda and Edward had arranged to take Georgiana and Selina in their carriage, an arrangement not entirely to Georgiana's satisfaction, since it obliged her to keep to whatever time Edward considered appropriate. She was surprised her brother and sister-in-law had accepted the invitation: she would not have imagined Lady Winters and her daughter to be the chosen companions of either. The thought crossed Georgiana's mind that they were keeping watch on her, a circumstance as inconvenient as it was irritating.

They called promptly, Edward looking very correct in well

tailored knee-breeches and a cravat tied neatly, without ostentation. He cast his eye over his sister's attire approvingly and assisted Selina and Georgiana into the waiting barouche.

A number of guests had already arrived at Lady Winters's establishment and were being regaled with refreshment. Edward took it upon himself to select something to drink for his ladies, but while Amanda and Selina seemed quite content with what was given to them, Georgiana immediately began to look for somewhere to lose the sickly red concoction. She had always hated raspberry cordial, even as a child. It irritated her that Edward should not have remembered.

"Perhaps this will be more to your liking, Miss Grey."

Georgiana turned her head to find Mr Lakesby holding a glass of Madeira towards her. Smiling gratefully, she accepted it, still looking for somewhere to leave the unwanted cordial.

"Allow me."

Lakesby relieved her of the glass and gave a quick glance about the room before tossing the bright contents in the pot of a nearby plant.

"I don't think you should have done that," said Georgiana, a gurgle of laughter in her voice.

"Probably not, but as Aunt Beatrice's only interest in foliage is for its decorative value at affairs such as these, I do not think she would be overly concerned." He smiled. "Can your relations spare you for a few moments?"

Georgiana glanced towards Edward, Amanda and Selina. She had been surprised her brother had not moved to her side immediately at Lakesby's arrival. She realised now that the three of them had been held in conversation by an acquaintance. She nodded and allowed Lakesby to lead her to another part of the room.

"You must allow me to tell you, you look quite charming," remarked Lakesby as soon as they were out of earshot.

Assuming he had wanted to speak to her about Sir Robert

Foster's murder, Georgiana frowned.

"Thank you," she said, "it is most kind of you to say so, but surely you did not take me aside to tell me that."

"I have a favour to ask," Lakesby said.

"Oh?" Georgiana's suspicions were aroused.

"It concerns my cousin. She confides in you, does she not?"

"Yes, up to a point." Georgiana was wary.

"I'd like you to talk to her. I think the silly minx is plotting mischief."

"And you'd like me to find out if that's the case?"

"Exactly," said Lakesby.

"Presumably to report it back to you?"

"Precisely."

"In other words," said Georgiana slowly, "you'd like me to spy on her."

"I would hardly call it that, Miss Grey."

"No, I daresay you wouldn't," said Georgiana. "Yet that is what it is, breaking her confidence."

"Miss Grey, I must protest." Lakesby paused, then lowered his voice. "I think Brandon Foster may be planning to elope with Louisa."

Georgiana looked at him in shock. "Surely she would not take such a step? She must know better."

"He might talk her into it," said Lakesby in a grim tone. "They have been on somewhat friendly terms."

"But even so," said Georgiana. She looked towards him speculatively. "Should I assume you would not look favourably upon his suit if he were to approach you?"

"I would not." The hard edge left Lakesby's voice when he addressed her again. "I beg your pardon, Miss Grey. You see, the timing is just too convenient. Under the terms of her father's will, Louisa inherits a substantial sum of money upon her marriage. Brandon Foster, as we know, was left nothing but a title and that ramshackle country house. As it is, I suspect Louisa has been lending him money out of her allowance."

"I see," said Georgiana, recalling her own thoughts on the subject.

"In view of his gambling debts, I shall own myself surprised if she ever sees it again."

"His father's death left Sir Brandon a clear path to Louisa," said Georgiana thoughtfully. "What does your aunt say? If she was in favour of the father, is she likely to accept the son?"

Lakesby shook his head. "I don't know. He wouldn't be her first choice, I'm sure."

"No, I know that." She looked at him quizzically. "I think you will end by having to marry her yourself, Mr Lakesby. It seems the surest way of protecting her from fortune hunters and will win your aunt's approval."

The hint of anger in Lakesby's expression startled her. "I think not."

Georgiana turned the subject to what she thought was safer ground. "I did not imagine Sir Brandon had any thoughts of marriage. Even if he is only acting from mercenary motives, surely he would have to be very certain of your cousin's acquiescence before taking any drastic step."

"I know. That is what concerns me."

"I rather gained the impression she was ready to accept Sir Robert," said Georgiana, seating herself in a nearby alcove. "Not eager, perhaps, but resigned to her fate." She glanced up at him. "Has she shown a degree of preference for his son?"

"No more than any other young blade," he said sitting next to her. He grinned suddenly. "Until the Crimson Cavalier rode into her life."

"I don't imagine the Crimson Cavalier's acquaintances are people with whom you would wish your cousin to associate," remarked Georgiana lightly.

"Perhaps the Crimson Cavalier should find a new set of acquaintances."

"Perhaps," said Georgiana quietly. "If Sir Brandon's interest in Louisa is sufficient for him to take the risk of eloping with her, do you think it possible he would take the risk of killing his father?"

"To remove him as a suitor?"

Georgiana nodded.

Lakesby frowned. "It's possible, I suppose, if he thinks her portion worthwhile."

"It must be very difficult for her to feel she should be suspicious of everyone."

Lakesby looked at her, the ghost of grin appearing.

"Well, after all, Miss Grey, one never knows what dark secrets one's acquaintance might have."

Georgiana threw him a baleful look. "Very true."

A shadow falling across them put an end to further conversation on the subject. Edward looked from one to the other.

"Here you are, Georgiana." He nodded briefly towards Lakesby, who had risen at his approach. "Lady Winters said dinner will be served shortly. Come along, I will escort you."

"Where are Amanda and Selina?" Georgiana knew her tone was not welcoming. However, with Edward's own voice sounding appropriate for use to a child, she was unable to pretend she was pleased to see him.

"They are talking to Lady Winters at present. Selina is going in with an acquaintance of her ladyship to whom she has just been introduced. I believe Amanda is seated next to Mr Laurence, so he will be taking her in."

"Really?" said Lakesby. "He must be about a hundred. Are you sure it is not the other way about, Grey?"

Edward Grey looked at Lakesby with an expression of deep disapproval. Lakesby was unfazed. He rose with a smile.

201

"I had better go to my aunt. I daresay she will have some venerable dowager she wishes me to look after."

"Good heavens, Edward, I cannot walk in to dinner on my brother's arm. Just think how much pity I should attract. I would rather go in on my own."

"Surely that will not be necessary," commented Lakesby.

Edward looked doubtful but rescue arrived in the form of Mr Laurence's son, expressing his pleasure at learning Miss Grey was a guest of Lady Winters and his earnest desire to escort her into dinner. She accepted readily, knowing him to be an inoffensive, if serious gentleman and one to whom Edward could hardly object, having already sanctioned his father's escort of Amanda. Her hand on the younger Mr Laurence's arm, Georgiana sailed off with a smile, leaving her brother with Mr Lakesby.

"I think my cousin would be glad of your escort, Grey," said Lakesby, nodding towards Louisa. "With so many undesirable characters dangling after her, I should be glad to know she was in safe hands."

The dinner was excellent, and not one of Lady Winters's ten guests could complain of the quality of the soup or the wine sauce adorning the sole. As the last of the covers were removed, her ladyship rose to lead the ladies to tea. Georgiana found herself hoping the gentlemen would not linger overlong with their port.

Having received her cup of tea, Georgiana looked for Louisa. Unable to banish from her mind Lakesby's words about Brandon Foster, Georgiana felt a degree of concern about the prospect of Louisa running off with Sir Robert's son. It was quite possible the girl would see it as an adventure. If it transpired he had killed his father, accusations of impropriety would be the least of her problems. As Georgiana spotted Louisa, she made her way towards a nearby empty chair, resolutely avoiding both Selina and Amanda.

Louisa smiled with pleasure at her friend's approach.

"I have not had a chance to speak to you all evening," the girl declared.

"I'm sure you have been busy with your mother's other guests," said Georgiana politely.

"It is not I who have been busy," said Louisa.

"Oh?"

Louisa looked slyly through her lashes at Georgiana.

"Max has been very attentive since the minute you arrived. I believe he has a *tendre* for you."

"Don't be absurd," said Georgiana, a little too vehemently.

"Why should it be absurd?" asked Louisa.

"Your cousin and I barely know each other."

"That could be remedied," said Louisa. "I think Max would like that."

"Louisa, you put me out of patience with you," said Georgiana, exasperated. "If you must know, he wanted to speak to me about you."

"About me? Whatever for?" Louisa was all innocent inquiry.

Georgiana could have bitten out her tongue. This was not how she had intended to approach the delicate subject with which Lakesby had entrusted her. She did not know whether she was more annoyed with Louisa for goading her into a reaction or herself for not controlling it. She looked at Louisa, who was watching her expectantly. Georgiana thought carefully about how to phrase her next sentence

"He is rather concerned," she said at last. "He is afraid Sir Brandon Foster has intentions towards you which are less than honourable."

Louisa paled. Georgiana continued, "I said, of course, I was certain he had nothing to fear, since you would never agree to anything improper."

"N-no."

"However, you know how one's male relatives assume the

worst," said Georgiana conversationally. "My brother is just the same. I have only to spend more than ten minutes in a man's company for him to be certain I am contemplating an elopement."

"An elopement!" said Louisa. "Did Max say that? Does he think I am planning to elope?"

"Oh, no, he did not say that," replied Georgiana, just about truthfully. "However, I think he is a little concerned you may be taken in by someone with few scruples."

"He must think I am very foolish," said Louisa, with an air of dignity more appropriate to her mother.

Georgiana thought it best not to answer this directly. She wondered about adopting a less obvious approach.

"How could Max imagine I would elope with Brandon Foster of all people? I am quite cross with him," said Louisa.

"Perhaps he had the impression Sir Brandon was a particular friend of yours," said Georgiana soothingly.

"That is no excuse," said Louisa, a slight blush appearing on her cheeks. "Brandon Foster indeed! He's hardly the Crimson Cavalier..."

Louisa left the sentence unfinished in a manner which left little room for doubt. She glanced towards Georgiana. "It is true he is a friend. He has had problems and I have helped him with a little of my pin money, but that does not mean I'm going to marry him."

"No, of course not," said Georgiana soothingly. "Although, Louisa, it is not altogether the thing to lend money to a man who is not to be one's husband."

"It's only now and again," said Louisa. "There are occasions when Brandon is in the suds. Sometimes he is quite comfortably off."

"Oh?" said Georgiana. "Does he repay your loans at such times?"

Louisa appeared nonplussed at this question, but was

spared the necessity of a reply by the entrance of the gentle-men from the dining room. Lakesby steered them towards the tea tray before moving to join his cousin and Georgiana. Louisa glowered at him.

"Whatever is the matter with you, Louisa?" said Lakesby.

"Nothing," she responded in a haughty tone.

Lakesby laughed, much to the girl's irritation. He looked towards Georgiana. "Have you been upsetting the child, Miss Grey?"

"I'm not a child," said Louisa, standing up angrily. "I am quite grown up. I wish you would realise that." She flounced away, leaving Lakesby staring after her in astonishment.

"What on earth was that about?" he asked.

"I'm afraid it's my fault," said Georgiana in apologetic tones. "I was trying to find out whether there was anything in this suspicion of yours about Sir Brandon. She seemed rather offended by the notion."

Lakesby frowned. "Do you believe her?"

Georgiana wrinkled her nose as she considered this.

"Yes, as a matter of fact, I do."

"Really?"

Georgiana nodded. "She seemed genuinely shocked when I suggested the possibility of an elopement. She does acknowledge they are friends, and it is true she has lent him money occasionally."

"I thought as much," said Lakesby. "Well, at least she knows I am keeping an eye on her."

"I don't think it's fair of you to tease her."

"Possibly not. But she'll recover."

Georgiana was thoughtful. "Louisa mentioned there are times when Sir Brandon is quite comfortably off."

"Really?" Lakesby looked surprised at this. "It's true there are occasions when he seems to throw money about more freely. I had not attributed it to anything more than recklessness."

"I assume he's not too successful at the tables?" inquired Georgiana.

Lakesby shook his head. "Mediocre at best. In any case, what winnings he does have are poured back into the game, or the more pressing of his debts."

"Perhaps he's been selling the contents of the family home."

"What concerns me more is that Louisa may be lending him more than she is willing to admit. I should hate to see her frittering away her inheritance on such a fellow."

"Yes," said Georgiana slowly. "Surely she cannot touch the principal?"

"No, of course not," said Lakesby. "Her mother and I control that. However, she does receive a fairly generous allowance – more than I would like, but her mother insists she has enough for any trinkets she takes a fancy to."

"You speak as though you grudged it," said Georgiana.

"Not at all," said Lakesby. "Tell me, do you mean to torment your brother about his liaison with Lady Wickerston?"

"That sounds rather harsh," said Georgiana, wondering if there was a reason for the sudden change of subject.

"The notion of you doing it or my having worded it so?"

Georgiana gave a shake of the head. "Why should it concern you?"

"It doesn't especially, but I thought you might be interested in Lady Wickerston's regular morning rides in Richmond Park."

"Oh?" said Georgiana. "Who told you that?"

"My groom."

Georgiana thought about this new piece of information, seeing two possibilities. She gave a quick glance towards Edward. Satisfied his attention was elsewhere, she lowered her voice, conscious of the dryness of her mouth.

"Does she meet my brother there?"

"That Brackett was too discreet to say. I believe they meet occasionally, but not on a regular basis."

Georgiana looked thoughtfully ahead of her. There was a glint of mischief in her eye.

"Lady Wickerston is careful," she said slowly. "I'm not sure I can persuade her to tell me anything. Besides, how can I ask my brother's mistress if he was with her on the night of Sir Robert Foster's murder?"

"Perhaps you should ask him."

The thought of Edward's expression were she to ask such a question was one Georgiana found extremely diverting. She cast a surreptitious glance towards him and smiled. "Perhaps I will."

The look on Lakesby's face dared her to do just that.

"By the by, what has become of that boy?"

Georgiana was evasive. "I don't think you need worry about him holding up any more coaches."

Lakesby grinned. "Read him a sermon on the evils of highway robbery, did you?"

"Something like that."

"I wish I could have heard it."

"I'm sure you would have found it very amusing."

With the approach of Lady Winters any further conversation on the subject was firmly closed. Lakesby rose, but her ladyship declined his offer of a seat, smiling graciously. She was clearly doing her obligatory circulation among her guests, although the thought struck Georgiana that she had decided the tête-à-tête between her nephew and his companion had lasted long enough.

"I must make you my compliments," Georgiana said to her hostess. "The dinner was excellent."

"I am so pleased you enjoyed it." Lady Winters turned her attention back to Lakesby. "Maxwell, do you know what is the matter with Louisa? Of a sudden she seems to be out of sorts."

"Perhaps she is in love," he said lightly.

Her ladyship looked unamused. "I wish you would speak with her and find out what is wrong."

"If I get an opportunity," said Lakesby, clearly bored with the subject.

Lady Winters looked anything but satisfied with this concession. She addressed Georgiana. "Louisa is very fond of her cousin, you know. He can always manage to lift her spirits."

"Indeed?" said Georgiana politely. She could not resist a quizzical glance at Lakesby. His answering expression promised retribution.

"She was quite distressed about poor Sir Robert's death," Lady Winters continued.

"Yes, I'm sure she was," Georgiana responded. "It must have been quite a shock."

"Oh, yes," said her ladyship. "I would have been so happy to see her respectably settled, knowing she would be generously provided for. Such matters are a constant worry to a mother."

"Yes," said Georgiana, who had never heard any reports of Sir Robert's generosity.

Lady Winters sighed. "I hear the bulk of Sir Robert's fortune goes to a distant cousin. I can only hope Louisa will not have to wait long for another eligible suitor."

"I shouldn't waste any more time thinking about it," Lakesby recommended. "Louisa will marry well enough sooner or later."

"I would prefer it was sooner, Maxwell," said her ladyship, "before some serious mischief befalls her." She turned and left them abruptly.

14

Amanda did not want to be away from her children too late so their party took leave of Lady Winters shortly after eleven o'clock. Since Amanda was anxious to check the nursery, the carriage called first at the house she and Edward shared. Edward insisted Georgiana and Selina came in for a glass of wine, an invitation which appealed more to Selina than Georgiana. However, her brother was already out of the carriage, waiting to hand her down. Since he would never countenance sending her home in his carriage without an escort, Georgiana had no option but to acquiesce.

Amanda went straight to the nursery, Selina at her side, having expressed an earnest desire to see the children while promising not to disturb them. A waiting footman helped Georgiana off with her cloak. Edward gave instructions to the footman to fetch some wine. Striding down the hall, he told his sister he would join her presently. Georgiana decided to wait in the library. She smiled at the footman, telling him there was no need for him to show her the way.

Georgiana cast her eyes over the rows of books, taking in no more than half of the titles. Her mind was on the words of Lady Winters. What mischief could she be expecting to befall Louisa if she was not soon married? Did she also fear her daughter was at risk of being persuaded into an elopement? Georgiana began to wonder whether she had been too easily convinced by Louisa's denials.

The door opened softly and the footman appeared bearing a decanter and glasses. Georgiana smiled her thanks and declined his offer to pour, saying she would wait for her brother. She moved away from the bookshelves as the footman departed. Despite her initial reluctance to enter the house, Georgiana was glad of the opportunity to stretch her legs and enjoy some quiet after what seemed endless raptures from Selina about Lady Winters's party.

Her eyes fell on a rectangular box which rested on a large mahogany desk. Its style was familiar and not something she would have expected to find in plain sight. She frowned. It was unlike Edward to be so careless. She gave a quick glance towards the door, then raised the lid. Georgiana found herself staring into a case empty but for the red velvet lining with its two distinct pistol shapes.

"Georgiana, what are you doing?"

Georgiana started. She had not heard Edward open the door. She moved away from the desk guiltily. Edward strode over and picked up the box, locking it inside a drawer.

"Isn't it a little late for that?" Georgiana asked.

"What do you mean by prying into my personal affairs?" Edward demanded stiffly.

Georgiana faced her brother unflinchingly.

"I was concerned that a set of pistols had been left out in the open."

"Really?" said Edward.

"Where are they?"

Edward began to look flushed. "It's late. When Selina comes down from the nursery I shall escort you both home."

"Where are the pistols?"

"That is hardly your concern, Georgiana."

Georgiana rolled her eyes. "For heaven's sake, Edward, do stop being so pompous."

"You are fond enough of telling me you consider your life to be none of my concern."

A fair point, she thought, still determined to have an answer. "Surely you haven't given them to your postilions?" The pistols were heirlooms, and this seemed unlikely.

Edward looked at her in irritation. His voice, when he spoke, was petulant. "Since you insist on knowing, they were stolen."

"Stolen?"

"Yes."

"Have you done anything about recovering them?"

"Certainly. I'm not a fool."

"You've found no trace of them?"

"No. Why are you interesting yourself in the matter?" said Edward.

"When did you miss them?"

"A few days ago."

"Before Sir Robert was killed?"

A look of horror appeared on Edward's face. "Surely, Georgiana, you are not suggesting they were used to kill Sir Robert? That's preposterous."

"Really?" asked Georgiana.

"It would be an outlandish coincidence. It's hardly likely they were stolen by Sir Robert's murderer."

"How can you know that? Where did you leave them?"

"I do not propose to justify my actions," said Edward haughtily. "You know I'm not a careless person."

"It seems I don't know you as well as I thought."

"What do you mean?"

"Lady Wickerston."

The two words hung in the room between them. Edward's face took on a corpse-like pallor. He walked quickly to the door and closed it quietly. When he returned he seemed more in control of himself.

"What about Lady Wickerston?"

Georgiana gave a slow smile. "I know she is your mistress, Edward."

Edward swallowed, evidently shocked. He sought refuge in brotherly authority. "Georgiana, this is hardly an appropriate subject for discussion."

"Spare me the sanctimony, Edward. It seems you're hardly in

a position to talk to me about what is and isn't appropriate." She paused, sauntering over to examine the bookshelves. "Ironic, when I think of the way you constantly lecture me, not to mention foisting Selina on me as a companion."

"I did not foist her on you," said Edward hotly. "I merely suggested Selina to bear you company, since you could hardly live alone."

"You wrote to invite her without consulting me. And your moral stance is no longer convincing."

Edward strode to the wine decanter and poured himself a glass. Georgiana shook her head as he offered her one. Disposing of his wine in one swallow, Edward poured another and took a deep breath. Silence hung between brother and sister, heated and anxious on his side, cool, almost amused on hers. The door opened, and Amanda entered with Selina close behind her looking nervous.

"For heaven's sake, the children are asleep. I could hear raised voices from the nursery," said Amanda.

"What?" said Edward, his colour draining.

"I wish you would try to be more amiable with each other," Amanda begged. "What was it this time?"

"Oh, the usual," Georgiana said lightly. "Edward thinks he knows best about everything."

If Edward was grateful to his sister for her discretion, he did not show it. Instead, he drank the remainder of his wine and spoke gruffly to his wife. "I shall escort Georgiana and Selina home. I do not expect to be very long, but do go to bed, you must be exhausted."

"Not at all. I'll wait," said Amanda, smiling affectionately. She embraced Georgiana and Selina, wishing each a fond goodnight.

The drive was accomplished in silence, with Edward avoiding his sister's eyes and she lost in thought. Selina sat miserably stealing glances at each. Reaching Georgiana's front door, Edward pressed her hand urgently as he helped her from the carriage, speaking in a strained undervoice.

"Georgiana, I must talk to you. May I come in for a few moments?"

"Certainly," she responded.

Edward's face was drawn, and Georgiana was surprised at the hint of desperation in his eyes. Entering the house, she wished goodnight to Selina, who looked eager to escape. Georgiana led Edward into the drawing room and closed the door.

"Well, Edward, what is it?"

Edward seemed to be struggling for the right words.

"I feel I should apologise for my behaviour."

Georgiana had not expected this. "Oh? Well, thank you, but should you not be apologising to Amanda?"

"You are right, of course." He paused. "Thank you for not saying anything to her."

"I have no wish to see her hurt."

"No." He fell silent for another moment. "How did you find out?"

"Your party. There passed a look between you which could not have meant anything else."

Edward let out a long-drawn breath and covered his eyes with his hand. Georgiana thought he seemed broken all of a sudden.

"It's not that I am unhappy with Amanda," he said, "or that I don't love her. I do, very much indeed." Edward sank into a chair.

Georgiana nodded. "Of course," she said in a tone which betrayed her tongue as firmly in her cheek. "I see, this is just a diversion, it doesn't mean anything."

Edward looked angrily at her. "You don't understand."

Georgiana laughed. "Nonsense, Edward, I understand only too well."

"It's complicated."

"Of course it is."

Edward glared in response to the mockery in her tone. Georgiana shook her head.

"Oh, for heaven's sake, Edward, your private life is no more my business than mine is yours. However," she continued, preventing any opportunity to protest, "Amanda doesn't deserve such treatment."

"Do you think I don't know that?" Edward said angrily. "Every time I think of it, I'm ashamed of myself. But if you understood all the circumstances…"

Georgiana looked at him, waiting for enlightenment.

"There are reasons… Lady Wickerston relies on me."

"Good gracious," said Georgiana. "Why on earth should she rely on you?"

Edward's tone grew lofty. "As I said, Georgiana, you do not know all the circumstances."

"I know. All gentlemen have their indiscretions."

Edward's chest swelled. "This is not an indiscretion."

Georgiana's eyes widened. "What? But you said…"

"Never mind what I said," responded Edward irritably. "I don't care to discuss it with you."

"Indeed?" said Georgiana. "Then what are you doing here, pray?"

Edward seemed at a loss. Georgiana went to the door and opened it.

"If there is nothing more, I shall say goodnight."

"No, Georgiana, wait, please."

Georgiana closed the door.

"Well?" she said.

Edward began to pace the room, seeming to search for what he wanted to say. Georgiana waited patiently.

"I know you think I am just amusing myself, but it is not that simple. Neither do I wish to betray Amanda." He paused.

"I know it is wrong, but it is the deuce of a tangle. I have tried to break it off, several times, but there are difficulties."

"What difficulties?" inquired Georgiana.

Edward was evasive. "Lady Wickerston has problems. I am not at liberty to discuss them."

"Oh, very well," said Georgiana. She looked towards her brother. "How can you be sure Amanda won't find out? I did."

Edward looked gloomy.

Georgiana's tone grew brisk, practical. "It would be very much worse if that were to happen."

"I am aware of that," he responded, "particularly in the present circumstances." The abruptness with which he stopped speaking drew Georgiana's attention.

"What do you mean, 'the present circumstances'?" she demanded.

Edward looked uneasy, as if he had been caught off guard. "Why, Sir Robert Foster's murder. It makes things a trifle awkward."

"Awkward? My goodness, Edward, what a description. What does Sir Robert's murder have to do with you and Lady Wickerston?"

"Nothing," he said hastily. "But he was her uncle; this is a difficult time for her."

"She did not appear particularly grief stricken," said Georgiana. "Tell me, do you know if Lady Wickerston had anything to gain by her uncle's death?"

"No, of course not," he said, a little too vehemently.

"No, she had nothing to gain, or no, you don't know?"

"This is absurd, Georgiana. Are you implying she had something to do with his death?"

"I'm not implying anything, I'm asking a question."

"Well, it's out of the question. In any case..." Edward paused, looking uneasy.

"In any case, what?"

Edward drew a deep breath. "I was with Theresa Wickerston on the night of Sir Robert's murder."

"You were?"

He nodded.

"So you weren't at Brooks's?"

"No. At least, I did look in there, but didn't stay very long."

"I see." Georgiana digested this information. A finger of doubt niggled at her. Edward's story did not quite ring true.

"Lady Wickerston will support what you say, I suppose?"

"What?" he asked. "You don't mean to ask her?"

Georgiana shrugged. "Not unless I have to."

"Why on earth should you have to?" he demanded. "I don't like the idea of you discussing this with her, Georgiana."

"I'd be surprised if you did." Georgiana said lightly.

"Sir Robert's murder has nothing to do with you, Georgiana. I must say, you're developing a very unhealthy interest in this business."

"Yes, well, it concerns a friend of mine," Georgiana said cagily.

"Lakesby, no doubt," Edward said with a grim note to his voice.

"Louisa Winters," said Georgiana promptly. "There was talk of her marrying Sir Robert."

"You're not serious?"

Georgiana nodded. "Indeed I am. I believe Lady Winters and Sir Robert had virtually arranged it."

Edward looked slightly nauseous. "I can't imagine Lakesby agreeing to it. Isn't he the girl's guardian?"

"Yes, with her mother. You're quite right; he wasn't in favour of the match." Georgiana paused and looked closely at her brother. "I understand you and Mr Lakesby are better acquainted than you led me to believe."

Edward pursed his lips. "I don't wish to discuss it."

"For heaven's sake, Edward, it was a lark. I don't imagine

anyone even remembers it."

The look on Edward's face left Georgiana unsure whether she had offended his dignity or his vanity.

"We were sent down, Georgiana."

"Yes, well, even so, I think it a trifle excessive that you should still not be on speaking terms." She paused, then continued tentatively, "I suspect he regrets it."

"No doubt you consider you know best," said Edward stiffly. "I must go. It's growing late." He hesitated, looking steadily at his sister. "It is not always wise to take people at their word, Georgiana. Since you are so interested in Sir Robert Foster's murder, I suggest you ask your friend Lakesby about his own motives. He had a grudge against Sir Robert, far greater than any Theresa Wickerston may have had. Goodnight, Georgiana." Refusing to say anything further, he left.

Emily was waiting for her when she retired.

"Are you quite well, miss?"

Georgiana smiled, trying to shake off her abstraction. "Yes, thank you, Emily. I'm sorry, my mind was elsewhere."

Georgiana lay awake for what seemed like hours, a jumble of thoughts tossing around in her head. Foremost in her mind were Edward's parting words. She was less surprised by his suggestion that Lakesby had a grudge against Sir Robert than by his assumption that she was accusing Lady Wickerston.

Georgiana slept fitfully and rose feeling little rested. Emily looked knowingly at her mistress when she brought her chocolate, but made no comment, merely inquiring what she proposed to wear that day. Georgiana felt a twinge of guilt that that she was not being entirely candid with Emily. The maid knew the worst about her and had been friend, confidante and protectress. It weighed heavily on Georgiana that she was holding information back from her.

Drinking her tea at the breakfast table, Georgiana found

herself watching James as he went about his duties. It was hard to imagine him as a murderer. Yet although Georgiana had known him as long as she had known Emily, in some respects he was hard to fathom. He had seemed to accept his imprisonment philosophically. Georgiana had never heard him complain about the cough he had acquired which seemed a permanent part of his life.

"James."

The footman turned towards her inquiringly, halting his progress out of the room.

"Yes, miss?"

Georgiana found herself unsure what to say. How could she ask her footman how he had spent his evening out? It was none of her business. To point out the coincidence of it being the night of Sir Robert Foster's murder denoted a lack of trust which was likely to wound him. Resolutely pushing away the guilt she felt, Georgiana smiled.

"How is Tom getting along?" she inquired by way of opening the conversation.

"Well enough, miss. He seems keen and willing to learn, but we're keeping him away from the china."

Georgiana frowned in puzzlement. She would have expected him to say the silver. James seemed to read her thoughts.

"Breakages seem more of a danger than theft, miss."

"I see. I trust no one's objected to his being here?"

"Not at all, miss. It was nothing more than a charitable impulse after all. In fact, Mrs Daniels has taken to mothering him. He – er – doesn't seem entirely comfortable with that. I suspect he's not sure how to take it."

Georgiana smiled. "Mrs Daniels is an excellent creature, but I can imagine her rather overpowering for a boy of his age."

"Quite so, miss."

"As long as he is not proving a disruption to the household."

"Not at all, miss."

"I'm very glad to hear it. By the way, I understand you changed your day out this week."

"Yes, miss. There was a matter I needed to attend to."

"I see. James, you would tell me if there was anything wrong, wouldn't you?"

"I beg your pardon, miss?"

"I'd like you to feel you could come to me if you needed any help."

"Thank you, miss, but I'd not wish to impose."

"It's hardly an imposition, James. After all, I have known you and Emily for rather a long time."

"Even so, miss…" James paused, looking steadily at her. "Begging your pardon, Miss Georgiana, but why should you imagine there's something wrong?"

"I was just concerned, James. It's not often you change your day out so I wanted to be certain nothing was amiss, particularly as…" Georgiana halted, wishing she could have bitten out her tongue.

"Particularly as what, miss?"

Pushing her empty plate away, Georgiana drew a breath and spoke steadily.

"Your evening out was Tuesday, was it not?"

"Yes, miss."

"I believe that was the night Sir Robert Foster died," she said in as light a tone as she could manage. "It occurred to me that you might have encountered some trouble, either heard something, or seen the person who carried out the murder."

"Or committed the murder myself?"

"James, no," Georgiana protested.

"It's all right, miss. Lord knows, I had reason to dislike the man. I can't honestly say I was sorry to hear he was dead, miss, but I promise you I had nothing to do with it."

"James, I am not trying to accuse you. I just want to find out what happened."

"I beg your pardon, miss, but shouldn't you leave that to the proper authorities?"

"I have my own reasons for wishing to see the matter resolved."

"I see."

Georgiana wondered whether he did. However, she did not pursue it and he did not elaborate.

"I visited a friend, Miss Georgiana."

"Oh?"

James seemed hesitant to volunteer any more. Georgiana waited expectantly.

"He's someone I met when…" James's voice trailed off. He took a deep breath before continuing. "He'd been sentenced to transportation."

"Then how did you come to be visiting him?"

"He escaped," said James uneasily, "before the sentence was carried out."

"So he was in hiding," responded Georgiana.

"Yes, miss. I took him some food and some spare clothing." He bowed his head slightly. "I beg your pardon, miss. I know it was wrong, but I took pity on the poor fellow. He was planning on going to France."

"It's quite all right, James. I don't need to know any more," said Georgiana. She paused thoughtfully. "Unless… Did Sir Robert by any chance sentence your friend?"

"I don't know, miss. It's possible, I suppose."

"You didn't see anything out of the ordinary?"

James shook his head.

"And your friend?" she asked.

"He didn't mention anything, miss, though I think he was too busy trying to avoid being seen himself."

"Yes. Thank you, James."

"Miss."

James departed. Georgiana was surprised to see him return a few minutes later.

"Mrs Grey has called, miss."

"What?" Georgiana laid down her napkin. "Please show her in, James."

"Very good, miss."

Georgiana's first thought, that Edward had confessed his indiscretion to his wife, was soon dismissed by her sister-in-law's appearance. Amanda looked concerned but not upset, and was immaculate in a cream morning dress. She laid down her reticule on the breakfast table as she came forward to embrace Georgiana.

"Amanda, I trust there is nothing wrong?"

"No. That is, I'm not sure."

"Shall I ask James to bring some fresh tea?"

Amanda shook her head. "No, thank you. I won't stay long. Where is Selina?"

"Gone to do some sewing," replied Georgiana. "Shall I send someone for her?"

"No, I'm glad to find you alone. I wanted to speak to you about Edward."

"About Edward?" Georgiana was wary. She poured herself a second cup of tea to avoid her sister-in-law's eye.

"Yes. You see I am a little worried about him. He does not seem quite himself."

Georgiana refrained from suggesting this could be an improvement. "In what way?" she inquired.

"He seems preoccupied, worried about something. Has he said anything to you?"

Georgiana took a sip of tea while gathering her thoughts.

"Edward is not given to confiding in me," she replied.

"I know," said Amanda. "But I had hoped perhaps if there

221

was something he did not wish to worry me about…"

Her voice trailed off. Georgiana's heart went out to her. Impulsively she put her hand over Amanda's.

"I'm sure it's nothing. It's probably just the extra responsibilities of his magistrate's appointment."

"I suppose so," Amanda sighed. She smiled. "Thank you, Georgiana."

"Has he made any progress with the inquiries into Sir Robert's death?" Georgiana asked as casually as she could.

"I don't know. He hasn't really talked about it."

Georgiana was unsurprised. Amanda drew on her gloves. "I must go," she said. "I have a few errands. I don't suppose you'd care to accompany me?"

"No, thank you," responded Georgiana. "I have some matters of my own in need of attention."

"Very well," said Amanda, rising. "Give my love to Selina, won't you?" She moved towards the door just as James entered the room.

"Yes, James?" prompted Georgiana as he looked towards her.

"Mr Lakesby is here, miss."

Amanda looked at her sister-in-law in some surprise. Georgiana did not blink.

"Already? Very well, I suppose you had better show him into the drawing room. I will be there directly."

"Yes, miss."

The footman withdrew. Georgiana turned and bade her sister-in-law goodbye, making no attempt to explain her visitor.

Lakesby stood in the middle of the drawing room, looking out of the window, his driving gloves in his hand. He turned and smiled as she entered. "My curricle is outside; your stable-boy is walking the horses. I assume he can be trusted with them?" He looked at her attire. "Had we not arranged to go driving today, Miss Grey?"

"Yes, but I am afraid my sister-in-law called and has just this second left. I will not keep you above a few moments while I fetch a pelisse."

"Of course," said Lakesby, turning his attention back to the window.

There was no sign of Emily, so Georgiana reached quickly into the wardrobe for a pelisse, hastily tying the ribbons at her throat. The bonnet she chose was the first one which came to hand and she ran lightly down the stairs clutching it, putting it on her head when she returned to the drawing room. Not being certain where Tom was, Georgiana wanted Lakesby out of the house with all speed. She was not ready to run the risk of the two meeting.

"There was no need to rush," said Lakesby with a smile as he came towards her.

"I do not wish to delay," said Georgiana straightening her bonnet. "I mean to call on Lady Wickerston later this morning."

"Do you?" asked Lakesby as they stepped out to his curricle. They fell silent as they reached earshot of the stable-boy. Lakesby tossed him a coin. They did not speak again until the horses were moving.

"What do you intend to say to Lady Wickerston?" Lakesby inquired. "Surely you do not mean to tax her with her liaison with your brother?"

"Good gracious, no," said Georgiana with a laugh. "Besides, I have already spoken to Edward about that."

"What?" Lakesby was momentarily startled. "You're not serious?"

Georgiana looked towards him, an impish grin appearing. "Was it not your own suggestion, Mr Lakesby?"

"Well, yes, but I did not imagine..." He stopped and looked at her sternly. "I ought to box your ears."

"Hardly your responsibility, Mr Lakesby," she said lightly.

"Very well, what did your brother have to say?"

Georgiana hesitated. Edward's infidelity was a family matter which she felt uneasy discussing with Lakesby. Besides, she was not fully convinced of his innocence in the matter of Sir Robert's murder, especially after Edward's suggestion that he had a motive.

"You might as well tell me, you know," he remarked. "If Lady Wickerston is Sir Robert Foster's niece, it could have some bearing on his murder."

"How so?" said Georgiana, knowing he was right.

Lakesby gave her a baleful look. "Stop trying to pretend you have the intellect of my cousin. I know perfectly well you have a first class brain and all this has already occurred to you."

"What makes you so certain?" Georgiana demanded.

"Because if you were bird-witted you would have been on the gallows after you had held up your first carriage."

Georgiana did not answer. Lakesby looked exasperated. "Miss Grey—"

"Mr Lakesby," she interrupted, "my brother seems under the impression you had a motive for the murder of Sir Robert."

Lakesby was silent for a moment or two. When he did speak, he was not casually dismissive as she had expected.

"I take it you mean apart from my supposed desire to remove him from the path of marriage to my cousin," he said grimly.

"Yes," said Georgiana, her mouth suddenly dry.

Lakesby turned and looked fully at her.

"Your brother is right, Miss Grey. I did."

"What – what was it?" She found the words dragged out of her.

"Sir Robert Foster was responsible for the death of my father."

15

Georgiana stared at Lakesby's grim expression, thunder-struck. "But – but, how? What happened? I beg your pardon. This must be very distressing for you."

Lakesby shook his head. His hard eyes were fixed on the road ahead although Georgiana thought she could detect the ghost of an ironic smile.

"No matter," said Lakesby.

"What happened?" Georgiana asked again, more gently.

Lakesby did not answer immediately. Georgiana watched him closely.

"I was in Europe at the time," said Lakesby. "I always wondered whether it would have made a difference if I had been in England." He smiled at her. "Probably not, but I suppose one always asks these questions."

Georgiana did not speak, waiting for him to continue. When he did, his tone was brisker.

"After Louisa's father died, his will gave my father joint guardianship of Louisa with my Aunt Beatrice, a responsibility I inherited."

Georgiana nodded.

"She's not a bad girl, really," he continued with a smile, "but one has to be on the alert."

"I can imagine."

"Sir Robert Foster was showing an interest in Louisa almost as soon as she left the schoolroom, barely a year and a half ago. My father favoured the match no more than I." Lakesby's voice dropped slightly. "Sir Robert arranged a weekend house party and invited Aunt Beatrice and Louisa. I don't know what my aunt was thinking, accepting that invitation. My father decided to go, to put a stop to any ideas Sir Robert

225

might have had about pursuing Louisa."

"Sir Robert had your aunt's encouragement?"

"Oh, yes," said Lakesby, his tone hardening. "My aunt has been very focused on Sir Robert's wealth and the extent of his estate. My father knew if left to their own devices, Aunt Beatrice and Sir Robert would have the whole business settled."

"But, surely, as joint guardian he could have forbidden the match?" said Georgiana.

"Certainly," replied Lakesby. "But he thought it better to nip any pretensions in the bud. Besides, Miss Grey, you have seen Louisa with Sir Robert. I do not imagine you were under the impression she enjoyed his company."

"No," said Georgiana slowly. "I felt quite sorry for her."

"So did my father," said Lakesby. He gave a slight smile. "Louisa can be as foolishly flirtatious as any other girl of her age. However, she is also vulnerable. She's always been very nervous around Sir Robert Foster. My father saw no reason for her to be subjected to his attentions, whatever her mother's ambitions."

"So he ensured she wouldn't be left alone with Sir Robert?" said Georgiana.

"He tried," said Lakesby, the hard note returning to his voice. "Unfortunately, Fate, and Sir Robert, conspired against him."

"I can well believe it of Sir Robert," said Georgiana. "What did he do?"

"He arranged a day's shooting," said Lakesby crisply. "Nothing unusual about that, but my father was suspicious. He confided his concerns to me in a letter, although of course by the time I received it, it was much too late. He planned to keep watch on Sir Robert. No one seems entirely sure exactly what occurred, but two things are clear: Sir Robert broke away from the main party, and my father – presumably

concluding his host intended to pursue his designs on Louisa
– followed him."

Lakesby paused. Georgiana watched him carefully.

"Sir Robert walked towards the main house. I understand
my father was some distance behind – I imagine he did not
want Sir Robert to realise he was there." Lakesby paused. His
next words seemed to require some effort. "Sir Robert did not
return to the house. He stopped some way from the rest of
the party, and his gun went off."

Georgiana felt an eerily sick sensation rise in her throat.
Lakesby grimaced.

"You realise, of course, the shot hit my father. He was killed
immediately. Sir Robert always swore it was an accident. I
daresay it was. It was impossible to prove otherwise. No one
else in the hunting party saw exactly what happened, and he
certainly put on a convincing show of sorrow and contrition.
At the very least it was abominably careless."

"Yes," said Georgiana. "Surely there was an inquiry?"

"Indeed there was. They found it was accidental death;
there was no evidence to suggest anything else."

"I see. Mr Lakesby, I am so sorry."

"Thank you, Miss Grey. You are very kind." He gave a little
twisted smile. "So you see your brother is quite right. I had no
reason to love Sir Robert Foster."

"Your mother must have been very distressed," said
Georgiana gently.

"She was." Lakesby made no further attempt to elaborate.

"I am sorry I pressed you to tell me," said Georgiana. "It
must have been painful to go over it again."

"It is no matter," said Lakesby. He fell silent for a moment,
his face clouding. "It does still make me angry. Accident or
not, it shouldn't have happened." He sighed. When he spoke
again, his tone had softened. "I beg your pardon, Miss Grey,
you are not to blame. My mother was never the same after my

father's death, you see. Oh, I don't mean she retreated into gloomy widowhood – it is not in her nature – but her life lacked something. She is surrounded by friends, forever visiting people in one part of the country or another: she's been in Northumberland for the last two weeks, as a matter of fact. Yet a part of her remains distant, untouchable – almost gone."

"I see," said Georgiana. "I'm so sorry. But surely your aunt knows of all this? Why was she so anxious to promote a match between Louisa and Sir Robert?"

Lakesby shrugged. "My aunt will see no further than what is of advantage to her. Sir Robert was no pauper." He glanced towards Georgiana. "There is no point in pretending. You know, of course, she initially had other plans for my cousin."

Georgiana nodded. "Yes, Louisa told me."

"I thought she had," said Lakesby. "I never knew a girl whose tongue could rattle so."

"You are hard on her."

"No, I'm not," said Lakesby, unrepentant. "You know as well as I, she has no idea of discretion." He looked at her shrewdly. "Though I daresay you have not objected to that."

Georgiana did not deign to respond to this observation. With hands folded, she fixed her eyes on the road ahead. Lakesby laughed softly.

"I imagine she's been a valuable source of information in your inquiries," he observed.

"Not at all." Georgiana glanced towards him mischievously. "Do you think your aunt had an idea the prospect of a marriage between Sir Robert and Louisa might prompt you into a declaration?"

"Possibly," said Lakesby shortly. It was clear he was bored with the subject.

The sharing of Lakesby's confidence had come as a surprise to Georgiana, leaving her in a state of puzzlement.

Although he had told her of his father's death, she felt it had been with some reluctance. She wondered whether this was because it was painful for him to speak of it, or because he knew it gave him a strong motive for Sir Robert's murder.

The return to Georgiana's home was a little later than she had expected. However, she was in time to do justice to an excellent luncheon, if a little preoccupied. Nibbling a piece of apricot tart, she listened with half an ear to Selina's chatter, making appropriate responses although her mind was elsewhere: a skill achieved through long practice.

Turning her mind to others with a reason to kill Sir Robert, Georgiana ventured forth in the afternoon to call on Lady Wickerston.

Despite Lady Wickerston's claim that she was not close to Sir Robert, Georgiana was not sure whether her ladyship would be receiving visitors in view of the recent bereavement. Neither had Georgiana any idea what she would say to Lady Wickerston if invited into the house. She was fully prepared for a rebuff and more than a little surprised to be granted admittance.

Lady Wickerston met Georgiana in the small salon. Her ladyship came forward with a gracious smile, moving elegantly, hand outstretched.

"My dear Miss Grey! What a charming surprise. You'll take some tea with me, of course?"

"Thank you, Lady Wickerston, you are very kind."

While Lady Wickerston rang to give instructions about the tea, Georgiana had leisure to look about the room. It was small, attractively furnished with simple yet exquisite taste. The Sèvres bowl with freshly cut flowers near the large bay window was one of the few concessions to ornamentation.

When the tea was ordered, Lady Wickerston settled herself in a chair opposite Georgiana and smiled.

"It's very kind of you to call, Miss Grey. I have so little

company these days."

"Really?" Georgiana was genuinely surprised. It was the sort of statement one expected from someone elderly, living in seclusion. Her ladyship seemed near Georgiana's own age and could not have been described as an invalid. However, she did look rather pale. Georgiana took a guess.

"Your uncle's death?" she asked in a sympathetic tone.

Lady Wickerston shook her head, giving a slightly sad smile.

"No, not really. As I said, he was not a very close relative, although it would hardly be seemly to venture into society until after a suitable period of mourning."

"No, of course not," said Georgiana, unable to banish from her mind the fact that Lady Wickerston apparently saw nothing unseemly about venturing out to meet Edward. She smiled sweetly. "I had heard you were in the habit of going riding in Richmond Park. Have you had to discontinue this?"

Georgiana was surprised to catch a fleeting look of alarm in Lady Wickerston's eyes.

"Who told you that?" asked her ladyship.

"I really can't remember," said Georgiana. "Does it matter?"

"Perhaps not," said Lady Wickerston. "But I beg you will not mention it again. My husband may come in, you see, and he does not approve of me riding out."

"I see," said Georgiana.

The door opened and a neatly dressed maid entered with the tea tray. Her ladyship smiled and thanked the girl, waiting for her to pour before dismissing her from the room.

"Would you care for a scone, Miss Grey?" asked Lady Wickerston.

"Yes, please."

Georgiana studied her hostess as she picked up a small pair of silver tongs and used them to put a scone on a china plate.

She found it strange that Lady Wickerston should bother to make her welcome. Perhaps she was trying to allay suspicion.

"Your uncle's death must have come as a shock to you," said Georgiana, accepting the plate her ladyship held out to her.

"Yes," said Lady Wickerston, with a small sigh. "It was quite dreadful for him to have met his end in that way, especially since–" She broke off suddenly, flushing slightly.

"Since?" said Georgiana, trying to mask her curiosity.

"No matter," said her ladyship quickly. "Would you care for some bread and butter?"

"No, thank you." Georgiana forced herself to hold back the questions on her tongue. What had Lady Wickerston been about to say, and how could she be persuaded to divulge it? Georgiana realised she would have to try forging a closer relationship with Lady Wickerston than anticipated. Despite the difficulties of the situation, Georgiana could not help appreciating its irony.

As Lady Wickerston handed Georgiana a fresh cup of tea, her hand brushed against the arm of her guest's chair. Georgiana had the fleeting impression her ladyship flinched slightly.

"Are you quite well?" asked Georgiana.

"Yes," said her ladyship with a smile. "I burned my wrist on the teapot this morning. It's nothing, very foolish of me."

Recalling her own mishap with the teapot, Georgiana was unconvinced. However, she decided to shrug it off, reminding herself that her own occupation drew out an instinctive suspiciousness in her nature which was in most cases probably unwarranted. She imagined it extremely unlikely Lady Wickerston would be trying to camouflage stolen jewels about her person. She brought her mind back to the main point of her visit.

"Has my brother told you he has been appointed magistrate

in your uncle's place?"

"I believe he mentioned it to my husband."

"Really?" said Georgiana. She wondered if Lady Wickerston was attempting to cover any direct conversation she may have had with Edward.

"Yes," said her ladyship, seeming quite surprised at the hint of disbelief in her guest's tone. "I gather the gentlemen discussed it at your sister-in-law's party."

"I see." Georgiana paused, looking reflective. "I understand my brother is acquainted with a Bow Street Runner who is going to investigate."

"I'm sure that will be a help."

Her ladyship was far too discreet. Georgiana tried a different approach.

"Tell me, Lady Wickerston, are you not the least bit curious as to who could have killed your uncle?"

Lady Wickerston looked rather startled. "I understood it was that highwayman, the Crimson Cavalier."

"Not necessarily," said Georgiana. "I believe he was in the area, but that doesn't make him guilty of the murder."

"Why, that is absurd," said Lady Wickerston, showing the first signs of animation Georgiana had noticed. "Who else could have had a reason to kill him, pray?"

"It would be interesting to find that out," said Georgiana. "I believe your uncle was not, I beg your pardon, a very popular man. There could have been others more comfortable with him dead."

Lady Wickerston looked at her guest without speaking. For a moment, Georgiana thought she would be ordered from the house.

"Why, that is quite horrible," said her ladyship at last. "One expects that sort of behaviour from highway robbers, but to think anyone else could… I do hope you are mistaken."

Georgiana took exception to the definition of all highway

robbers as murderers, but resisted the temptation to take issue with her hostess.

"I've no wish to cause you pain, but there were people who stood to gain from Sir Robert's death, more so than the Crimson Cavalier. Why, my own brother has done so."

Lady Wickerston's eyes flew to Georgiana's face. Her countenance had paled. Georgiana watched her carefully. Her ladyship seemed aware of the scrutiny and composed herself.

"I am sure your brother would not have killed my uncle for the sake of his seat on the magistrates' bench."

"I imagine not," said Georgiana.

It was Lady Wickerston's turn to study Georgiana. "Do you doubt him?" she asked in what her visitor considered a slightly challenging tone.

"Not at all," responded Georgiana. "I was merely pointing out that others may have had reason to kill your uncle."

"Well, perhaps," said Lady Wickerston. "I daresay my uncle met any number of low creatures during his time as magistrate. However, it seems in rather poor taste that you include your brother with them."

"You mistake me, Lady Wickerston, indeed I do not." She weighed her next words carefully. "I did not realise you were so well acquainted with him." Georgiana knew she was on dangerous ground. The chances of persuading Lady Wickerston to admit to an affair with Edward were slim, but Georgiana could not resist pursuing it.

The barest hint of wary suspicion crossed Lady Wickerston's face, to vanish as quickly. "One does not have to be well acquainted with your brother to see what kind of man he is," said her ladyship evenly.

"That is very true." Georgiana gave a sorrowful sigh, which she hoped would prompt Lady Wickerston to come to Edward's defence, but though a flash of annoyance flickered in her ladyship's eyes, she seemed inclined to follow the course of discretion.

A sudden noise in the hall took the attention of both ladies. As Georgiana turned towards the door, she noticed a look of anxiety cross her ladyship's face. By contrast, her voice was cool.

"I imagine that will be my husband."

The opening of the door to the small salon showed her ladyship's surmise had been correct. Lord Wickerston stood on the threshold for a moment staring at his wife and her visitor. He met Georgiana's smile with a dark look she found vaguely frightening.

"I didn't know you had anyone here," said Lord Wickerston.

"Yes, Miss Grey was kind enough to call," said Lady Wickerston in her collected manner. "We are just having some tea, if you would like to join us."

"No, I don't think so." His lordship turned abruptly and left them. Georgiana suppressed a shudder of relief. She looked towards her hostess. Lady Wickerston seemed disinclined to react to her husband's interruption, but Georgiana thought she sensed equal relief at his departure. It occurred to her that Lady Wickerston was likely to be less communicative with her husband in the house. Georgiana decided it would be politic to remove herself.

Taking leave of Lady Wickerston, Georgiana was glad to get into the fresh air and sunshine. She stood on the pavement and took a deep breath before mounting the steps of her waiting carriage.

"Georgiana!"

With one elegantly slippered foot on the bottom step, Georgiana turned her head. Edward seemed as startled to see his sister as she was to see him.

"What on earth are you doing here?" he demanded.

"I might ask you the same question."

He responded in a hissed whisper. "I was coming to deal with that matter we discussed last night."

"Well, you could not have timed it worse," Georgiana informed him. "Lord Wickerston has just arrived home, in no genial frame of mind."

Edward looked towards the house, an expression of concern on his face.

"Perhaps I should check..."

"No, you should not," said Georgiana firmly. "I gather you have walked?" Edward nodded.

"Well, then, you can escort me home."

As he hesitated, her voice grew more insistent.

"You can only make matters worse if you go in now."

Edward sighed. "I suppose you're right." He handed his sister into the carriage and followed her. Closing the door behind him, he looked at Georgiana with eyes narrowed in suspicion. "Why were you there, anyway? Prying into my personal life again?"

"I visited Lady Wickerston on entirely another matter," responded Georgiana in a dignified tone.

"What?"

"Prying into my personal life, Edward?"

He glowered and did not attempt to pursue the issue.

"Amanda came to see me this morning," said Georgiana after a few minutes.

Edward looked surprised. "Did she? What for?"

"She was concerned about you." His expression became puzzled. "Yes, I could not understand it either."

Edward looked uneasy.

"What did you talk about?" His voice was hoarse.

"Don't worry," said Georgiana. "I didn't mention your secret."

Edward flushed. "That's not what I meant," he said indignantly.

"Of course it was," retorted Georgiana. "You must think me a great simpleton if you imagine I do not believe that to be your first concern."

Edward drew in his breath. "Yes, well, what did Amanda want?"

"I told you, she was worried about you. She said you'd been preoccupied and thought you had something on your mind." Georgiana paused. "I suggested to her it was probably your new responsibilities as magistrate."

"That is true as well, of course."

Georgiana threw him a baleful look.

"Thank you, Georgiana," Edward said in a low voice.

Georgiana acknowledged his gratitude with a nod. As they sat in silence, she gave him a quick, thoughtful glance. She had a fair idea of what his reaction would be when she spoke again.

"Edward, how are your inquiries into Sir Robert's murder progressing?"

Edward gave her a disapproving look. She decided to turn her knowledge to her advantage.

"Do you not think it would be wise to humour me, Edward, given the fact that I know you are not quite perfect?"

"What?" Edward looked intently at his sister as he sought to comprehend her meaning. "Georgiana, that's blackmail!"

"Count yourself fortunate I ask so little in exchange."

"Georgiana!"

"Oh, for heaven's sake, Edward, spare me the 'holier than thou' nonsense," said Georgiana. "You know full well I'm not going to discuss your indiscretion with Amanda. The least you can do is indulge my curiosity without sermonising about the impropriety of it."

Edward continued to look disapproving. "Very well," he said finally, in an exasperated tone, "though I fail to understand why you are so concerned."

"I want to see justice done," Georgiana said promptly.

Edward eyed her suspiciously.

"Really? Well since you are so interested in this sordid business, you may as well know we hope to have it concluded soon."

"You do?" Georgiana was startled.

Edward nodded proudly. "You remember me telling you I am acquainted with a Bow Street Runner?"

"Yes," said Georgiana.

"Well, he – um – that is…" Edward coughed uncomfortably. "He has had occasion to come into contact with some rather disreputable people. It seems one or two of them are prepared to lay information. We shall have the Crimson Cavalier by the heels in no time."

Georgiana was unimpressed. Most of those who frequented the Lucky Bell had a fair idea of who the informers were. She herself had noticed conversations cease when certain characters came into earshot.

"It seems there is a tavern known as a haunt of highwaymen and other such cut-throats," Edward was continuing enthusiastically. "We intend to put one or two Runners in there to see what they can find out."

"How resourceful."

"They will soon fit in, and by keeping their eyes and ears open, they should find out quite a bit."

While common sense told Georgiana she would need to be on the alert, part of her felt she should tell her brother not to waste the Runners' time. Although informers always posed a potential danger, she knew anyone unfamiliar to the Lucky Bell would stand out too readily to be trusted.

"You think someone will tell them where to find the Crimson Cavalier?" she inquired.

"For the right price."

"What is that price?" Georgiana could not prevent herself

from asking.

Edward smiled. "Why should you wish to know that, Georgiana? Are you going to tell me you know his whereabouts?"

Georgiana hated Edward's humouring tone.

"I imagine I might know as well as anyone else," she retorted.

Edward's eyes widened. Georgiana instantly regretted the impulse.

"Have you been held up by the Crimson Cavalier?" Edward inquired in surprise.

"No," she responded, deciding it more prudent not to make the admission she had to Louisa about encountering the notorious highway robber.

"Well, I'd advise you to be careful when travelling about," he recommended. "Make sure you have two armed postilions."

"Yes, Edward," she said meekly. She ventured a glance at him. "I understood he had been fairly active. Have you questioned any of his victims?"

"Oh, yes," he said. "But no two people say the same thing. Some say he is short, others tall. He's been described as dark, fair, brown eyes, blue. Can you imagine, one person even thought he had hair the colour of yours? Did you ever hear such nonsense?"

"Unbelievable," said Georgiana in colourless tone.

Edward was frowning. "The Runners heard he had recently held up Lakesby so were hoping he could tell them something. However, it was of no use."

"Really?"

"I understand Lakesby wasn't any help at all when my acquaintance went to see him," Edward said in disgust. "He said he didn't get a good enough look. You'd think he was trying to protect the fellow."

"Imagine that," said Georgiana, hoping her relief was not

too apparent. She was about to ask what Lakesby's groom had said when she recalled she was not supposed to know anything about the incident.

They had by this time arrived at Georgiana's front door. Edward stepped out of the carriage and handed her out, declining the offer of refreshment she felt obliged to make. As the coachman took the carriage to the stables, Edward began to walk on his way, leaving his sister to wonder just how safe she was from his Runner.

Horton opened the door to his mistress looking even more correct than usual, something she found disconcerting in the extreme. Georgiana looked at him uneasily.

"Is everything in order, Horton?"

"Yes, miss."

It was not enough to reassure her. She eyed him warily. "So there is nothing I need to know?" she said, drawing off her gloves. "Nothing out of the ordinary has occurred?"

"A small matter, miss."

"Very well, Horton, tell me, what is it? I am prepared for the worst."

Horton hesitated. However, the sight of the determined expression on Georgiana's face made him capitulate. "Very well, miss. It is the young boy you engaged as a page."

"What about him?" Georgiana was feeling increasingly uncomfortable.

"He has run away, miss."

16

Georgiana summoned Emily to her room. The maid arrived as Georgiana was stripping off her pelisse. She tossed it on to the bed to join her gloves.

"What is all this about Tom?" Georgiana demanded as her maid rescued the garment and put it carefully in the wardrobe. "Horton says he's disappeared."

Emily nodded, frowning as she picked up the gloves, which Georgiana had left turned inside out. "Yes, miss. No one's seen him since you went out."

"Are you sure he's not hiding somewhere in the house?" said Georgiana, conscious of the absurdity of the question even as she asked it.

"No, miss. James and I checked everywhere. He's gone."

"Then he has to be at the Lucky Bell," Georgiana said thinking aloud. "I'll have to go down there."

Emily looked horrified. "Begging your pardon, miss, but isn't it better left as it is? I mean, it's a risk having him here, knowing what he does."

"He doesn't know, I'm sure of that," said Georgiana.

"Even so, he's seen the Crimson Cavalier enough times to guess, maybe not right away, but sooner or later, and if you go down to that tavern again…"

"In which case, it's more of a risk having him on the loose." Georgiana shook her head. "No, I'd rather have him under my eye, at least until Sir Robert's murder is resolved. Then there's Mr Lakesby. I shudder to think of his reaction."

"But Mr Lakesby doesn't know you've met Tom before," said Emily. "Why should he say anything about it?"

"I made myself responsible for the boy," Georgiana said. "Left to his own devices, Tom could start holding up coaches again. He may not be so fortunate next time."

"That would hardly be your fault, miss." Emily looked thoughtful for a moment. "But there are others he might talk to, though. Curious housebreakers, perhaps."

"I doubt that will be a problem," said Georgiana. "Unless one found his way here and recognised Princess..." She paused, biting her bottom lip thoughtfully. A quick glance out of the window told her it was too early to think of riding to the Lucky Bell. In any case, what could she say? She supposed the Crimson Cavalier could inquire whether anything had been heard of Tom there. However, if he had returned to his former haunt, it would look odd were she to try persuading him to abandon it.

"Where was Tom last seen?"

"This morning, miss. I believe Mrs Daniels sent him to the chandler."

Georgiana raised an eyebrow at this.

"It's paid with the household accounts, miss. She'd not given him any money."

"I didn't think so. Still..." Georgiana's voice trailed off as she thought. Fetching candles lacked the excitement of highway robbery, although Georgiana knew from her visits to the Lucky Bell that Tom was not afraid of hard work. She thought it unlikely Bess and Cedric would pay him as high a wage as she had offered. She suspected that the bulk of his income there depended on the generosity of the tavern's patrons.

"He could sell the candles, miss. The wax ones would fetch a good price," offered Emily.

"True," said Georgiana, "but what would he do then?" Another thought occurred to her. "Is anything missing?"

Emily shook her head. "Not so far as James and I could tell, miss."

Georgiana sat at her dressing table, drumming her fingers on its surface.

"I trust no one's sent the Runners after him?"

"No, miss. I think Mrs Daniels was worried, and fretting about the candles, of course, but Mr Horton seemed to think we'd go on better without him." She paused. "He may be right, miss."

"He may." Tom had certainly not been a calming influence since joining the household. "What of my cousin?"

"Not said much, miss, but I think she seemed relieved, though a bit fearful."

"I daresay she thinks he's made off with the silver."

"What is it, miss?"

Georgiana glanced towards her maid. The concern she saw on Emily's face made it clear she had not been able to conceal that a further thought niggled at the back of her mind.

"I was wondering whether Tom saw an opportunity to escape the search for Sir Robert's murderer. He won't know that Mr Lakesby took his pistol, of course, but he may fear its discovery."

"I suppose it would look bad for him."

"It looks bad for anyone with a pistol, especially if they can't account for it," Georgiana replied, thinking of Edward. Frowning, she toyed briefly with the notion of looking for Tom on the road. However, it would not be feasible until darkness had fallen. She stood to face Emily, speaking decidedly.

"We had best wait a while and see if he returns. If he hasn't done so by dinner time, I'll consider what's to be done. In the meantime, I'll go and see my cousin."

Georgiana listened with half an ear to Selina pouring out her anxieties. She made appropriate responses to her cousin's declarations that she had never trusted the rogue and had checked her few pieces of jewellery on hearing he'd gone, relieved though she was, and made soothing noises over her fears that he could still come back and murder them. With one eye on the clock and her mind on Tom's possible whereabouts and what to do if he did not return, Georgiana was startled by her cousin's voice growing suddenly sharp.

"Georgiana!"

Georgiana started guiltily under her cousin's reproachful scrutiny.

"I declare, you've not heard a word I said."

Georgiana smiled apologetically. "Indeed, I have, Selina. I beg your pardon. I was just a little distracted for a moment."

Selina seemed mollified; Georgiana thought relief at Tom's apparent departure had inclined her towards forgiveness. She herself was growing increasingly uneasy, consuming her dinner with what Miss Knatchbull considered unbecoming haste, in her anxiety to excuse herself and ride out in search of the errant boy. Georgiana was about to rise from the table when James approached.

"Excuse me, miss, but the boy has returned."

There was a stunned silence for a moment, broken unexpectedly by Selina.

"Well, tell him to take himself off," she cried in a shrill voice. "The ungrateful wretch has lost his opportunity."

"Selina, please," said Georgiana calmly. "I will take care of this." She addressed her footman. "Has he offered any explanation?"

"No, miss. Looks guilty as sin, but seems to want to stay."

"Very well," said Georgiana. "Ask him to wait in the small saloon. I'll be down directly to speak with him."

Georgiana ignored the angry disappointment she felt coming from her cousin and walked to the small saloon. Tom stood, hands behind his back, facing his judge. Georgiana looked at him without speaking for a moment or two as she decided on her line of attack.

"Well, Tom, what have you to say for yourself?"

"Nothin', miss."

"Nothing?"

The boy shook his head. James's surmise had been accurate: he did look as if he had something to hide. Georgiana was not inclined to offer an easy escape.

"You disappear for most of the day, without leave, and have nothing to say?"

"No, miss."

"Can you think of any reason why I shouldn't dismiss you immediately?"

The boy looked down and shuffled his feet. "Suppose not, miss."

"You suppose not." Georgiana paused, looking at him sternly. "Have you forgotten I am responsible for you, or that Mr Lakesby still has the power to order you into prison?"

The boy looked at her fearfully.

Georgiana continued without mercy. "Perhaps you would prefer a spell in Newgate? My footman has been there, he can tell you about it."

"No, miss. Please, miss."

"Then you will answer my questions. Where have you been?"

Tom looked at her indecisively. "You won't like it, miss."

"I like your silence little better. Tom, I am rapidly losing patience."

"I – I went to the Lucky Bell, miss," he said in a rush.

Georgiana took a deep breath. "You went to the Lucky Bell?" she said without raising her voice.

"Yes, miss."

"After I told you not to?"

"Yes, miss. Sorry, miss, but I had to."

Georgiana's first thought was to determine whether this visit could endanger her secret. She had to find out who he had seen and what he had said.

"Why did you have to go there, Tom? I thought we had an agreement."

"Well, yes, miss, I know, but – but, there's people as knows me there and I had to…" His voice trailed off. He was clearly expecting the worst.

"What did you have to do?" Georgiana asked patiently.

"I had to tell them I wasn't a gallows-bird. I know some of them don't care, but there's Harry and – and the Crimson Cavalier. They'd worry."

"I see." Georgiana looked steadily at the boy. "Did you see them?"

"I saw Harry," said Tom. "But the Cavalier wasn't there."

Georgiana forced herself not to smile at the forlorn note in his voice.

"I've heard of the Crimson Cavalier, of course," she said unemotionally. "But who is this Harry?"

"A cove I know."

"Is he also a highwayman?" Georgiana pursued.

Tom proved stubbornly loyal, however, refusing to be drawn on this point. Georgiana realised she might have underestimated him.

"Very well. What did you talk about?" The casual note in Georgiana's voice concealed her burning need to know.

"Nothin' much," responded the boy.

"Nothing much. Oh, pray, Tom, let us not go through that again," Georgiana begged.

"Ain't nobody's business," Tom said in surly accents.

Georgiana did indeed find it difficult to justify her curiosity to Tom. She could hardly tell him she wished to assure herself of her own safety by discovering whether or not he had been indiscreet. Or could she? Perhaps she just needed a different approach. What was that phrase Emily had used?

"I have no wish to find you have disclosed details of my home and personal belongings to some curious house-breaker," she said haughtily.

"Oh." It was apparent this aspect had not occurred to Tom.

245

"I ain't done that, miss."

"No?" said Georgiana, an eyebrow raised interrogatively. "Really?"

"I'm not a liar," said Tom indignantly, "and Harry's no kencracker."

"I see," said Georgiana dryly. "So you told your friend Harry where you were, did you?"

Tom looked uncomfortable. "Not exactly, miss. I didn't tell him where this ken was, just that I was safe."

Georgiana gave him a measured look. "I only have your word you can be trusted," she said. "I have not forgotten there was a murder a few days ago. How can I be certain neither you nor your friends were involved?"

Tom looked uneasy. "I weren't," he said in a strangled tone.

"My cousin is convinced you are going to murder us in our beds."

"Well, she's daffy," he muttered.

Repressing a desire to laugh, Georgiana responded with severe disapproval. "Tom, I must insist you show some respect."

He hastily begged pardon, looking down at his shuffling feet.

"Did you know Sir Robert Foster?"

"Who?" he asked.

"The gentleman who was killed."

"Oh, aye, had me round for tea, he did."

"Tom." There was no mistaking the warning note in Georgiana's voice. Tom gave way before it.

"Beg pardon, miss."

"I'd like a truthful answer, please. Did you know the gentleman who was killed on the road?"

"Not to speak to."

"But?"

Tom remained silent for a moment or two, the sweat on his

forehead showing increasing uneasiness.

"I – I held him up, miss. Didn't get nothing, though."

"That's all?"

Tom nodded vigorously.

"When did this incident take place?"

"Dunno."

"Really?"

Tom shrugged but remained obstinately silent.

"The night he died, perhaps?"

"Dunno."

"Tom, if it was, you'd best tell me right away. It will be all the worse for you if someone saw you there."

Tom's response was swift. "No, there weren't no one there."

Georgiana raised an eyebrow. "Go on," she invited.

Tom glowered but continued, "I just wanted to stop him for some gewgaws, like the Crimson Cavalier. Only he wouldn't give me anything, said something about being took by a highwayman the night before."

"That's quite true," said Georgiana. "Sir Robert and his party called here after the robbery."

Tom's eyes widened. "Lor'! Really, miss?"

Georgiana's expression brought him back to the point.

"The pistol went off and the old cove fell. Took to me heels back to the Lucky Bell. Didn't know if I'd hit him, thought I'd just spooked his horse, only then I heard he was dead."

"I see. Have you told this to anyone?"

"Just my friend Harry." Tom moistened his lips. "He said they been looking for me. Reckoned I should come back here."

"Really?" She paused but received no response. "Very well. Please don't mention it any further," she said. "You can go." Georgiana needed time to think.

Tom looked at her apprehensively. "Are you throwing me out, miss?"

"No. Get back to your duties. But Tom," she said as he turned to depart.

"Yes, miss?"

"I mean it. Don't go back to that tavern, or you shall leave this house and very likely Mr Lakesby shall hand you over to the authorities."

"Yes, miss."

As soon as the door closed behind Tom, Georgiana sighed. It was the scenario she feared. Faced with it, she had to determine her course of action. Foremost was establishing the truth of the incident. It was possible Tom's original surmise had been correct, Sir Robert's horse had thrown its rider on being startled by the noise of the pistol. However, it was equally possible Sir Robert had been hit by a mis-firing weapon, which left Georgiana with the problem of whether protecting Tom would put her own neck in the noose. She would have to speak to Harry.

While to all appearances, Georgiana received no different a reception from usual in the Lucky Bell, she thought she could sense some surreptitious glances and the odd whisper as she walked through the taproom. There was clearly as much speculation here as in Polite Society as to whether or not the Crimson Cavalier had murdered Sir Robert Foster. She noticed one or two faces she didn't recognise and wondered whether they were Edward's informers, glad she had decided against wearing the identifying badge of the bright red scarf. Even without enough evidence to charge her with murder, there was no sense in encouraging anyone to follow her home.

Georgiana found Harry in their usual parlour. She paused on the threshold, noticing he was not alone. Sitting comfortably on his knee was the saucy tavern maid who had shown such an interest in Georgiana at their earlier encounter.

"Ah, here we are," said Harry as Georgiana entered. "Fetch

us another bottle, lass. This young cove and I have business."

The girl bounced off, casting a look of mischievous flirtation at Georgiana. Her cold glance apparently had no discouraging effect; the bubbly, curly-haired girl gave her a wink as she left the room.

Harry laughed. "You've made a conquest, there, my lad. A fine blow to me, that is."

"You're welcome to her, Harry. I've no time for that now," said Georgiana, striding over to Harry.

"Lord, it's only a bit of fun," said Harry. "No one's asking you to wed the girl."

Georgiana ignored this. "Have you seen Tom?" she asked.

"Aye, that I have," said Harry, growing serious. "The lad's had a stroke of luck." He paused, scratching his stubbled chin. "That carriage he held up, you know you thought one of the nobs felt sorry for him?"

"Yes," said Georgiana cautiously.

"Seems she's offered him a place."

"What?" Georgiana hoped she managed to inject the right amount of surprise into her voice, not wishing it to sound overdone.

Harry nodded. "Would you believe it? The boy's her page. Right smart he looks, too. Cleaned up, I almost didn't know him."

"Well, well," said Georgiana. "He's been lucky."

"That he has," agreed Harry. "Still managed to get himself shot in the shoulder, but I suppose that's better than dancing at the end of Tyburn's rope."

"Is that all he said?" asked Georgiana, her back to Harry as she looked out of the window into the darkness. The heavy black cloak she wore masked her trim, too feminine figure.

"That was all," Harry responded. "Didn't say who she was or where the ken was." His eyes narrowed in amused suspicion. "So if you're thinking of taking a crack at it…"

"Not my line," said Georgiana briefly as she turned around.

"Nor mine. A man's safer on the high toby. Easier to get away in a hurry."

Before Georgiana could respond, the door opened and the curly-haired maid entered, bearing a tray with the wine Harry had ordered.

"You took your time," he complained.

"Sorry, sir," the girl replied. "It's been that busy since that rascal Tom went off."

Georgiana refrained from comment.

"Yes, well, never mind," said Harry. "Put it down and be on your way. We've business here."

The girl obeyed. Harry waited for a moment after the door had closed before speaking again, seemingly wanting to be certain no one was within earshot. He held up the bottle and looked inquiringly at his companion. Georgiana shook her head.

"At least Tom's all right," she said.

"For now," said Harry.

Georgiana looked closely at her companion. "What is it?"

Harry seemed reluctant to speak for a moment, then relented.

"Tom told me – the night the old beak was killed, it seems he took it into his head to turn bridle-cull."

"Oh?"

Harry nodded. "Popped the old gent, knocked him off his horse. Didn't even seem sure how. Took off and said he's been worrying ever since."

"I can imagine," said Georgiana, feeling the coldness of the blood running through her.

"I told him to stay in this new ken of his and keep quiet about it."

"Seems a sensible course."

"He wasn't even sure the old man was dead, seemed as

though he'd just been thrown off his horse and winded."

"Where did Tom get the pistol?"

"Oh, it was Sid's. One of those jailers slipped it to him for a few glasses of rum." Harry laughed. "It's a good job Cedric or Bess didn't find out."

"Indeed," said Georgiana.

"People been looking for him anyway. Cedric saw him today and didn't grudge the boy his luck, but we thought it best to say nothing, not even to Bess. Tom's better off where he is."

"Yes," said Georgiana, conscious of the compliment Harry paid her in passing on this information. "Have you heard anything else?"

"Some. A couple of strangers've been asking questions. Narks, I reckon. Don't know as anyone's told 'em anything, but keep your daylights open."

"I will. Obliged to you, Harry."

Harry raised a glass in acknowledgement.

"You won't do anything foolish, will you?" said Harry, taking a couple of coins out of his pocket as he stood.

"Such as?" said Georgiana, her eye on Harry as he tossed the money on to the table.

"Getting yourself hanged," Harry retorted.

"I shall certainly try to avoid it."

Unthinkingly, Georgiana had slowed Princess to a ladylike pace wholly unsuited to the animal's temperament. In the overpowering quiet, she gradually realised she was not alone. Georgiana sensed rather than heard a near presence, and instinctively picked her way into the cover of the trees, eyes scanning the darkness for some sign of life. An uneasy sense of a trap took possession of her. Despite her caution in omitting her scarf, could someone have pointed her out to the informers? There was no sense in turning back; she would

251

probably be no safer in the Lucky Bell.

Georgiana held her breath, forcing herself to think clearly as she tried to slow her speeding heartbeat. Before she had a chance to make a decision, she became aware of a new factor in the game. Experience of the road enabled her to pick up the vibrations of wheels before the carriage came into sight. She wondered whether she could use this to her advantage. She drew her pistol and cast her glance cautiously to the road.

The shot rang out before Georgiana could judge its direction, closely followed by another in response. The blow to her shoulder knocked her off balance, and she kept her seat with difficulty. She was dizzily aware of the cold trickle of blood on her skin before she registered the burning pain.

Keeping tight hold of Princess's reins, Georgiana concentrated on escape. The carriage was bearing down upon her, preventing all possibility of crossing the road to freedom. She pulled further back into the cover of the trees, casting her eyes towards the road as she went, fighting against growing nausea. Staring with blank astonishment at a blurry shape appearing from the opposite side of the carriage, Georgiana wondered if she was delirious. Forcing her eyes to focus, she saw a masked, dark-caped figure astride a horse. He pulled up at the edge of the road, seemingly awaiting the carriage, pistol at the ready. As it drew level, the rider pointed his weapon upwards and fired. It was enough to scare both beasts and passengers and Georgiana was surprised to see the hand with the pistol gesture along the road, sending the coach hell-for-leather onwards. Georgiana did not move. As the noise of the carriage wheels receded, she saw the masked figure looking in her direction.

17

Georgiana held her breath, not daring to move, but not sure how much longer she could keep still. She did not recognise the horseman, although this was a popular area for the clientele of the Lucky Bell. As he moved towards her, Georgiana found the lightness in her head had spread to her knees. They seemed in danger of giving way. She couldn't urge Princess on, and the pain in her shoulder was growing worse. It took every strain of effort to hold fast to the pistol.

"Be calm. You have nothing to fear." A vaguely familiar voice cut through her hazy state.

She made no protest as the newcomer took hold of Princess's bridle and led her further into the cover of the trees. They found a quiet clearing where her companion dismounted. Georgiana felt herself eased from the horse's back and seated against the support of a nearby tree. A flask which smelled of brandy was held to her lips. She pulled away and shook her head.

"No, please…"

"Drink it," he commanded.

His tone clearly brooked no argument and feeling too weak to dispute the matter, Georgiana obeyed. The brandy sent a reassuring warmth through her, and she felt sufficiently restored to object when he started to unbutton her coat.

"You're losing a lot of blood," he said peremptorily. "We've no time to waste."

Georgiana was beginning to feel weaker, and allowed herself to be eased out of her coat. A handkerchief was folded into a pad with businesslike efficiency. He commanded her to hold it against her wound. A second handkerchief was used to secure the pad, tying it around her shirt sleeve tightly but with a gentle touch. The activity around her shoulder aggravated the throbbing. Georgiana began to feel dizzy again and leaned back against the tree, closing her eyes.

"Stay with me. Nearly done."

Georgiana opened her eyes and smiled.

"Excellent." He nodded encouragingly. "Do you think you can ride?"

Georgiana nodded, then rose a little unsteadily, holding the tree for support. "What are you doing here?" she asked.

"Looking for you."

"What?" Georgiana screwed up her eyes, trying to absorb this information. "I don't understand."

"Never mind that now. Time enough for explanations when you've had a chance to recover. I think perhaps you should ride with me, and I will lead your animal."

"Certainly not! I am not such a poor creature," said Georgiana scornfully, although she did accept the hand he held out for support.

With aid, Georgiana managed to re-mount Princess, sitting straight on the animal as she faced determinedly ahead. Her wound still pained her with its sickly throbbing, but felt slightly easier now the bleeding was stanched by the hurriedly fashioned bandage. He handed her the brandy flask again. She took a grateful sip, conscious of an anxious glance cast in her direction. There was no further comment, however, and Georgiana took up Princess's reins briskly. As her companion set forth to check the road, she nodded her thanks and rode away quickly before he could stop her.

The ride home was longer than Georgiana had ever remembered it. The pain in her shoulder and increasing blurriness of her head gave a heaviness to every step Princess took. Holding her balance was a gargantuan effort. She sat up straight in the saddle, refusing to succumb to her injury.

The reassuringly familiar light in the back window rallied

Georgiana's spirits when at last it came into view. Sliding off Princess's back, her legs acquired a disturbingly jelly-like quality when she attempted to put her weight on them. Emily gave a stifled cry at the sight of blood on her mistress's clothes. As Georgiana sank on to a chair just inside the door, she became aware of Emily leaving the room briefly and returning with James, looking as if he had dressed in haste. Emily held a cup of water to her lips. She drank gratefully then leaned against the wall, eyes closed.

"We must get her to her room," said Emily, picking up the candle from the window ledge.

"Can you walk, miss?" asked James quietly.

Georgiana nodded and with her footman's aid, stumbled up the stairs to her room. She sank gratefully on the bed, closing her eyes as the blessed softness of feather pillows and mattress melted against her bruised body.

The whispered conference between James and Emily sounded unnecessarily loud in her throbbing head. A moment or two later the door opened and closed again. One of them had gone out. Georgiana found she didn't care. She heard the splash of water in the basin and then felt Emily's capable hands laying a cold compress on her head. She smiled her thanks at the maid and cried out in protest as Emily began to unbutton her shirt.

"Leave me, Emily. Just let me sleep."

"I have to get you out of these clothes and cleaned up, miss. Come along, you'll be more comfortable."

Georgiana knew her maid was right, but her injury protested at further disturbance. She bit her bottom lip as the fire raged through her shoulder. Georgiana saw a fleeting look of shock cross Emily's face as she began to clean the wound, noting in a detached way that it must be worse than she had thought.

It seemed an eternity later when Emily finished her task

and Georgiana settled gratefully against her pillows in a fresh nightgown. She was glad of the chance to rest at last and closed her eyes. She was not sure how long or indeed if she had slept when she became aware of the murmur of voices in the room again. She thought one was Emily's, but she did not recognise the other. A moment or two later, she felt a touch on her wrist; she decided her pulse was being checked, and raised no objection to this. However, she thought she would resist strongly if anyone were to attempt touching her injured shoulder again.

This was tested almost immediately. Georgiana groaned. The hands which examined her wound had a gentle but firm, almost professional touch. The murmur of indistinguishable voices came to her ears when the examination was finished, and a moment or two later she felt herself lifted from the pillows, a glass containing some evil-smelling brown liquid held to her lips. Emily's gentle insistence overcame her reluctance, and she finished the draught obediently. Georgiana noticed the unknown figure on the other side of the room rolling up his shirtsleeves in businesslike fashion. It occurred to Georgiana through her disorientated state that the bullet was probably still in her shoulder. She assumed the strange man to be a surgeon. Just before drifting into unconsciousness, concern gnawed at her over the advisability of this unknown person being admitted to her predicament.

Georgiana woke just about able to make out the daylight through the curtains. Emily stood by her dressing table folding a towel, a prosaic action Georgiana found oddly comforting. As she stirred, the stiffness in her shoulder gave way to pumping pain and the almost forgotten incident came flooding back. She winced and Emily turned.

"Oh, miss, you're awake. Thank heavens! We've all been so worried about you."

"All?" The shock of her injury having begun to wear off,

Georgiana's practical caution reasserted itself. Just how public was her present situation?

"James and me," said Emily, straightening the bedclothes. "Oh, and the surgeon, of course."

"There was a surgeon here?" said Georgiana, struck by how unnecessary her question was as soon as the words had left her lips. Of course there had been a surgeon. She vaguely remembered being probed in professional fashion by someone she did not know. "Where did you find this surgeon?"

"James knew of him," said Emily. "He didn't ask any awkward questions. Neither did James." She paused, her eyes scanning Georgiana anxiously. "You were very bad, miss. You'd lost a lot of blood. The ball was still in you. We had to get someone to attend to you."

Georgiana rubbed her forehead with the palm of her good hand. "How long have I been unconscious?"

"Two days."

"What?"

Emily nodded. "Delirious, too. I didn't dare let anyone near you in case you said something you shouldn't. Miss Knatchbull wasn't too happy about it." She paused. "We've given it out you've had an attack of influenza."

Georgiana tried to sit up. Emily leaned across to assist, propping the pillows against her back.

The story about her having influenza would keep away any curious well-wishers. It sounded as though it had even had the desired effect on her cousin. She looked up to find her maid regarding her intently.

"What happened, miss? Do you know who did this?" Emily asked.

Georgiana shook her head, an impulse she regretted almost immediately. She put her hand up against it.

"I don't know," said Georgiana. "I thought I had been followed from the Lucky Bell. I did wonder if it was Edward's informants, but the shot came so fast, I'm not sure."

"You didn't see whoever it was?"

"No" She hesitated a moment, not certain how Emily would react to what she had to say next. "There was someone on the road, a highwayman, I thought. He said he was looking for me."

"What?"

"It was odd. He was on the road and when a carriage approached, he fired a shot that seemed intended to frighten them away. Then he came to help me, bandaged the wound."

"I wondered," said Emily. "I didn't think you could have done it yourself. You don't know who he was?"

Georgiana thought she did know but preferred not to air her suspicions. "I didn't recognise him."

"But you came back alone."

"I didn't dare wait. He was far too solicitous. I rode away as soon as I got an opportunity."

Emily looked thoughtful for a moment. "Well, without him you'd have lost a lot more blood."

"Yes."

"By the way, Mr Lakesby's called round two or three times," said Emily. "Seemed quite concerned when he heard you were ill."

"That was good of him," said Georgiana.

"Yes, I thought so."

"I suppose James knows everything?" said Georgiana.

Emily wrinkled her nose. "He's not asked anything and I've not told him."

"Oh?"

"You need not worry about James, miss. He'll hold his tongue. Now, do you want something to eat?"

Georgiana found she was quite hungry, and accepted gladly.

"But no invalid food, please, Emily," she begged. "Something a bit more substantial than a bowl of gruel."

Emily smiled and said she would see what she could do. Georgiana leaned back against the pillows and closed her eyes. She was surprisingly tired considering she had been unconscious for two days. She still felt weak, but better than she had on the night of the shooting. A certain amount of discomfort was inevitable for a few days at least.

Georgiana chafed at time lost in her search for Sir Robert Foster's killer and her inability to do anything confined to her bed. She found herself wondering what Lakesby had learned, if she was correct in her supposition that he was her rescuer. Screwing up her eyes, she tried to recall the moments just before the shooting. She was still puzzled over the sudden appearance of an ally on the road. He had said he was looking for her. It was clear some sort of trap had been set, but how anyone else could have learned of it was something of a mystery. She was sure Edward and his fellow magistrates would not confide their intentions. The man on the road had not told her anything when she had asked him. He'd said it could wait until she had recovered; had he been afraid it would be too much of a shock to her? She found herself slightly resentful at this notion.

Georgiana considered the possibilities. The notion of Edward out on the road shooting at highwaymen late at night was too ridiculous to be borne. Yet he had seemed confident of capturing the Crimson Cavalier imminently and informers, taking the easy option of disclosure for payment, would hardly have the courage to lie in wait and ambush a notorious highway robber. She wondered how she could have been recognised without her red scarf, and whether all robbers on that road were being pursued. Edward had told Lady Winters he intended to do something about the highwaymen. Yet word of such a trap would soon spread, making the area one to avoid. Recalling the two strangers in the tavern, Georgiana frowned. While most of the Lucky Bell's clientele were discreet, she knew a few would talk for the right price. In any case, she thought she had been careful in ensuring she was not followed. She had certainly heard nothing behind her. She recalled the moment of hesitancy as she had slowed down her horse. That would give an attacker the opportunity needed, or allow anyone following to signal to a waiting compatriot.

A feeling of unease niggled Georgiana as she pushed herself more upright in the bed. Something about the arrangement did not make sense. If the trap had been set by Edward and the Bow Street Runners, why had she not been taken or killed? There had been enough time for both her and her ally to be captured. Her injury had held them for a few minutes and slowed progress. Surely any decent Runner would have been able to discover her? Besides, a trap argued the presence of a few. The capture of the Crimson Cavalier would be a feather in any cap. Why would they have given up the hunt so easily?

One possibility stood out to Georgiana more than any other. The trap was not set by anyone on the side of law and order. The intention had not been to capture but to kill her.

Georgiana closed her eyes and shook her head. She was growing fanciful. Emily said she had been delirious. Trying to pull her thoughts together, Georgiana realised that without the red scarf on her hat, anyone finding her body on the road would be unlikely to associate her with the Crimson Cavalier. She would be Miss Georgiana Grey, dressed in highwayman's clothes, certainly, but that could be taken as a prank. Questions would be asked. Would the murderer expose her, and so expose him- or herself?

"Here we are," said Emily, entering the room with a tray which held an appetising spread. Georgiana found her hunger had lessened. However, with no wish to admit this to

Emily, she made an effort to smile as the maid carried the tray over to her bed.

"Mr Lakesby called," said Emily.

"Oh?" said Georgiana feeling her face pale as she took up her napkin.

"Yes," said Emily, looking at her mistress with a slightly puzzled expression. "Is anything wrong?"

"No, of course not," said Georgiana picking up a chicken wing. "I am just a little more tired than I thought."

"Oh. Well, Mr Lakesby wondered how you were. He was pleased to hear you were awake."

"Is he still here? Perhaps I should see him."

"Indeed you should not," said Emily. "Receive him in your bedchamber, would you? You'll do no such thing."

"No, of course not," said Georgiana. "But I could go downstairs and–"

"You'll do nothing of the kind," said Emily. "You're weak as a kitten. Besides, he has gone. He said he would call tomorrow."

"Well, I shall see him then," said Georgiana.

"We'll see." There was a mischievous look in Emily's eyes. "Of course, if you see Mr Lakesby, I will not be able to deny Miss Knatchbull."

"Oh, very well."

Despite Emily's doubts, Georgiana did get her own way the following day and sat in the drawing room to receive Mr Lakesby. She was arrayed in a satin dressing gown of pale blue, her luxurious hair held back with a matching blue ribbon. Miss Knatchbull, having been denied entry to her cousin's sickroom, was determined to make up for it now Georgiana had left her bed. She fussed endlessly over Georgiana, insisting she ought to have a blanket over her knees and asking numerous times whether she needed a hot brick. By the time Lakesby arrived, Georgiana was driven to distraction by this solicitude. She only succeeded in getting rid of Selina by asking if she would make up a cold compress.

Lakesby greeted Miss Knatchbull as she fluttered from the room to carry out this errand. He held the door open for her before turning his attention to Georgiana. He paused momentarily on the threshold and visibly drew in his breath before advancing to greet her. He bent over her hand and Georgiana noticed his eyes flicker towards her bandaged shoulder. The household had been told she had taken a tumble from her horse when starting to sicken with the influenza.

"I am glad to hear you are better," said Lakesby, taking a seat in the armchair opposite her. "A fall from your horse as well as influenza? Most unfortunate."

"Thank you for your concern, Mr Lakesby."

The door closed behind the maid who had served their tea. Georgiana smiled.

"Please don't give it a thought. I understand Sir Andrew Gainston has been attending you. He is a fine surgeon and a friend of mine." Lakesby paused. "He is very discreet."

"Indeed? I would have thought that a requirement of a surgeon, in any case."

"Very true. But Andrew finds it less of a struggle than certain others." It was a moment before he spoke again. "Your cousin seems very concerned for your welfare."

"Yes. She is a good creature, but Emily thought it best to keep her from my room while I was ill. As you can imagine, this has not pleased her, hence I am being overpowered with kindness now."

Lakesby smiled but Georgiana was aware of him looking at her intently. "You are very pale still," he said. "Are you sure you should be out of bed?"

"I am well enough," said Georgiana.

Lakesby shook his head slowly. "No, there is something wrong. Won't you tell me?"

Georgiana was wary. Lakesby spoke again, his tone lighter.

"I imagine you won't have heard, there was a scuffle on the Bath Road a few evenings ago. There is talk the Crimson Cavalier was involved."

"Really?" Georgiana felt as if she had swallowed a biscuit whole.

"Apparently he managed to escape. There is a story he had some help."

"Fortuitous for him."

"To have someone conveniently on the road to lend aid as he was shot? I should say so."

His voice grew serious again. "There's been talk of the Crimson Cavalier getting caught, talk in very odd quarters."

Georgiana looked puzzled. "But there are always rumours. All sorts of people think they know what to do."

Lakesby leaned forward and shook his head. "This was different. I was in Jackson's Saloon. There were gentlemen talking as if they knew something, not ones given to boasting. It wasn't an odd one or two, nearly everyone seemed to have heard something, though no one could quite remember where the story originated. There was a definite air of anticipation, everyone seemed certain the Crimson Cavalier was on the verge of capture."

Georgiana looked thoughtful. "Edward said he expected to capture the Crimson Cavalier before too long."

"I daresay," said Lakesby. "But would he have been discussing it in Jackson's Saloon?"

"No, of course not," said Georgiana. "I can't imagine Edward or the Runners waiting on the road to mount an ambush. Surely they would take him into custody properly?"

"Quite. Neither would they let their plans be known to half of London. That tale had to be put around by the murderer."

"But why? What could it possibly achieve?"

Lakesby stood and took a turn about the room towards the

hearth. "It seems to me he – or she – must be feeling threatened. When Sir Robert was killed, everyone immediately put the blame on the Crimson Cavalier."

"I know," said Georgiana.

"But you've been asking questions, raising doubts."

"I don't know," said Georgiana. "It seems everyone I've spoken to still thinks it is the Crimson Cavalier."

"Not everyone," Lakesby reminded her.

"Perhaps. But the general opinion still seems to be in that direction."

"Possibly. But in any case, the murderer can't be sure," said Lakesby. "The longer an investigation continues, the more people may start to wonder about the Crimson Cavalier's guilt. What if he is brought to trial and has an opportunity to defend himself? What if the Crimson Cavalier can prove he didn't kill Sir Robert?"

"Maybe he can't," said Georgiana. She looked at Lakesby, as the full implication broke. "But the murderer doesn't know that."

Lakesby leaned on the back of the sofa where Georgiana sat and shook his head. "No. His best chance is for the Crimson Cavalier to be killed, either attempting a robbery or with someone trying to effect a capture."

"The investigation into Sir Robert's murder would end," said Georgiana slowly. "The murderer would be safe." Her brows knitted. "Or Sir Robert Foster would be safe?"

"I beg your pardon?" Lakesby looked all at sea.

"His memory, his good name, his family." Georgiana laid emphasis on the last word.

"Yes, I see." Lakesby looked thoughtful. "Lady Wickerston?"

Georgiana nodded.

"Edward may be thinking about scotching a scandal. He does seem to have other loyalties at present."

"Don't be too hard on him," said Lakesby to Georgiana's

surprise. "I know his involvement with Lady Wickerston came as a surprise, but I believe there was a reason for it."

"It isn't that," said Georgiana. "Edward seemed very quick to defend Lady Wickerston. He said he was with her when Sir Robert was killed."

"Surely you didn't accuse him of Sir Robert's murder?"

"No," said Georgiana. "Neither did I accuse Lady Wickerston." Lakesby raised an eyebrow.

"You think he felt a need to defend her?"

"Edward was very eager to tell me she had nothing to gain from her uncle's death."

"I wonder, did she?" Lakesby mused. "She may get a legacy, but I would hardly imagine it worth killing him. In any case, it would go straight to her husband." He glanced towards Georgiana. "I'm sure you have seen how she fears him."

Georgiana nodded. "There is something frightening about him."

"Yes," said Lakesby. "I cannot say more. My information is from idle rumour and speculation. Speak to your brother; I imagine he knows more than I do. It is difficult to believe he would subvert justice for her. I've always known him very strait-laced."

"Yes." Georgiana sounded thoughtful.

"I believe Sir Robert persuaded his niece to marry Wickerston. If I remember rightly, he was her guardian and he provided a sizeable portion for her."

"Really?"

Lakesby nodded. "On the understanding she would receive no more from him. Wickerston was considered a good match, he'd just come into a decent inheritance himself. I don't think anyone expected him to drink his way through it in less than five years."

Georgiana gave a rueful smile, shaking her head. "Do you think Sir Robert's refusal of further funds included his will?"

"I've no idea," said Lakesby. "To be honest, I suspect it's a point of conjecture even with Lord and Lady Wickerston."

"Perhaps a bequest would give Lady Wickerston a way out of her marriage, if she could get hold of the funds before her husband," Georgiana said.

Lakesby frowned. "She'd hardly expect your brother to leave his wife and family for her, would she?"

"I wouldn't think so. But a bequest from her uncle might allow her to live independently."

"And ostracised," said Lakesby, picking up his driving gloves. "She'd be better suited having her husband killed."

"To inherit the bills from his wine merchant," quizzed Georgiana.

"Touché," said Lakesby. "Try to get some rest, you need to get well."

"Indeed you do," said Selina, entering the room in time to hear Lakesby's last words. "Today is your first day out of bed and you mustn't exhaust yourself. Isn't that right, Mr Lakesby?"

"Most certainly. I should go. You are looking tired."

"Here is your compress, Georgiana," said Selina, trotting over to her cousin's side.

Georgiana eyed the item with disfavour.

"Thank you, Selina, just leave it. Would you mind fetching my shawl, please?"

"Not at all. I shall be back in a trice."

Georgiana spoke as soon as Selina was out of earshot.

"One other thing concerns me," said Georgiana. "No one seems to know why Sir Robert was out on the road that night."

18

Georgiana was infuriated by her enforced idleness. For some time after Lakesby left, she sat thinking about what she could usefully do. Selina, on returning with the shawl for which Georgiana had sent her, made approving noises that Mr Lakesby had kept his visit short, since she was certain it must have tired poor Georgiana. Poor Georgiana paid little heed, her mind occupied with the more pressing matter of Sir Robert Foster's murder. Selina eventually gave up, busying herself with some household tasks. Shortly afterwards, the maid came and cleared away the tea things, giving her abstracted mistress a mildly curious glance.

Georgiana's mind went round in circles, lighting on Sir Brandon Foster. Not yet satisfied of his innocence, she tried to think of a way of approaching him. Not only was there the difficulty of convincing her well-meaning jailers she was fit to leave the house, she needed a plausible excuse to speak to him.

The thought of soliciting Louisa's help entered her mind, to be rejected almost immediately. It did not sit well with her conscience, knowing Lakesby's concern over his cousin's friendship with Sir Brandon. The fact that Georgiana had spoken to Louisa about it herself would make it difficult to enlist the girl's assistance in trying to obtain information from him.

Before another idea could present itself, the young parlourmaid returned, closely followed by Edward. The girl was new to the household, and it had clearly not occurred to her that her mistress would refuse to see her brother after receiving Mr Lakesby.

Very much shocked by his sister's appearance, Edward

bombarded her with questions. She was glad to have her excuse ready to hand, the lingering grogginess caused by her wound hampering her usual inventiveness. She trotted out the tale of influenza and injuring her arm in a fall from her horse with ready aplomb, standing up tolerably well to Edward's interrogation. Knowing his sister was an excellent horsewoman, he was anxious for details.

"You haven't fallen off a horse since you were fourteen," he said.

"I know," responded Georgiana. "I must have been starting the influenza."

Edward looked unconvinced. Georgiana decided to try diverting his mind into another channel.

"Have you caught the Crimson Cavalier?"

Edward shook his head. "What made you think of that now?"

"I just wondered," said Georgiana. "I thought you were expecting to lay hands on him quite soon."

"We were," said Edward a note of gloom entering his voice. "He seems to have disappeared."

"Really?" said Georgiana. "Have your informers learned nothing?"

"Not a sign of him anywhere. I don't know if those fellows are even trying, or whether they just spend their time drinking. I suppose it's possible he's decided to keep out of sight. Well, he can't stay hidden forever. In any case," he continued loftily, "It's hardly a fit matter for me to be discussing with you, particularly in your present condition. Where is Selina?"

"Upstairs. And speaking of matters not fit for discussion with me, have you managed to talk to your friend?"

Edward flushed. "Yes, as a matter of fact."

"And?"

Edward looked acutely uncomfortable. "Georgiana, really."

"Spare me the Cheltenham tragedy, Edward."

"I thought you said my private life was not your concern."

"No more than mine is yours," she agreed cheerfully.

He sighed. "Oh, very well. Since you are already so well-informed on the subject, you may as well know. I have ended it. She wasn't happy, but seemed resigned. I was rather relieved. I must own I expected more of an argument."

"Really?" said Georgiana dryly. "I trust you won't be offended, Edward, but I have never considered you one of Society's more accomplished flirts."

"It's all very well for you to mock," said Edward angrily, "but you don't know the full story."

"Very true," said Georgiana. "Do you think Amanda would understand if you were to explain?"

"I imagine I would find Amanda a great deal more understanding than you have been," retorted Edward, "especially once she knew Lady Wickerston was being beaten by her husband."

The silence hung between them. "What?" Georgiana said finally, her voice husky with disbelief.

Edward sat down in the chair lately occupied by Lakesby, head in his hands.

"Lord Wickerston has a violent temper." Edward seemed to be weighing his words carefully. "He has on more than one occasion laid hands on his wife in anger."

Georgiana felt the colour drain from her face. Lakesby's words about Lady Wickerston's fear of her husband returned with disturbing clarity, along with the tale of injuring her hand on the teapot. As well as shock, Georgiana felt shame at blindness to the trouble of one of her own sex. Edward was right. Amanda would have been more sympathetic.

"How – how did you come to learn of this?" Georgiana thought she could hear her voice shaking.

"It doesn't matter," said Edward. "When I learned of it, I was angry. You know I am not given to calling men out,

Georgiana, but I came perilously close. Theresa persuaded me not to."

Georgiana remained silent.

"I felt sorry for her, of course. Any right thinking person would. She came to me for comfort. Gradually, it came to be more than that."

Georgiana offered no answer, consumed with guilt over her own behaviour. While concerned over the possibility of Amanda being hurt, she had mocked Edward over his affair with Lady Wickerston, never questioning what could have drawn her respectable brother into such a liaison.

Georgiana thought about her visit to Lady Wickerston. She herself had been uneasy in Lord Wickerston's presence. On top of her own problems, the whole situation served to depress her thoroughly.

"I'm sorry, Edward."

Edward looked at her in some surprise.

"Well, it couldn't have gone on forever. I've been thinking so for some time. There was an opportunity to end it, so it was the right moment to do so. Besides, if Amanda had found out…" He shook his head. "I don't think I could have borne that. I'm sure there would have been no recriminations, but to have her grow distant, as I know she must have…"

Yes," said Georgiana quietly. She looked at him with a frown of puzzlement. "What do you mean, an opportunity to end it?"

Edward froze. "I beg your pardon?" he said, the dryness of his mouth apparent in his rasp.

Georgiana closed her eyes, forcing herself to be patient.

"What was this opportunity to end your affair with Lady Wickerston?" Georgiana grew impatient of her brother's hesitation. "Oh, for heaven's sake, Edward, I assume it was something out of the ordinary for you to mention it specifically."

Edward seemed to be struggling with his thoughts for a

moment or two, then let go a heavy sigh.

"Theresa has been talking wildly, saying she can't bear to be with her husband any more. She – she has spoken of killing him." Edward stopped and closed his eyes, moistening his lips as he did so. "I didn't take her seriously; I thought she was just upset. But when my pistols disappeared…"

Georgiana's eyes widened. "She took them?"

Edward dropped his head in his hands. "I think she may have done. I don't think it would have occurred to me if it hadn't been for her uncle's death."

"I don't understand," said Georgiana. "When could she have taken them? She could hardly smuggle them out of your house following afternoon tea."

"They were in the chaise, under the seat. I kept them there for protection." He smiled ruefully. "I'm afraid Amanda's good nature may be partly to blame. She suggested we take Theresa home from Almack's one night, after Wickerston had gone off with some of his cronies. Perhaps Theresa picked them up when I took Amanda to the door."

"Perhaps? Edward, haven't you asked her?"

Edward looked horror stricken. "Georgiana, how could I make such an accusation? Imagine how she would feel."

Georgiana rolled her eyes. "Do you think she killed her uncle?"

"I don't know. It's possible. I believe he virtually pushed her into her marriage. She may have got upset, or it may have been an accident. I really don't know."

Georgiana regarded him steadily. "So you said you were with her on the night of the murder. Oh, go home, Edward, it seems to me your brain is in a muddle."

To Georgiana's surprise, Edward stood, accepting his dismissal meekly. "Very well. I shall pay my respects to Selina and be on my way. I was going to ask if you would have tea with Amanda one day." He paused awkwardly. "I've been

271

rather busy lately. I think she's feeling rather lonely with only the children for company. However, with your present state of health, perhaps it would be better for her to come and see you?"

"Yes, of course," said Georgiana. A thought suddenly struck her. "She won't bring Lord Bartholomew, will she?"

"I don't expect so. He is still staying with us, but has not spent much time at the house lately," replied Edward stiffly. "He seems to have made some friends among the Macaroni set."

"I see," said Georgiana. This struck her as odd, but Lord Bartholomew's behaviour always struck her as odd one way or another. She wasn't sufficiently interested to dwell on the matter.

Edward bent down and kissed his sister on the forehead.

"Goodbye, Georgiana," he said. "Take care. I will call to see you again."

Georgiana gave her brother a weary smile and wished him goodbye. After he had gone, she leaned back against the cushions thoughtfully provided by Emily. Fighting the inclination to doze, she tried to focus her mind. She found it difficult to concentrate. Edward's information about the state of Lord and Lady Wickerston's marriage had seriously disturbed her.

The door opened and Emily looked around cautiously. She entered when she saw Georgiana was alone, and went to draw the curtains.

"How are you feeling, miss?" Emily asked.

"Fine," replied Georgiana. "Very much improved."

Emily eyed her suspiciously.

"Oh?"

"Yes, indeed," said Georgiana brightly. "I am glad I decided to leave my room today, one starts to feel too sedentary lying in bed."

"Of course," said Emily. "Will you be having your dinner with Miss Knatchbull, miss? Cook wasn't sure if you'd feel up to it and suggested a tray in your room."

"In my room, I think," said Georgiana.

"Yes, miss," said Emily, suppressing a smile. "I'm sure Miss Knatchbull will understand."

Selina, when the decision was put to her, was all concern and affability, her solicitude prompting her to offer to plump dear Georgiana's pillows and read to her if she desired. Dear Georgiana did not desire but thanked her cousin solemnly, assuring her she had no wish to burden her with this programme. She recommended Selina get some rest herself.

Safe in the haven of her own room, Georgiana at last felt able to relax, more tired than she had realised. She agreed readily enough to Emily's suggestion that she undress before her supper was brought. Georgiana decided the best thing she could do would be to retire early, in the hope that the following day would see her with energy renewed to pursue her investigation.

It was as Georgiana was tying the belt of her dressing gown that Emily's voice drew her attention from her own thoughts. She looked up to see her maid holding the ring which had been stolen from Sir Robert Foster.

"Good grief, Emily, where did you find that?"

"In your drawer, miss. Were you meaning to keep it?"

Georgiana recalled how she had said she was tempted by it. On finally removing it from her hand after the teapot incident, she wanted rid of the thing. In her hurry to bandage her hand and return to her uninvited guests, she had tossed it in the corner of a drawer, where it had lain forgotten until this moment.

"No," Georgiana responded with a shudder. "I'd forgotten I'd put it there."

Emily looked uneasy as Georgiana came to take it from her.

"What do you mean to do, miss? Take it to the Lucky Bell on its own?"

Georgiana shook her head. "No, it's not worth the risk of riding down there with one item, especially now. I'll give it to Sir Brandon, tell him his father lost it the night he stopped here." She frowned as she held it, studying the gold of the setting around the stone. "Emily, am I imagining things, or does this look dull?"

Emily looked unsure. Georgiana peered more closely, scratching the edge slightly with her thumbnail. Flecks of gold paint came away to reveal a grey band underneath. Emily gasped.

"Well, well," said Georgiana. "It's paste."

"I don't understand," said Emily. "Why would Sir Robert wear a piece of fake jewellery? His pockets weren't to let, were they?"

"No, but those of his son were. Perhaps Sir Robert didn't know. Fetch me some notepaper before my supper, would you? I mean to ask Sir Brandon to call upon me tomorrow."

A rather puzzled Sir Brandon Foster waited upon Georgiana shortly after eleven o'clock the following morning, Miss Knatchbull having been conveniently despatched to procure some barley. The discovery of there being none in the house led Georgiana to declare, through gritted teeth, that barley water was just what she needed to make her feel more the thing.

"Sir Brandon, thank you so much for calling on me," said Georgiana with her most charming smile. "I do hope I haven't inconvenienced you?"

"No," he responded. "Your note said you had some personal business you needed to discuss?"

"Yes," said Georgiana. She held out the ring on the palm of her good hand, noting the pallor of Sir Brandon's face as he sank into an armchair. "I believe this is your father's," she continued smoothly as if she noticed nothing amiss.

"Where did you get that?" Sir Brandon asked, his voice hoarse.

"One of my servants found it while dusting. Your father must have lost it the night he came here. I'm sorry for the delay in returning it to you."

"It was my mother's."

"Oh." Georgiana was unprepared for that. She looked at the ring again. The single stone could be worn by either a man or a woman. Georgiana had been attracted by its simplicity. She recalled it had been a loose fit when she had tried it. Sir Robert had worn it on his little finger, but now that she thought about it, the late Lady Foster had been on the plump side.

"I – I didn't know my father had it. I thought it had been lost."

"Really?" said Georgiana. "Since your mother's death?"

Sir Brandon looked ill at ease. "What? Well, I don't know, just that it wasn't among her things."

"Oh? It's unusual for a gentleman to be so familiar with his mother's jewellery."

"She wore that ring often. It belonged to her mother."

"I see. Then of course it would be important to her. You never noticed your father wearing it?"

Sir Brandon shook his head. "No."

"Well, perhaps he only wore it occasionally," Georgiana said, turning the ring around in her fingers as she studied it.

"Yes. Thank you for returning it."

Sir Brandon rose, reaching out his hand as he moved towards Georgiana to take the ring. She made no attempt to give it to him but continued to study it, a slight crease appearing across her forehead.

"Sir Brandon, I've just noticed, the ring seems to be damaged." Georgiana held it out for inspection. "Look there, the gold is flaking away; there seems to be some other metal beneath it."

The muscles around Sir Brandon's mouth grew noticeably taut.

"I expect it's a trick of the light."

"No, I don't think so," said Georgiana, examining the item more closely. She looked up at him with eyes wide with innocent surprise. "Sir Brandon, this appears to be a cheap bauble. It can't be your mother's ring."

"No, it's just old. You forget it's been handed down."

Georgiana shook her head. "No, Sir Brandon, this is clearly paste. The original must have been stolen and replaced. How shocking! You should notify the authorities. My brother is a magistrate. Perhaps he can help."

"No!"

Georgiana raised an eyebrow.

Sir Brandon drew a breath. "It was my mother's idea at first," he said, looking up to face Georgiana. "I was in Dun territory. My father refused to pay my debts. I was desperate, so my mother gave me a piece of jewellery to sell. She thought if it was copied, my father would never know. It worked; he didn't find out. She gave me a few more baubles after that."

"A practice you continued after her death?" observed Georgiana.

"My mother wouldn't have minded. I didn't touch anything of my father's, so I didn't think he'd notice. I didn't know he had this ring. It was one of the first pieces my mother gave me."

"I see."

"It hardly matters now," said Sir Brandon.

"Now your father's dead."

"I didn't kill him."

Georgiana made no comment.

"I didn't," insisted Sir Brandon, his voice taking on a petulant quality. "In fact," he continued, "I can prove it. I was with friends – well, acquaintances – at a card game. They will remember I was there."

"Did you see your father on the day he died?"

"No."

"So you wouldn't know what he was doing on the Bath Road that night?"

Sir Brandon shrugged. "He was robbed on the previous night, wasn't he? Maybe he thought he could get his trinkets back. Perhaps he offered a reward."

"Perhaps," said Georgiana. "Though would someone with such strong views on highwaymen negotiate for the return of his property?"

Sir Brandon shrugged again and said in a surly tone that he had to go, thanking Georgiana for the return of the ring as though the words were forced from him.

Georgiana lay back against the cushions of her couch as Sir Brandon departed. She could not rid herself of the feeling she was missing something. Her face wore a thoughtful frown as she rang for Emily.

"What is it?" Emily looked at her mistress in some concern.

"I don't know," said Georgiana frankly. "Something doesn't fit and I can't think what it is."

"Did Sir Brandon have anything useful to tell you?"

"I'm not sure," said Georgiana. "It seems the ring was his mother's, although Sir Robert was wearing it. Sir Brandon's been selling her jewellery and replacing them with paste to pay his debts. He said it was his mother's idea."

"Oh?"

"I believe she was a doting mama," said Georgiana. "He claims Sir Robert didn't know – that he kept to his mother's pieces."

"If Sir Robert had married Miss Winters, he might have started giving her some of those pieces."

"Perhaps. Louisa might not have recognised a piece of paste, but I daresay someone would, very likely her mother. And Sir Brandon might not have been able to borrow money from Louisa so easily."

"No."

"Sir Brandon said the ring was left to his mother by her mother, so if she gave it to him, I don't see that his father had much claim on it. And since most of Sir Robert's estate goes to some cousin, I can almost feel sorry for him."

Georgiana considered Sir Brandon's suggestion that his father went out alone in the hope of retrieving the property which had been stolen. She could easily reconcile the sanctimonious magistrate with a self-interested person willing to take any opportunity to find what belonged to him. Her difficulty was that she knew his property would not have been available to him on the night he died. Georgiana wondered how many people would have known of the robbery early enough to use this information against Sir Robert. If someone had lured him out on to the Bath Road with the promise of returning his goods, he must have received a note. Was it too much to hope he had not destroyed it?

Emily looked aghast at Georgiana's pronouncement that she needed a pretext to get into Sir Robert's house. With darkness falling, stretching the Crimson Cavalier's skills with some housebreaking seemed her best chance of finding what she needed. Emily's reaction to this proposal showed Georgiana a stubborn side she had never before seen. At Emily's insistence she sent a note to Mr Lakesby. She was less than pleased by his reply that he would deal with the matter.

"If he had said I should not worry my pretty head over it, he could scarcely have been more insulting," said Georgiana, screwing the note into a ball and throwing it into the fire. She scribbled another hurried note.

"Come along, Emily, help me change."

Emily's face still radiated disapproval, but she complied. Not many minutes later, Georgiana crept cautiously down the stairs, for once using the main staircase because the back area was occupied with working servants. Luck smiled on her as she opened the front door. Cavendish Square looked deserted as she slipped out, melting against the side of the house to make her way to the stables.

Keeping watch, Emily accompanied her to the stables. Emily begged her again to reconsider. Georgiana shook her head. She looked towards James.

"Give me half an hour, then go to my brother and give him this note. He told me that his Bow Street Runner would be calling on him this evening. Tell him I had a thought about Sir Robert's murder after Sir Brandon left, and ask him to bring the Runner to Sir Robert's house."

"Oh, miss." Emily looked convinced her mistress had lost control of her sanity.

"I will be out of there by then," Georgiana assured her servants. "You must believe me, it is imperative you follow my instructions. Promise you'll do as I say."

Brother and sister looked at each other before nodding. Satisfied, Georgiana tied on her mask and bundled her long auburn hair into her hat, from which she had again prudently omitted the red scarf proclaiming her identity. Mounting Princess, she moved slowly away, walking the animal towards her destination so as not to attract too much attention.

Georgiana's knowledge of some of the less salubrious streets proved a godsend, enabling her to reach Sir Robert Foster's house without encountering anyone she knew. As expected, she saw lights burning, and counted two rooms having the appearance of occupancy. Tying Princess to a tree at the back of the house, she began to scout for an unobtrusive door or window which would allow her to effect entry unnoticed. Her search was soon rewarded with a side door; it looked like one used by tradesmen or servants. Georgiana prayed it would not be locked. Her prayer was answered as she saw a scullery maid come out to empty a bucket, giving her the opportunity to slip in as the girl's back was away from her. She negotiated her way along a corridor wall, away from the sound of servants' chatter. She was aiming for the lit area she had noticed at the front of the house. It was not many minutes before she realised she had been right. A door, slightly ajar, gave her a full view of Edward's pistol, held in a slim hand that was shaking slightly. Georgiana drew her own weapon, her breath suddenly loud in her ears.

"My dear fellow, you don't seriously imagine you are going to get away with this, do you?" drawled Lakesby's unmistakable tones. "A murder on the road which one can blame on a highwayman is one thing, but in your own home – do be reasonable. There is no one else who could be accused."

"Be quiet!" Georgiana recognised Lord Bartholomew's high-pitched, petulant tones. "I've a right to shoot a house-breaker, haven't I?"

"But I'm not a housebreaker," said Lakesby calmly. "I came through the front door." His voice acquired a mocking edge.

"You had to interfere, didn't you? It was nothing to do with you, but you had to ask questions. I had to kill that wretched man. I'd have lost my inheritance if he'd had another son. I couldn't let him marry that cousin of yours."

"Now, there at least we are in agreement. However, you needn't have killed Sir Robert. There was no way I would have permitted my cousin to marry him."

"Quiet!" A note that was almost pride entered the voice. "Despite all his posturing about highwaymen, he couldn't resist when it came to a chance of getting his own property back. But all those questions poor Georgiana's been asking, and then you. Soon enough even dear dull Edward would realise I'd taken his pistols from his carriage, and might start wondering why."

Lord Bartholomew's voice had risen to a shriek. Georgiana expected a servant to come and investigate at any minute. His lordship was clearly panicking, liable to shoot. Her pistol was cocked. She moved towards the door, her eyes alighting on a vase of freshly cut flowers on a small table. She transferred her pistol to her left hand, wincing slightly at the shaft of pain that came from her bullet wound. The fingers of her right closed around the vase. Anger sharpened her determination. She found she resented anyone but herself referring to Edward as dull, and the phrase 'poor Georgiana' was not one she could easily forgive.

Georgiana seized her moment. She threw the vase with impressive force, hitting the pistol in Lord Bartholomew's hand. He whirled round to see who the new assailant was, a little off balance, but managing to hold tight to the pistol. Lakesby, recovering from his astonishment, made a grab for it while Georgiana pushed the door hard against Lord Bartholomew. As the two men struggled, the pistol went off. Inside the room, Georgiana closed and locked the door behind her, looking to see if one of the combatants had been hit. They continued to struggle; it appeared neither was injured. She gave Lord Bartholomew's leg a sharp kick. He cried out as he started to topple over. Georgiana hit Lord Bartholomew hard with the pistol handle, then pointed it steadily at him. He was lying on the floor, all fight seemingly gone out of him. Lakesby stood, breathing heavily. He glanced towards his rescuer, then gave a smile and an exaggerated bow of thanks.

"There's a Bow Street Runner on the way," Georgiana said to him, hoping Lord Bartholomew's winded condition and the servants now banging on the door would prevent him recognising her voice.

"Then you should go," said Lakesby. "I'll take care of matters here. Thank you."

Georgiana gave him a nod, noting he held Edward's pistol in businesslike fashion over their quarry. Hearing her brother's voice out in the hall, she made speedily for the window. She saw Lakesby waiting to see her safely out before he opened the door.

19

"I can't believe you're going through with this." Emily's voice was heavy with disapproval as she watched her mistress tie the red scarf on her hat.

Georgiana shrugged.

"Why not? Sir Robert's murderer has been caught. He has even confessed."

"Even so…"

"What do you expect me to do, Emily? Settle down to a life of paying morning calls until Edward finds me a suitable husband?" She grinned at this, a mischievous twinkle in her eye as she looked at her maid. "Though something tells me Edward won't be doing any more matchmaking on my behalf, at least not for a while. Had I accepted his last suggestion, he would be the brother-in-law of a murderer."

"Instead of the brother of a highway robber," Emily retorted.

"Yes, well, he doesn't know that," said Georgiana as she checked her pistol.

"That bullet wound isn't even healed properly yet," said Emily.

"I shall do well enough." She paused, looking steadily towards her maid. "Don't worry so. There's no more risk now than there was before Sir Robert's death."

"Well, there was enough then," said Emily. She picked up Georgiana's reticule, and continued putting away the more feminine items of clothing in her wardrobe. "It's still hard to believe Lord Bartholomew Parker is a murderer."

"I know," said Georgiana. "He seems to have had more ingenuity than I would have credited."

"I expect Mr Edward was shocked."

"Oh, yes," said Georgiana warmly. "Especially with the way

283

Lord Bartholomew turned on him. I thought Selina would have an attack of the vapours when she heard." Georgiana paused. "Edward thinks he ought to resign his seat on the magistrates' bench."

"Really?"

"It would be more convenient," remarked Georgiana, "at least as far as I'm concerned. However, to be honest, Emily, I find myself in some sympathy with him. I know how much it means to him, and he was so proud of having achieved it."

Emily was shaking her head. "It's not his fault his wife's cousin is a murderer."

"No." Georgiana was thoughtful. "I don't feel I ought to try to influence Edward's decision."

"Perhaps not, miss," said Emily. "What made you realise about Lord Bartholomew?"

Georgiana tilted her head slightly. "When I asked Sir Brandon why he thought his father had gone out that night, he suggested Sir Robert had gone to get his property back."

"On the road?"

Georgiana nodded. "Oh, yes, a word in the right quarter can often secure results. The robbery was no secret, but I'm sure Sir Robert would not have wanted such a meeting known. It would not accord with his public face of a magistrate determined to make examples of the criminals who came before him." She paused. "However, a family member, even a distant one, would be well enough acquainted with him to realise he could be lured out."

"And Lord Bartholomew was a cousin."

Georgiana nodded. "Between that and his new curricle and new friends, I'm ashamed I didn't put it together sooner."

"What happens to his inheritance?" asked Emily.

"I believe it now goes to Sir Brandon. Ironic, isn't it?"

"I imagine Mr Lakesby was surprised when you arrived at Sir Robert's house."

"He certainly seemed to be, at first," said Georgiana. "Yet he took it in his stride somehow. After him trying to make me wait patiently at home, it was very satisfying to go to his rescue."

"Well, you shouldn't have gone dashing off like that," said Emily severely.

"Yes, Emily you've made your point."

"As for going out now–"

"I have to let Harry know Tom's adventure on the road did not kill Sir Robert."

"He was just injured?"

Georgiana nodded. "Knocked off his horse, Edward said. I imagine Tom's attempt at robbery was a gift to Lord Bartholomew. He would have found him struggling to his feet, groggy and swearing. It gave him an advantage. Sir Robert would be in no position to fight, and would look battered and bruised when he was found. Easy to blame on a highwayman."

"A particular highwayman."

"Yes," said Georgiana with feeling. "You know, I believe Edward was almost as shocked by Lord Bartholomew stealing his pistols as committing the murder. Apparently, he'd seen them there when he went with Amanda to call on some acquaintance, and went back to the carriage fussing about dropping his handkerchief. He hid them in some excessively caped greatcoat."

Georgiana pulled on her tightly-fitting gloves and picked up her hat and mask.

"There is no need to wait up," she said, "although I do not expect to be very late."

Georgiana led Princess out on foot, mounting some way from the house where she thought it unlikely she would be seen. There was still some aching in her shoulder, but she decided she would be better for some exercise. The night was clear and, fortunately, the road quiet. Georgiana smiled to herself under the mask. She had more caution than Emily credited. The Crimson Cavalier would be back soon enough, but Georgiana knew she had to let the dust settle first.

Georgiana again found Harry in the company of the curly-haired maid. As Georgiana entered the tavern, the maid was summarily dismissed. Georgiana shook her head at Harry's offer of wine and followed him to the parlour.

"I hear that problem of yours has been solved," said Harry without preamble as he closed the door.

Georgiana nodded.

"One of the quality, wasn't it?" Harry continued.

She nodded again.

"Well, well," Harry said, rubbing his chin. "It just shows you. You never know, do you? I expect Tom's abandoned any idea of the high toby?"

"I imagine so," said Georgiana.

"Just as well," said Harry. He looked at Georgiana shrewdly. "So the Crimson Cavalier will be back on the road soon?"

"Soon enough," said Georgiana. She looked steadily at her compatriot. "Thank you for your help, Harry."

Harry brushed her words aside. "We all have to stick together. What's bad for one's bad for another, and as I said, I'd be sorry to see you hang."

Georgiana glanced curiously towards Harry. There had been something in his tone which made her uneasy. It was unlikely that he had guessed the truth about her. Yet she could not repress the feeling he knew more than he was prepared to divulge. She could only be glad he seemed inclined to show her friendship.

Untying Princess from behind the tavern, Georgiana breathed a sigh of relief. At last, it was over. The whole thing had seemed unreal somehow. Standing in the quiet of the night behind the Lucky Bell, it would have been all too easy to convince herself it had been no more than a bad dream.

Georgiana mounted Princess and began to pick her way across the yard towards home. She had not realised how tired she was. She knew Emily had probably been right. It hadn't been sensible for her to venture out with her shoulder still weak. But Georgiana could not abide inactivity, and could not feel easy until she had spoken to Harry about Tom and thanked him for his efforts on her own behalf. Georgiana flattered herself she had never underestimated his shrewdness. However, it was beginning to occur to her that there was an omniscient quality about him eerily reminiscent of Lakesby.

The cool air brushing against her cheeks refreshed Georgiana, and with the reassuring sensation of Princess's invigorating canter, she began to feel more like her old self. Her mind moved forward, planning the Crimson Cavalier's next piece of work. It would be wise to wait a while. The slightest vulnerability would take away any advantage she might have. However, Georgiana had no wish to delay too long before resuming her work. It would not do for the Crimson Cavalier to lose her touch through lack of practice.

Emerging on to the road, Georgiana reflected on the irony of her recent habit of checking to ensure there were no travellers. It was long past the hour when all but the most determined of revellers would be setting out for home. The distant sound of approaching wheels caused her to frown. She began to draw back when something familiar about the equipage made her pause. Looking into the distance, her eyes gradually made out the shape of the chaise. Georgiana gave a slow smile under her mask as she drew her pistol. She took up her position on the road.

The chaise came slowly to a halt. Georgiana saw the coachman's eyes roll heavenward as he caught sight of her levelled pistol. Lakesby's eyes met hers, an unholy amusement in their depths.

"Your valuables, sir," came Georgiana's muffled voice.

Lakesby tossed her his coin purse and drew off his signet ring.

CRÈME DE LA CRIME PERIOD PIECES

GRIPPING DEBUT CRIME FICTION FROM DAYS GONE BY

**A new strand from the UK's
most innovative crime publisher.**

BROKEN HARMONY   **ROZ SOUTHEY**

Charles Patterson, impoverished musician in 1730s Newcastle-upon-Tyne is accused of stealing a valuable book and a cherished violin. Then the apprentice he inherited from his flamboyant professional rival is found gruesomely murdered.

As the death toll mounts Patterson starts to fear for his health and sanity – and it becomes clear to characters and readers alike that things are not quite as they seem…

ISBN: 978-0-9551589-3-3
£7.99

TRUTH DARE KILL

GORDON FERRIS

The war's over – but no medals for Danny McRae. Just amnesia and black-outs: twin handicaps for a private investigator with an upper-class client on the hook for murder.

Newspaper headlines about a Soho psychopath stir grisly memories in Danny's fractured mind. As the two bloody sagas collide and interweave, Danny finds himself running for his life across the bomb-ravaged city.

Will his past catch up with him before his enemies? And which would be worse?

Fast-paced post-war noir, with a grimly accurate London setting.

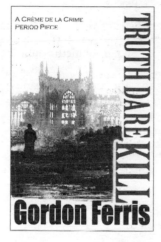

ISBN: 978-0-9551589-4-0

£7.99

NEW TITLES FROM OUR BESTSELLING AUTHORS

From ADRIAN MAGSON: a fourth rollercoaster adventure for Riley Gavin and Frank Palmer

NO TEARS FOR THE LOST

A society wedding…

A crumbling mansion…

A severed finger…

For once, Riley Gavin and Frank Palmer are singing from different hymn books. As bodyguard to former diplomat Sir Kenneth Melrose, it's Frank's job to keep journos like Riley at bay.

But Sir Kenneth's dubious South American past is catching up with him. When he receives a grisly death threat involving his estranged son, the partners-in-crimebusting stop pulling against each other.

Helped by former intelligence officer Jacob Worth, they discover Sir Kenneth has more secrets than the Borgias, and his crumbling country house is shored up by a powder which doesn't come in Blue Circle Cement bags.

ISBN: 978-0-9551589-7-1   £7.99

From MAUREEN CARTER: Birmingham's feistiest detective is finding things tough again

HARD TIME

An abandoned baby…

A kidnapped five-year-old…

A dead police officer…

And Detective Sergeant Bev Morriss thinks she's having a hard time!

Bev doesn't do fragile and vulnerable, and struggling to cope with the aftermath of a vicious attack, she is desperate not to reveal the lurking self-doubt.

But her lover has decided it's time to move on and the guv is losing patience. And her new partner has the empathy of a house brick. But she can scarcely trust her own judgement, so what's left to rely on?

Just when things can't get any worse, another police officer dies.

And the ransom note arrives.

And hard doesn't begin to cover it.

ISBN: 978-0-9551589-6-4 £7.99

From LINDA REGAN: a sizzling follow-up to
BEHIND YOU! (ISBN 978-0-95515892-2-6), the sell-out
debut from a popular actress turned crime writer.

**DI Banham and DS Grainger take a walk
on the seedy side of Soho in**

PASSION KILLERS

A convicted murderer has recently come out of prison, to the horror of six women who were involved in his crime.

Twenty years ago they were all strippers in a seedy nightclub.

Now some of them have a lot to lose.

Two of the women are found dead – murdered, and each with a red g-string stuffed in her mouth.

Enter D I Paul Banham, ace detective but not so hot when it comes to women. He focuses his enquiries on the surviving women, and finds that no one has a cast-iron alibi.

Everyone is a suspect and everyone is a potential victim.

And Banham is falling in love…

ISBN: 978-0-9551589-8-8   £7.99

MORE EXCITING DEBUT
CRIME FICTION

A KIND OF PURITAN   **PENNY DEACON**

Claustrophobic futurecrime chiller, first in a gripping series which nods towards J D Robb.

A subtle and clever thriller - Daily Mail

ISBN: 978-0-9547634-1-1   £7.99

IF IT BLEEDS   **BERNIE CROSTHWAITE**

Chilling murder mystery with authentic newspaper background.

Pacy, eventful… an excellent debut. - Mystery Women

ISBN: 978-0-9547634-3-5   £7.99

A CERTAIN MALICE   **FELICITY YOUNG**

Taut and creepy crime novel with authentic Australian setting.

a beautifully written book… draws you into the life in Australia… you may not want to leave.
- Natasha Boyce, bookseller

ISBN: 978-0-9547634-4-2   £7.99

PERSONAL PROTECTION   **TRACEY SHELLITO**

Erotic lesbian thriller set in the charged atmosphere of a lapdancing club.

a powerful, edgy story… I didn't want to put down…
- Reviewing the Evidence

ISBN: 978-0-9547634-5-9   £7.99

SINS OF THE FATHER   **DAVID HARRISON**

Blackmail, revenge, murder and a major insurance scam on the south coast.

… replete with a rich cast of characters and edge-of-the-seat situations where no one is safe…
- Mike Howard, Brighton Argus

ISBN: 978-0-9547634-9-7   7.99

Withdrawn

**Indianapolis
Marion County
Public Library**

**Renew by Phone
269-5222**

Renew on the Web
www.imcpl.org

For General Library Information
please call 269-1700